PEACE SHALL DESTROY MANY

Rudy Wiebe

PEACE SHALL DESTROY MANY

INTRODUCTION: *J. M. Robinson*
GENERAL EDITOR: *Malcolm Ross*

New Canadian Library No. 82

McClelland and Stewart

Reprinted, 1982

The Canadian Publishers
McClelland and Stewart Ltd.
25 Hollinger Road, Toronto

0-7710-9182-6

Manufactured in Canada by Webcom Limited

CONTENTS

TO THE SCATTERED MEMBERS

OF

The Coffee Club

FOREWORD

The Anabaptists of the sixteenth century were the extreme evangelical wing of the Reformation movement. The name "Mennonite" was early attached to them, after Menno Simons, their sole early theological leader to survive persecution. Because the group's literal biblicism expressed itself in believers' baptism, a life of discipleship, separation of church and state, non-participation in war or government, the "Brethren," as they preferred to call themselves, were savagely martyred by Catholic and Protestant alike. Restrained from open proselytizing, they could do no more than teach their faith to their children; what in 1523 began as a religious movement became in time a swarming of a particular people from various nationalities bound together by a faith: like ancient Israel, they were a religious nation without a country. They were driven from Switzerland to America, from Holland and northern Germany to Prussia, then Russia, finally to North and South America. Wherever they went they carried peculiar customs, a peculiar language, a peculiar faith in the literal meaning of the Bible.

Over the four hundred years of their existence, the Mennonites have divided into several fairly distinctive groups. Their extremely individualistic approach to religion could hardly have other results. In one form or another, they still hold essentially the principles which forced Conrad Grebel and his companions to part with the reform of Zwingli in Zurich.

The Mennonites portrayed in this book belong to no particular faction; they could belong to any one of several groups that came to Canada from Russia in the 1920's. All characters and situations are fictional.

And in the latter time, a king
shall stand up.
And his power shall be mighty
and he shall prosper.
And he shall magnify himself in his heart,
and by peace shall destroy many:
But he shall be broken without hand.

DANIEL 8

INTRODUCTION

The setting of Rudy Wiebe's first novel, *Peace Shall Destroy Many,* is a community which has cut itself off from the world to follow in the steps of Christ. The scene is the wilds of Saskatchewan, and the year is 1944. The outside world seems to be the source of evil, its tank tracks desecrating the earth which here is rightly turned by the plow, its war planes overhead tearing the serene sounds of a farm-yard at evening. But the story told is of the inner strains that threaten this community and of the awakening of one of its sons to the need for a new way. The first view of Thom Wiens is of him plowing, following the traditional path of the fathers; the final view shows him driving, reins in hand, seemingly (in the mind of one of the characters) towards the brightest star in the east. Left behind, broken, is the former leader, Peter Block.

Peter Block, the founder and "rock" of the community, is the most interesting figure in the book. This is a didactic novel, and the analysis of Block is central to the intention of the author. Through the probing of this character is probed, too, the origins of the community and the motive beyond the apparent ones holding it together. Two events are central in Block's life, the time the descending axe brought him face to face with his mortality, and the time he killed a man. Both have to do with his "son-necessity." (p. 126) That "son-necessity" is the driving motive of his life and the measure of his worldliness. Mrs. Block condemns his subterfuge during the Russian famine in hiding food for his son. Her will is resigned to God's. Not so, Block's. To escape earthly oblivion is his need, his son his hope. Work for that son is his "only religion." (p. 127) Block's true relation with his community in Canada, too, is questioned by his conduct in the old country. When he has to choose in Russia between the community and his son, there is no conflict. That other villagers will have to make up for the grain he withholds, "he cared not at all." (p. 127) Moments before he beats the Bashkir to death, the thought of his son without milk feeds his fury.

Years after that killing, Block, now in Canada, founds his community; to be alone in the wilderness with the thought of his past act threatens to undo him utterly. Desperate personal need and the resolve to protect his son drive him to create a colony which will be wholesome and clean, from which the evil of the world will be barred. To shut out the world is an exacting task. Rules gain ascendant power. The effects of Block's intense dedication are seen in his family, Mrs. Block always silent, Elizabeth listless, "all the bloom gone" (p. 25), Pete, mechanical, replying to Thom's invitation to let go, " 'How would that get the work done?' " (p. 139). When Block shows a moment's tenderness for his daughter, she looks "dully at him, as at a lump of mud" (p. 137). His wife, at the funeral, shudders at his touch. Block's faith in the saving power of work is ironically commented on as Elizabeth lies dying amid the busy sounds of harvesting. She is buried on the day set aside for the Thanksgiving Festival. Perhaps Block, reaping death, failing to redeem his sins of Russia is a figure of pathos; if so, the pathos emerges despite his readiness to repeat the sins of the past. When he learns of Elizabeth's fall, he thinks: "If the man had stood before him, he would have bare-handedly torn him limb from limb" (p. 145). Protection of his son is still an obsessive concern. He visits Louis, and when he leaves, "erect in the withering cold . . . he did not care . . . that he had, by every standard he ever believed, damned his own soul eternally. Wapiti was clean for his son" (p. 185).

Block determines that as a consequence of what has happened to Elizabeth, "the breeds must go" (p. 153). It is characteristic of him in coping with "evil" to focus on the external situation. Mrs. Wiens suggests that the evil within must be experienced to a degree if it is to be mastered. Block seeks to protect by limiting awareness. Too simple or rigid a concept of evil and how to cope with it can yield an ironical harvest, the novel seems to suggest.

The other major character through whom the author explores the life of the community is Thom Wiens, the youthful protagonist of the novel. Thom, starting guiltily in the first scene at his pause from work, begins orthodox; since the coming of Joseph, the teacher, however, doubts have jolted his mind like the stones impede his plow. As the story progresses, he comes, through a series of moments of seeing, to question his community's expression of its belief.

The meeting at which Joseph challenges their use of German (it prevents them carrying the gospel to their neighbours) and their non-participation in the war is one such moment. At the start of the meeting, Thom is confident of the church's ability to deal finely with its problems. When, however, a reconciliation is sought by forcing an apology from Joseph, he questions the kind of "peace" aimed at, one to be gained by ignoring the issues raised. The crooked figure of the grizzled old caretaker which holds his attention embodies a growing distrust in Thom of his elders. Torn between Joseph's influence and his faith in his own community, he is left at the end wandering "alone where guide-posts bearing the same legend pointed over horizonless dunes in opposing directions" (p. 63).

The meeting scene is explicit in stating its issues. A more satisfying moment portraying Thom's awakening is the scene in which he stumbles over the skull of a wood-buffalo and pulls it up "moss and roots dangling" (p. 82), more satisfying because more subtle and because to an extent the reader has to "see" for himself. Pulling up the skull, Thom is arrested by a sense of the past, and he gains in a flash a new consciousness of this country, Canada, which his community ignores and of the dignity and mystery of its native people, the Indians, who have a history of their own. Pete scoffs at Thom's moment of humility and wonder, and Thom is further isolated. The dwindling of the friendship of the two young men is a measure of Thom's development. This episode along with others of similar effects, his glimpse of two Poles at the picnic, for example, enlarges Thom's awareness of what lies beyond his community's limits and plays its part in altering his relation to the community.

Thom's moments of insight do not alone motivate him, however. When he confronts the marriage of Herman and the "half-breed" girl, Madeleine, he feels revulsion: "A Christian can't just up and marry any person the storm blows into his house," he spits out at his sister. "There have to be rules" (p. 109). The author's portrayal of his hero is not uncritical. Thom is tellingly exposed in the scene that juxtaposes the radio broadcast of the liberation of Paris with his brooding over the relation of Herman and Madeleine. Flowing from the radio is a great human experience. Thom is as good as deaf to the swelling sound "like the prayer of an innumerable multitude" (p. 103). When "the great voice of the Parisian people blossomed in the room," we are told ironically, he "could not help but listen" (p. 106). But he is uncomprehending before the massive human emotions, childish. The juxtaposition of the great event and the local preoccupation in this scene and the kind of response Thom makes to each provides one perspective on the effects of withdrawal.

Thom's baring of his thoughts about Herman and Madeleine's marriage, however, leads him to face "monsters" (p. 110) in his subconscious. He is capable of confronting the self within. Later he realizes that at the Bible class he gives for the Indian and Métis children, he is avoiding one of the girls who appears ready to make a commitment. He does not really want to convert the child; he prefers to evade the problems she would create in a community ordered the way his is. Contradictions of this order lead Thom to a crisis; for him the choice seems to be one of following tradition or following Christ. Ironically, the community has become the "world" which he must overcome. He is brought, however, when he learns what happened to Elizabeth to yet another kind of crisis.

Stepping into Elizabeth's grave at her funeral to effect the final placing of the coffin, Thom had been strangely affected viewing "all Wapiti" (p. 157) from that vantage point. Not until later, however, does he really "see" from the perspective of Elizabeth's grave, when he learns how she died. Then he reacts in horror against Block and his rules. His faith itself trembles; he breaks with his principles he decides to leave and go to war. Here, then, is one possible ending of the story, Thom's quest bringing him to this point of rupture. In fact, this is not his final position.

At this time of intense hostility to Block, Thom is, in a way, like Block. He is disgusted with an evil he places outside himself. The position he takes up in this state, his decision to leave, is for him an unbalanced one. In the final chapter, he finds another position, does so, in part, because he views evil in rounder terms; he glimpses the darkness within himself.

Under the taunts of Herb Unger the night of the Christmas concert, Thom lets his thoughts for a moment dwell on Razia in a way that startles him: "Such wells of depravity yawned in his empty self that he could only shudder . . . . " (p. 227). Later that night, for the first time in his life, Thom smashes a man in the face, brute strength surging to assert itself in the "void" left by his "splintered dogmas" (p. 235). The references to Thom's "empty self" and to the "void" within him at these moments describe the condition in which he has lived since reacting so violently against Block, a condition of "fearful vacuum" (p. 226), the principles on which he has based his life (non-violence among them) disowned by him. The night of the school concert, forces operate upon him to draw him back from the point he has earlier reached. The moments noted above are among them; so is the figure of Hank Unger, back from the war, boasting of his killings. Thom, listening to him remembers that Hank is one of those who has deserted the "law of the fathers"

(p. 226). If some of the forces operating on Thom that night of the concert, then, restore his sense of need for the values his community has taught him, others lead him to see new terms on which to live with his community.

The play wins Thom's earnest identification with the quest of the three kings. The Indians' living conditions have always aroused aversion in Thom's community, but in the play Christ is found in lowly conditions, in "an old barn . . . about to collapse" (p. 232). And Jackie Labaret leads the way to Christ. The Three Kings find their answer in that barn. Perhaps in an ironic way the barn scene that follows helps Thom to find his way. He sees the darkness within that must somehow be met. Not the war abroad but the confrontation with "one's own two faces" (p. 238) becomes of first consequence. An external war, too, waits to be fought here in Wapiti, the war to secure a right relation with the Indians and Métis. Just as "war" is not necessarily bad, so "peace" is not necessarily good. The peace based on neglect and evasion will destroy.

The society portrayed in this novel is a highly particularized one, a community which has isolated itself from the world, but elements of the story are universal — youth's clash with established ways, the discrepancy between ideals and attainment. The author interests us in the issues which involve this community. The attempt to shut out the evil of the world sets up its own contradiction. That there is no escape is one theme, and in a sense this is a "war novel." To an extent, too, it is concerned with the "heart of darkness." Canada is a theme, and the relationship of different races. Motives are probed effectively. Contrived effects and conversations mar, but the story has good dramatic moments, Elizabeth's last day, for example. Pete and Joseph are colourless characters; Pete's blankness, however, is justified – Block is his father. There is awkwardness in the presentation of Razia and of Hank. Razia, however, is used thoughtfully to control tone, once at the funeral, a second time at the end to counter the earnestness of Thom in following the school play. Herb Unger serves many functions. There is effective patterning in the use of thunder at the beginning and end of the "Summer" section. The most arresting parts of the work, however, are those involving Block.

The degree of impartiality the author achieves is a question the work poses. Is, for example, Thom, the hero, probed as acutely as Block? One can say that the author's perspective is larger than any pride in sending a missionary to India, the genuine hurt this brings to Rempel is noted. The young people voice their "nobility," but there is sympathy, too, for Mrs. Wiens' simple acknowledgement of human limitation. A glimpse of Block's inner conflict is allowed; Thom is not left uncriticized. *Peace Shall Destroy Many* is a first novel of considerable interest. Since its publication in 1962, Mr. Wiebe has brought out two other novels, *First and Vital Candle,* 1966, and *The Blue Mountains of China,* 1970. It is to be expected that this author will gain increasing attention.

J. M. Robinson
University of Manitoba

Spring 1944

PRELUDE

The school stood at the crossroads in the valley, its loggish face southward. Flanked by teacherage and sagging barn, it waited with its door yawning in the spring morning as the children neared on four roads cut like slashes through the bush. Reluctantly they came, listening to the spring frog-song, touching the buds on the slim poplars, snuffing the freshness. Soon the yard rang with their running shouts and tumbled hills' re-echo.

The teacher stepped through the door and his bell clanged. When the distant measures of "O Canada" had faded over the tree-tips and the stirring flag on its pole was the only movement near the school, two overalled figures arose from behind a bush on the east hill and ran down its bare face. Where the white-puffed willows hid the school, they eased to a walk, shoes dangling over their shoulders, arms swinging syrup-pails tight with peanut-butter sandwiches.

They halted just out of sight of school where a brook sluiced under the moss-rumpled beams of a culvert. The taller boy placed his pail on the ends of the wooden planks and lay down, dark head over the edge. The other dropped his pail, shrugged off his shoes and trotted to the opposite side. Here the brook foamed between willows smothering a barbed fence. The boy worried a rotten bit of wood off the culvert, dropped it into the stream, ran back and sprawled beside his companion. The wood floated beneath them, swooshed through a little dip, hesitated an instant, and then sailed regally past the rushes into the wide expanse of the slough. They watched the water's eternal refolding over the rocks.

The tow-headed boy jerked suddenly erect. "Let's go!"

"Okay."

They rolled up their pant legs and, after grimaced testing, eased their feet into the frigid water. Shoes and sandwiches were hastily stowed in a recess under the culvert. Brandishing his empty pail, the fair boy edged farther, eyes wild with the pushing life of spring.

"The eggs should be out today—oogh!" he gasped, the water numbing his knees.

"Yah!" The dark boy pushed gurgling by towards the sprouting grass of the slough-flats. The frogs were croaking loudly.

CHAPTER ONE

The yellow planes passed overhead swiftly and in thunder. Thom Wiens had heard their growing roar above the scrape of the plow on stones, but the trees hedged them from his sight. Then suddenly, as he twisted on the halted plow to look back, they were over the poplars, flying low and fast. The sense of the horses' sweated trembling was in his rein-clenched hands as he stared the yellow planes out of sight to the north.

Fly, you heathen, he was thinking. Fly low, practise your dips and turns to terrify playing children and grandmothers gaunt in their rocking chairs. Practise your hawk-swoops, so you can gun down some equally godless German or bury a cowering family under the rubble of their home. To get paid for killing. To be trained to kill more efficiently. If you shoot down five Germans you get a medal. If you kill twenty at once, you get a Victoria Cross and the King himself shakes your hand. What will you do when all the Germans have been killed and the only work you know is shooting men? Acclaimed murderers everywhere!

They were gone, flying in a tight triangle like ducks going north for nesting. Thom slid to the earth and worked his short crow-bar under the stone which had staggered the plow just before the planes appeared. Loosened, it came easily and he walked across the plowing, holding the heavy stone against his stomach. The heap of rocks along the fence ground together as he dropped it. With the edge of his hand he knocked at the dust on the white-worn front of his overalls.

Before him the fence stretched tight over the humped land.

He could see a third of a mile of it bordering the open field, every post belly-deep in stones. The planes passed so quickly and, standing there with his hand raised for a last brush, Thom suddenly experienced, like a water-bucket emptied over him, the weeks and months spent gathering rocks from the field and piling them, one by one, along the fence until only enough post showed for a top wire. To grow something took a long time, and the machines for it were slow. There were no machines to pick rocks. But the machines for death were wind-swift. For a moment he felt he had discovered a great truth, veiled until now: the long growing of life and the quick irrevocableness of death.

The heaped rocks recalled him, and he turned to stride rapidly towards the plow. To just stand, thinking! He glanced about, happy for the rugged world that had hidden his dreaming. Pulling his feet up hard with each step, he sensed within himself the strength of his forefathers who had plowed and subdued the earth before him. He, like them, was working out God's promise that man would eat his bread in the sweat of his face, not pushing a button to watch a divine creation blaze to earth.

As the four horses moved under his urging, he settled his broad limbs to the jolting ride. He cringed then as, with a flare of conscience, he recalled Brother Goertzen's clipped German phrases: "We are to follow Christ's steps, but we do not have pride. By God's Grace we understand what others do not. As we cannot imagine Him lifting a hand to defend himself physically, so we, His followers, conquer only by spiritual love and not by physical force. Always only love: for those who love us, for those indifferent to us, for those who hate us, for those who would kill us, which is the same thing; *all* are included when He says, 'This is my commandment, that you love one another even as I have loved you.'"

Thom could not doubt such sermons. He had grown up hearing these statements and if someone had asked him when he had first known that Christ bade his disciples love their enemies, he could no more have answered than if he had been asked to consciously recollect his first breath. All week the stentorian voice had ruled the hushed church: "Have you not heard our country loudly proclaim that we must protect the innocent from the 'trampling boots of tyranny'? The whole land is geared to destruction so that it will not be destroyed. The glorious end justifies any means we use to attain it. For the Christian, the righteous means are more essential than comfortable and apparently necessary ends. What do we gain if we retain our bodies here on earth an hour longer, but lose our everlasting souls? We can ignore the black power and his fiendish earthly workers who can destroy our bodies but cannot touch our souls." There was no argument against that.

And truth necessitated following.

The horses were wheeling in their awkwardness at the corner of the field and stopped at his touch. Home was beyond the hill and a line of trees. Thom felt the ground warming with expectation, the ripeness of the earth's belly pushing itself up against the steel of the shares. When he lay with his face in the sandy loam, arms and legs yearning, he was beyond himself. It seemed to Thom that every man must feel the smallness and the greatness, his face in the dirt when the clouds were sheep with their heads down in the sunshine of the open sky and the larks chanting from their post-perch and the burdened horses nodding their heads to earth with sweat black in straggles down their thighs. Lying there, he felt doubts settle in his mind like mud in the hollows of the spring-soaked land. He could not actually imagine that men should wish to kill one another; yet they must, for how else could they give themselves into the murder that was the Army? The earth holding him, he thought, If only there were enough trees and hills and rocks in all Saskatchewan or all Canada or even all the world to hide us from a Hitler who has tasted power like a boar's first gulp of warm blood. But once a man has tasted power, you cannot pen up or dispose of him like a blooded boar, and he the greater danger. And Thom felt the persistent, recurring prick: sometimes you think you should help try, anyway.

He rose quickly and the horses heaved in unison. He knew the shape of every tree along the rock-heaped fence without lifting his eyes from Jerry's hocks treading the furrow. Why must something as remote as being required to kill another human become as forcibly real as the plow's hump against stone beneath him. But it had become so. Could he but know himself strong, like Peter Block! To stand alone before the judge in a courtroom crowded with gimlet-eyed women whose husbands and lovers and sons were flying like yellow hawks, somewhere over the bend of the world, and to say clearly, "It is against my conscience." Never having considered even for an instant that there might be another way. If he could but know himself strong!

The whoop behind him perked the horses' ears. As Thom turned on the iron seat, the tow-headed "Indian" transformed himself into a small fighter-plane, and with arms outstretched, lunch-pail rattling, bare feet flashing in the turned earth, came soaring in gasps to trip and sprawl beside the slow plow. The boy was up even as he rolled.

"The planes—we saw 'em, Thom! Three big ones flyin' low and makin' the biggest noise! Boy, they were 'way longer than Wapiti School—longer than Beaver even—and they were bangin' like anythin'. Maybe they'll bang apart, huh? When I'm real big I'll fly some—wow!"

Thom looked down on Hal walking in the following furrow. He said, brotherly casual, "Why do you want to fly one if it might bang apart?"

"Oh. I'd get one that goes smooth, like *brrrsssh*—" and the small boy spread his arms, made several rolling swoops with the upper part of his body, and then, to avoid running into the plow, threw himself beside it as he tipped forward.

"You'll spread your nose all over the plow-wheel if you don't watch. You were to wear shoes to school."

Hal was up and behind the plow again. He rattled his battered syrup-pail. "It's too hard walkin'. An' the Indians came past today—I saw 'em first through the big window, even before Jackie Labret, and I put up my hand real fast an' Mr Dueck saw it even before Jackie raised his hand—"

"Were the Indians packed for the summer?" interrupted Thom.

"Uh-huh. Mr Dueck said, 'All right, Helmut,' before he saw

the wagons an' I went out an' all the other kids had to sit down again to read their books an' Jackie was real mad after school 'cause he got hardly one look an' almost—"

"Who was moving?"

"Ol' Two Poles. An' Hankey was there on the wagon. He waved. There were lotsa squaws an' more wagons. But Ol' Two Poles an' his pinto were on the front wagon goin' to the Point."

"The pinto wasn't *on* the wagon, it was hitched *to* it, not? Fishing will be good if they move this early."

"Uh-huh. Jackie said the muskrats have been real good. We would ha' followed their trail back but they just use the main road now an' don't go on the trails like they used to—Jackie says they're mostly fenced shut anyhows an' we were comin' home by Martens an' we saw the planes goin' north like hell Jackie sa—"

Thom swung round on his seat. "Don't you say that or I'll trim you. Not once more!"

The little boy's eyes dilated with sham innocence. "But I didn't. Jac—"

"Okay, okay! Never mind that. And tell Jackie he needn't talk like that. It's bad—for him as well as you. If you say that again, you'll walk home by yourself from school. You're not going to swear like a half-breed."

"Half-breed" to Hal was merely a species of being that did certain things he himself was not allowed to do because they were "bad." Usually when talking near his elders, he was careful to avoid phrases that might catch a sensitive adult ear but then he always forgot what they had termed "bad" before. Puzzling now, no really good method of describing the thunder of the planes struck him—except Jackie's way, with a pleasurable push on the "bad" word. The furrow was cool to his toes. He curled them as he walked, leaving bunched ridges of sand behind the scoops where his toes had been. He stopped and lifted one foot carefully. Like a row of tiny pigs sucking. He ran to catch up.

"Anyway, we're gonna fly 'round in yellow planes when we're real big an' just fly an' fly. Why don't you fly, Thom?"

The difficulty Thom found in answering his brother's simple

questions always reflected to him his unstable faith. Like his elders, he believed life's answers explainable to a child; even if the answer grew more complicated as the child grew, it could never basically change, for the basic answers were known. So he said, on his confident level, "Because the people that fly those planes do nothing good with them. They fly in the war and try to kill as many people as they can. And remember what you learned in Sunday School? How the Lord Jesus said we weren't to bother anyone, but love them all, like you love Mom? We are to do good, not hurt."

"Why do they want to hurt and kill people?"

"I suppose because the others are trying to do it to them first."

"Why?"

So Thom explained as he had known it himself since he was a child, working the religious idea, among Mennonites always expressed in High German, into the unaccustomed suit of workday English. Somehow, while he was plowing, he could not suddenly speak to his small brother in the smooth German of the church, not even regarding non-resistance. "The Bible says that when men live in sin they do sinful things. They do not love but hate. They don't trust each other. They turn around quickly and hurt you when you're not looking because they care only for themselves and wish to get all they can without working for it. Finally, if they can't get away with their evil any other way, they try to kill the other person."

"Why don't the police get 'em?"

What next! Yet why not? A long-submerged argument rose in his searching mind. He spoke before he thought, sensing his deviation only as he proceeded: "Because there are whole countries of these people, and the police are few. So other countries feel they have to join together to kill those who are doing bad, so that they themselves and their families won't be hurt and killed—"

Hal did not sense his hesitation. "Does Hank Unger fly a plane to kill people so we won't be hurt and killed?"

The horses began their turn at the corner where, through the white stems of the poplars, the house looked south and east. Hank Unger. Thom pulled out his watch.

"What with snooping after Indians and watching planes and gabbing, you're late for the cows before you get to the house from school. Now move."

"Is Nance in the barn?" The question broke across Hal's serious face.

"I got her in at noon."

"Oh boy!" the lad fled over the plowed land. "An' maybe it'll rain tomorrow so I can ride to school!" He was out of hearing among the trees.

The sky was empty as a tipped cup. As the horses eased their pull edging down a small ridge, over their backs Thom could see hills of poplar and birch, with coned pines among the willows along the creek between them. There was no longer enough bush between themselves and the world. There had once been, for during the first nine years of their settlement at Wapiti when, as the English were bought out and moved away, as the breeds settled back farther into the wilderness, only an occasional RCMP officer, coming the thirty miles of dirt road from Hainy to check their passports or eventually to bring their naturalization papers, had even reminded them of the world. But now into weather and crop reports the radio blurted statistics of people killed. Children could not walk home barefoot from school without a plane shadow crossing their faces, and people like Hank Unger sent pictures of themselves casual against fighter planes with the level waste of Africa beyond and left the faith of their fathers to do—what?

There was a point of thought beyond which Thom could not go. Since Joseph Dueck had come to teach at Wapiti School the fall before, his friendship with Thom had unlocked new thought possibilities of which Thom had formerly had no conception. He had been astonished to find that, with arduous effort, he could follow most of Joseph's thinking. On a winter Sunday afternoon, as the heater glowed red and the peaceful sounds of Pa's afternoon sleeping drifted through the curtain of the bedroom door, Thom had stumbled after Joseph's rambles regarding the meaning of existence, the nature of Christianity, the Christian's relationship to his fellow men. During the week, while cleaning the cow-barn or hauling hay to the stock, he would grope through the newly-discovered labyrinth of his mind, alternately enchanted and intimidated, but, despite the varying paths he chose, he always arrived at the same ultimate point. He could no more have denied what he held to be the basic tenets of his belief than he could have straddled the sun. He was at that point again: he had been told the truth. The church—the Deacon—they knew. Believe; questions were often simplest if not answered. When the plow jerked in the earth you could truly know, but when a man went his way, the surmise of whether for good or evil, if perhaps correct, told little of why. And Joseph said the "why" was most important. But why not leave simple at the simplest? Must he always wonder and try to explain? Why not accept like Pete Block? It was probably better not to know not to have to think about it. Perhaps no one could know, anyway. Joseph! "Leave it to the fathers," he said abruptly in German. He kicked the plow-frame and flexed his cramped legs forward so that they dangled nearly to the ground. It was sheerest comfort.

His head hung, dulled from plowing all day alone with his mind. On the last round, when the horses moved with the knowledge of coming rest, he liked the earth as it unfolded itself like the roll of a filleted fish to a thin knife. Packed by the snows, it twisted free and lay open, crumbling at the edges, intruding no questions, offering itself and its power of life to the man who proved his belief with his calloused hand. And the believers went on turning its page, while round the world it was wounded to death by slashing heathen tank-tracks. Plowing, he watched the furrows turn and settle.

The best of the day for Thom was when he drove the unhitched horses towards home and, above the jingling of harness and shuffling of feet, heard the last birds chirp themselves to rest on their branches. Faintly the sounds of the world shutting itself away for another day, a dog barking, the call of a boy to his cows, a calf bawling, the slam of a screen-door, drifted on a breeze now warm on the hillock, now cool in the coulee. He turned the corner of the hay-yard with the worked horses and looked north past the edge of the barn to the house facing him on the knoll. To the right stood the summer-kitchen; tin milk-pails blinked on the points of the slab fence separating the two buildings from the yard. As he closed the wire gate behind him, he could hear the pigs oink-ing to be fed in their huge pen. When he stopped the horses by the horse-barn, he was already in the smooth groove that was "doing chores."

For the past five springs, since he had finished grade eight, Thom Wiens had followed the same evening pattern of unharnessing the horses, watering them, stacking their manger with hay, dumping chop into their boxes, filling the trough for the coming cattle. Every spring he knew his bare arms and the drip drip of the rising bucket. Except for more land to plow each year, there were few changes. Across the well-mouth, Thom could now see the bent figure of his father re-shovelling a heap of grain, his face half-covered with a red handkerchief against the formaldehyde. Thom dumped the bucket over into the trough, gripped by the consciousness that his family was carrying on their ancestors' great tradition of building homes where only brute nature had couched. Saskatchewan, in the spiraling heat of the Depression, had acted wisely in opening up this rock-strewn northern bush to the Russian Mennonites.

He caught back the bucket with about a cupful of water left, lifted it, and drank without dripping as his older brothers had taught him years before. The water tasted pure as ice.

"Thom." He turned to see his mother outside the kitchen. "We need some water."

His mother watched him a moment as he came towards her; then she turned back into the log kitchen. He was her son. To her, despite the fact that she had four sons, tall dark Thom was different and, somehow, more important at this moment than the others. She had first known this feeling of special importance with young David, when coming to Canada on the crammed ship. Then it had been Ernst in the early back-breaking years in the Wapiti district. Now David was in India, across more oceans than she could imagine, Ernst was married and had his own farm two miles away, but Thom was at that age. And she felt more than ever that she was helpless before new manhood's unshackling of itself. Thom, stooping wide-shouldered to enter the door, reaching for the water pails on the wash-stand, had little notion of the prayers breathed for him in the heat of the kitchen wood-stove. He saw the fresh bread and dropped the pail-handle, eyes searching for the knife.

"Cut the cooler one—this will burn you."

He cut a chunk carefully. "What did Carlo bark about just after dinner?" They talked in Low German. The peculiar Russian Mennonite use of three languages caused no difficulties for there were inviolable, though unstated, conventions as to when each was spoken. High German was always used when speaking of religious matters and as a gesture of politeness towards strangers; a Low German dialect was spoken in the mundane matters of everyday living; the young people spoke English almost exclusively among themselves. Thought and tongue slipped unhesitantly from one language to the other. Now, as the pale butter melted into the bread and its warm aroma rose to Thom's head, his teeth crunched through the crust as his mother answered.

"Mr Block came to collect for that new church in Alberta. Even in the busy season he always does church work first."

"We haven't anything to give now."

"We promised when the hogs go. We have to help, others helped us. And you know Mr Block; he would never leave his farm now except for the church."

"Uh-huh." With his mouth full, he heard the cow bells nearing; he picked up the pails and went out. Deacon Peter Block had been the first Mennonite to come to Wapiti : he cleared the way for the others. When he had come, the wilderness, now thinned every winter for firewood and better grazing, stood as forest, and the only settlers were several Englishmen grubbing a few acres from the fastness. The Wiens family came three years later, in 1930, and together with Block and the others who followed, formed the Wapiti Mennonite Church. Swinging the pails to his stride, Thom thought of the good land that was left. The hamlet of Calder was only twelve miles south of the church, but to the highway on the east, Poplar Lake on the west, and to the Indian reservation across the Wapiti River to the north, all around the Mennonite settlement lay virgin sections, heavily wooded, enough for children's children. And there would be more, when the last breeds were bought out.

"How much left?" his father asked, passing towards the kitchen.

"Half a day maybe. Is the disc ready to take out tomorrow morning?"

"You'll have to use the hitch from the plow—I haven't fixed the other."

A grimace flicked over Thom's face, but David Wiens had already walked beyond hearing. Forty years before, Wiens had been Thom's age, unstooped and husky, serenely at ease in the Mennonite community life of Central Russia. The upheavals of Russian life after 1917 that drove him to America with his family had wrenched him from his roots. He had lived his lifetime in Russia: his sons built the farm in Canada. For him, the Canadian bush disrupted the whole order of things, for though one could succeed with some Russian Mennonite farming methods, most past standards seemed barely authoritative. Farming villages were impossible, married children had to settle far and farther from their parents, the family was splintered, the English language intruded itself. Yet if practical difficulties alone had been involved, Wiens might have regained himself. There was more, however. In Russia behaviour for him, the last of eight boys, had always been clear: right was right and wrong was wrong. Any situation could be quickly placed into one or the other category. Here, the people scattered in the Canadian bush lived, according to accepted Mennonite standards, such nonchalantly sinful lives that when Wiens was among them, even on his infrequent visits to Calder, he felt as if the foundation of all morality was sliced from beneath him.

For Wiens, as for his third son, there was one rock in the whirlpool of the Canadian world. They were both thinking of him at the same time. Deacon Peter Block. Where even the middle-aged Pastor Lepp was at a loss, the Deacon held the church community solidly on the path of their fathers. He seemed to understand how the newness of Canada must be approached. It was at his insistence that they had bought out all the English years before, despite the deeper debt it forced upon them, that they might have a district of Mennonites. Now, there were only four breed families left, and war prices had almost cleared them of their debt.

The first cattle ambled through the gate as Thom turned with the brimming pails. He glanced at the trough. With the cattle drinking at the full sloughs, there should be enough. He walked up the path, and then he heard the rumble of approaching planes, coming from the north-east this time. There were only two, and they came roaring directly over the yard, the tiny figures of the men, one behind the other, bumped in each plane, the motors hammering. The whole yard burst into a chaos of squealing pigs, flying squawking chickens, Carlo barking, Hal screaming "Bang! Bang!" and the cattle stampeding, milk jetting from swinging udders, towards the safety of the barn to crash against its closed door in a convulsion of bodies. Wiens, Mrs Wiens, Margret before the summer-kitchen, Hal astride Nance by the gate, Thom on the well-path: they could only stare in apprehension as the cattle bunched against the cracking door. In a minute the rumble had died over the flickering poplars to the south, and then Boss, her lead-bell clanging, broke through the bunching and galloped to the trough, circling crazily as she over-ran her mark. Others followed, one by one, to drink in gasps of slurping water. Wiens, shouting Carlo to silence, strode down the path to the few still strained against the cracking door, his wife behind him, both soothing with voice and then hand. From where Thom stood, one cow looked very bad.

Godless heathen, he thought. With all the sky to fly in, to come messing here twice on one day! He could see Pa feeling Nellie slowly. Her calf would be dead after that. Nowhere was there peace from them; after you were nineteen you could be sure it was coming. Pete Block's came when he was twenty. The judge would not feel that his staying home would be necessary: they did not have enough land. But to Thom's thinking that aspect of war was of no significance at the moment. He thought, If it comes on Friday, I will go to court on the day and say with the same conviction as Deacon Block's son, "It is against my conscience!" In the spirit and in the faith of the fathers. Murdering heathen!

CHAPTER TWO

It was almost summer, and Thom received no call.

The far shore of Poplar Lake slid a thin line between water and sky. With the breeze on the lifting lake, the sunlight darted up at Thom in broken pieces wherever he looked. They spoke no word while fishing, except in the tumult of the catch. Holding the bamboo binder-whip he used for a pole, he reached his long arm under his seat for the can and dipped out the seeping water, careful not to disturb the balance of the stubby boat. Pete rowed steadily, the line tied to his belt, stark feet flat in the sloshing water. Pete rowed every year: he never had his own tackle.

At the prow of the boat Ernst hissed, "He's hooked!"

Pete shipped oars and leaned back to grip Ernst's twitching willow-pole. Ernst's hands clenched the taut line and he pulled the fish hand over hand. Thom watched him, the line flipping back without tangle, and then he turned to see the pike break surface behind them, mouth plowing, to vanish again. Ernst muttered, "He's big. And going deep." For an instant the line was slack. The fish was going down off the rim of the bench along which they had been trolling, down to get ahead of the hook, but if caught well it could not escape and Ernst grinned as the line dripped stiffly again.

The fish came up hard, fighting with body and fins and mouth. Just alongside, it gave one last desperate slash, maw cavernous, and then Ernst's great hand clamped down on the middle of the speckled back. He held its twists aloft like a triumph, working with the pliers to get the hook free.

"Biggest of the lot. Look at that jaw! Hit it so hard he got it right back between the gill. Look how his eye moves—ha! Caught it right into the back of his eye! Greedy ol' brute." Thom saw the staring eyeball jiggle in the ridged head. Ernst said, "Well," and held the fish against a rib of the boat. He lashed twice with the pliers, expertly, and the fish twitched. After a moment the hook was free.

Ernst leaned to the water, washing his hands, contented. "That's eleven now. It's enough." Pete grasped one oar and turned in a tight circle.

Thom waggled his pole, having forgotten it in the excitement. "I'll leave mine out a bit."

"Pull mine in," Pete said.

"You're just like David was, Thom. Always the last in the boat and once you're fishing, you won't take in your line until you catch some kid's toe. 'Member how excited he got that last year and we were in on shore before he thought of his line and we had to shoo everybody away so he could get his hook in."

Thom laughed. "Sitting still for two hours in the boat always oiled his tongue for the rest of the day too."

"That was the last year he was home, eh?"

"Yah," said Pete. "I came with you next year."

"At least you do all the work for us now."

"Huh! It's your line."

Thom thought of the Deacon. It was typical of him that he had bought a truck anyone could use as needed, but he would not "waste" money on a fishing line. Such a—Thom could only think of "strong"—man. His thought slid away, in musing wonder at this one man's aggressive edge, his eyes vacant over the bleached water, when abruptly he comprehended the two other boats returning from the open lake to the west.

The short white-sand curve of bay enclosed by Cree Point merged bleakly to rocks. The women and older men, gathered this first Friday of June for the annual Wapiti-Beaver Schools picnic, lounged in the pine shade above the rocks while children shouted in the shallows. As the boat neared, Mrs Wiens and Mrs Block turned from their blazing fire in its ring of blackened stones. Hal came staggering through the water, "How many? How many?" slowing only as the sand-bottom faded into the rocks. Ernst stepped out; with a last heave from Pete, they were up and handing fish to the eager hands of the women. The June sun shone.

Margret, slim in her white dress, came down the trail through the pines with Elizabeth Block. Looking up, Thom felt a somehow nameless sorrow push in him at Elizabeth's squandered womanhood. Not actually squandered, he thought, for she seemed never to really have lived it. Neglected, rather. Why had she never married? She was at least ten years older than Margret; she worked always: the hard drudging labour of men, yet work never seemed to interest her beyond the point of its immediate necessity. As far back as Thom could recall, she had appeared exactly as now, dumpy, uninvolved, oddly wasted. As he handed up the last fish, his mother's gentle smile touched him. He remembered her words to him once on a last summer's evening when she stood in the kitchen door, sweat like jewels on her face and neck, the whiff of saskatoons boiling on the stove, and Elizabeth driving by on the road with a great hayload, rolling listlessly with the bumps, barely caring to wave: "That poor girl needs children. She's dying of old age and not thirty-five. At her age I had all of you except Helmut." Now, Margret ran towards the glistening fish, but Elizabeth stood afar, rounded as with weathering, all the bloom gone.

There was a tremendous shout and all turned to watch the other two boats in their race for the shore. Joseph Dueck, the Wapiti teacher, rowed to break the oars, Herman Paetkau mock-paddled with his hands, while Louis Moosomin, his position as Block's hired man forgotten, balancing in the stern, whooped to the world's echo. But the other boat was the sight: young Franz Reimer rowing, the Rempel twins laughing, and above all the yells of the watchers, Herb Unger's bellows, "C'mon, Franz, let's *go*, let's *go*!" The spectators screamed, "Head for the beach—the rocks here—the beach!" and the startled turn of the rowers, the hasty double-handed pull on one oar, and then the final effort with all the shouts coming as, with a roar, Herb leaped into the shallow water to hurl a tremendous heave against his boat in despair at not grounding first. But the other boat had run up with a lunge that sent Louis sprawling over Joseph in a welter of tackle and sloshing fish; the heavier boat followed on the instant with the twins laughing open-mouthed while Franz's gasps choked him into collapse over the oars.

"Not fair!" Herb was wading the last few yards, soaked to the hips. "They only had three! Besides, Franz is hardly used to his wife's cookin' yet."

Mary Reimer, white with apprehension, had run forward towards the boats but now halted abruptly in the roar that surrounded her, the memory of her wedding two weeks before written in blushes on her gentle face. Old Mrs Martens said in Low German, beside Thom, "With that Franz she'll have to get used to it. He'll do what he always has—if she sits worrying her pretty eyes out or not. When Martens was young he—"

Her voice was swallowed in the mass of the people surging forward to survey the tangled boats and aid, or impede, unloading. The family men remained aloof, as usual, watching from under the pines, arms crossed behind their backs. Only old Mr Reimer limped across the hard sand on his frost-stumped feet. "What a race! What a race! Like two stallions fighting to reach the chop-crib first! And look at the fish!" Food for the taking was ever a marvel to the Mennonites after the Russian famine of 1921-22. The old man stood near the boat, eyes shining, water inching to and fro at his boots.

Herb was shouting at the crowding half-naked bodies, "Gwan, you kids, you just get in the road here. Beat it!" while stringing his fish. The children eddied away towards their teacher. Herb looked up as Thom peered into the boat. "We got nine. You?"

"Eleven."

Herb's face darkened. "Lucky. But wait—we'll get you in the ball game after noon."

Against an inward prompting to drop the subject, quickly, Thom muttered, "We never wanted to beat you. Eleven's enough for us to eat."

"Course not. Did it just naturally, without thinkin'" Herb's voice spaded up sarcasm. "Your call 'll come naturally too—without you thinkin'. Just wait."

Thom knew then he should let it lie. Beyond the cheapness of a quarrel was the fact that Herb was older: he really belonged in Ernst's age-group. No man with his own farm, though a bachelor, bickered with anyone in his teens, yet the five years between them egged on Thom's answer; suddenly struck with the pettiness of the other's ire, and not to be outdone in wit, he spoke, and knew as soon as the words left his tongue that they were not witty, only malicious: "At least *you* needn't worry—you beat me there." For he could not keep his glance from sliding down to where Herb's ugly feet showed clear through the flicker of riled water: the flat feet that, despite a tough body and sharpshooting skill, forced Herb home; neither Air Force nor Navy nor Army would accept him. And Hank flying round the world, the younger brother by three years.

"At least I didn't sit around till they ordered me to report, and then hid behind my Pa's pants!" It was a hiss of rage.

"I know." And as Thom turned away he knew that even the last two words had the wrong inflection. Why did I go near his boat, he cringed. To quarrel with him, who does not hold to the belief of the fathers, who flaunts his scorn of all that is decent. To squabble about two fish! Heavenly Father, help me from myself.

The slap on his back shocked through him. Franz, his thin face gleaming above the sopping shirt, was beside him, wife hooked on his arm. "Sorry, Thom, that's a bit harder than I meant. Smell those frying fish! Let's go eat—I'm so hungry I could eat a horse between two mattresses."

Mary's laugh rang above the crowd.

The lake was immense about them like the sky; the black storm above had knocked them so long it seemed they had always been beaten bruisingly. The others had vanished; he alone was left to the waves' heave and drop, when he awoke and found someone shaking him. Thom sat up quickly in the surprise that after such a storm he should have to go for the cows, when he sensed the smell of the pine low above him, the lake beyond drained white in the sun, and then he comprehended that it was Pete and not Mom whose hand gripped his shoulder.

"The kids'll soon be through their ball-game. It's time we warmed up."

"Okay." Thom lay back on the moss, the quarrel crouched like blackness on the rim of his conscience. He stretched fiercely, arms grazing the gnarled roots, and then rolled out from under the tree. "Nice to sleep in the daytime, no work to bother. Thought for a minute it was morning and you were Mom waking me to get the cows."

The comfort of Pete was that he spoke just enough to suffice; if a grin would do, there was never a word. On a clear morning as the world began to stir, Thom felt that comfort when he heard Pete's thin whistle a mile away and the bark of his dogs starting the cattle from their cud. But now, the lake recalled the school picnic.

"Who's ahead?"

"Beaver School—127 to 103. Depends on the ball-game—winner gets forty-five points. Joseph's 5-3-1 point system sure is better than what we used to do. Every kid really wants that shield for his school."

"After lunch I just stayed for that race Hal was in—too tired. Of all the silly mornings for the cows to get out of the pasture. They know when you want to get through fast."

They had walked across the narrow neck of the Point from the fishing beach and now could hear the shouts of the children at ball in the clearing up the bank from the flat of sand used for racing. In the final turn of the road before the clearing, the dark pines leaned in the breeze against an occasional poplar or blanched birch. It was peaceful. Only the poking cry of a flicker in flight, or the jerk and scramble of a scolding squirrel, and the calls of the children far away. They passed teams of horses, dreaming by the wagons under the trees with barely a stamp of feet or shake of a head to show them alive to the droning flies. Then they saw the booth between the tree-trunks and the brightness of people beyond.

Pete said, unexpectedly. "It'd be nice to just stay in the bush—never go out."

After a moment, "Yah. Alone."

"No one to bother you."

They came to the poplar-pole booth, silent in agreement at the known impossibility. Old Lamont, bending among his cartons, straightened up as they neared and stood on the edge of the shade. Two years before, "Ol' Lamont's broke because of drink!" had startled the community. Block had bought the store then, but no man could be spared from work, so the Scot had to continue running it, albeit without liquor. Seeing the cherry radish-face, Thom remembered Hal's disappointment when, just after the "broke" news, they had gone for the mail and the old man had been quite usual in appearance. "Huh," Hal had scorned, "he's not even bent!"

"Not much left, young misters. Should ha' been here earlier when the boxes were fu'—ay, and I had the two prettiest girls in Saskatchewan helping me then—you missed it a'." The crumbled old voice dropped into confidence. "But I was waitin' for ye. I've got two bars left—the verra best, like before the War," and to the wonder of the boys, he pulled out two O-Henry bars. "Ye ha' to pay ten cents, but they're the real stuff."

"It was nice of you to remember us." Thom smiled at the friendly face.

They left the booth, the two bars in their pockets for after the game, chewing on the imitation gum. Gum and picnics were inseparable. "Tastes like truck inner-tube," Pete said.

"Probably would, if we had any to chew."

They neared the group of older men, under a clump of poplars, whose red-wristed hands hung awkward in idleness. Thom knew instinctively what they conversed about. After reviewing the parched spring, the War and politics would receive their ponderous attention. The men agreed on all matters, their opinions on any occurrence outside their own community being formed by general surveys of one Mennonite German weekly and by what Deacon Block told them. Block spoke English fluently and his business took him as far as North Battleford. The War intrigued the Mennonites, partly because they saw it as the culmination of world evil from which they had strictly, consciously, severed themselves, partly because Germany was the storm centre. In the 1920's Germany had been their stepping stone from the tyranny they fled in Russia (few considered that

Nazi Germany had little in common with the Hindenburg regime), but more than that, their own language told them that some 400 years before their own fathers had been German—and Dutch, which heritage they retained in their Low German dialect. They were honestly horrified at Hitler's ravage of Europe, but beneath often lurked the suspicion: "Only a German could set the whole world on its tail like this."

Joseph had once called Thom's attention to this undercurrent in Mennonite thinking. "Though Mennonites, because of their training, naturally abhor violence, yet they faintly admire it, somehow, in someone who without thought 'hews to it'! And if Germans are involved, this unconscious admiration is even bolstered a bit by our almost nationalistic interest in Germany. After all, we are displaced Germans, at least ethnically, and because we haven't had a true home for 400 years, we subconsciously long for one. It will take this war to knock any silly German ideas out of our heads." Joseph had laughed his big laugh, but not as if he were amused. "You'd be surprised how different some Mennonites in the south and in Manitoba sound now, compared to the middle thirties! They had no idea what Hitlerism was about."

Remembering Joseph's words, Thom listened hard as he and Pete passed the elderly men, but they were talking again of the weather: the abnormal drought that threatened to choke the barely germinated seed. Block was saying, "Burns Company said pigs should go up to about fifteen, maybe even sixteen dollars. Beef about seventeen. If we get rain in a week, we'll get a bumper, but . . ."

Then they were in the sunlight, beyond hearing, walking side by side. Thom looked across the diamond scurrying with children to where the tents of the Indians, camped at the Point for fishing, blinked between the trees. Dark, ragged forms squatted in groups or moved lanquidly among the tethered horses, far from the Mennonites, watching the children's game in rooted bush-like silence. Mennonites, when they passed nearby, stared as they would at any good land that needed clearing.

The spectators around the backstop exploded into cheers.

The ball flew far over the fielders' heads to send them dashing frantically as a dark boy raced around first base. Jackie Labret, in Grade three, though old enough for twice that. Joseph had once mentioned his initial wonder at the slowness of the non-Mennonite children, but winter had shown the teacher more than he wanted to know. In the cold when all moose moved across the river and rabbits supplied the only meat, existence, not study, became the problem for the Métis children. Their parents had no concept of planned farming: they ate until there was no more. Labrets, Razins, Mackenzies and Moosomins, the last the worst. Only a few Mennonites ever neared the Moosomin homestead, and they never went inside the four-walled shack or knew the mixture of common-law wives and husbands and children that were crammed there. Breeds lived as they lived: they were part of unchangeable Canada for the Mennonites. They associated, to a limited extent, only with Louis Moosomin, and that because in the war-shortage Block had hired him. Thom could see Louis standing with the men behind the Métis women, clean among their grimed gaudiness. Lean Herman Paetkau beside him was the only Mennonite on that side of the diamond. The two were talking, heads close, and Thom's mind hovered for an instant over the day last February when he had, in his hunting, happened unexpectedly on Herman's farm and —but he had promised Herman not to speak or even think of it. Let them find out. But it was four months now, and still no one —Thom turned sharply from his thoughts.

Jackie Labret had raced home to the cheers of all Wapiti and the children swarmed everywhere across the field. The game was over. As the two youths stepped among the people, the chatter of languages enveloped them. Across the diamond, Mrs Labret was calling to Jackie in Cree; a girl tripped over Mrs Unger's feet and stopped to apologize in High German; some older women stood in a tight circle whispering obviously in Low German; and then Thom heard a quiet voice say in English, "It's best that Wapiti School won the shield this first time. It was Mr Dueck's idea." Thom looked about and saw the profile of Annamarie Lepp as she gazed towards home plate where the children pushed around Joseph and Miss Friesen. The girls in their white print frocks looked like flowers, spread on the grass surrounding Annamarie, but hers was the only voice that reached clear beyond the pauseless titter that seemed to hover over them. He had not before noticed that, in contrast to the others, she seemed different. Her eyes were now on Block, who as head trustee was handing the shield to the Wapiti school children, his big voice unstumbling, though accented, on the English expressions. She looked at peace. He did not hear a word Block said, and later he could not remember a single detail about her, not even the form of her face. He did not seem to see what she looked like, rather he saw her, and he abruptly felt a lifetime would not be long enough to forget.

Pete jogged his arm. "Come on. We're next," and Thom jerked self-consciously, then followed through the crowd to where the wire backstop hung sagging from the leaning poles. The voice of Franz Reimer was announcing, "The final event of the afternoon: men's ball-game! Former Wapiti students against former Beaver!" And, always adding his bit, "Beaver won last year—can they do it again?"

"You betcher boots!" Herb Unger bellowed from somewhere beyond the backstop. Thom's mind stumbled against the remembered quarrel, but then Pete tossed a ball at him and he gratefully backed up the familiar distance, concentrating on the rhythm of pitching. With many gone in Alternative Service work, despite several young married men playing, the breeds made almost half the team. They were good players: despite his gun-shot limp, Louis was better than any Mennonite on their team; but it was not as it had once been.

Thom, pitching steadily now, could hardly have imagined how smoothly his thoughts slipped into traditional ways when he thought without concentrating. Occasionally, after long mulling and searching, when concentration would cause only more problems, he was wearily resigned to let tradition suffice. The War spoiled everything. Even Beaver's team, where they had no breeds, was half Russian and Pole. The poor white stuff that clung along the edges of Beaver district, as the breeds along Wapiti, could not have made a decent living anywhere. They too would be bought out when the men returned from camps.

That kind of people always sold when they got half a price, at the sight of bare money; so quickly forgetful of the agony of scrubbing; so ever hopeful of somewhere finding land where they would prosper like the successful neighbour they had long watched longingly; so ever clustered about by children whose goggle-eyes stared from their faces. As the older men hinted sometimes, it was God's judgement upon these godless people who never went to church, whose only pleasure was home-brew and bad whisky when they could get it, that they should wander destitute. The Bible clearly said of the righteous man that "whatsoever he doeth shall prosper." The Mennonites surveyed their own growing fields and sleek cattle. When you live decently, do not waste your money and health on tobacco, whisky, dancing, shows, fancy clothes, then prosperity comes. "Children, stay frugal and decent." Even in his most doubtful moments, Thom could not see how there might be a better formula for life.

"Let's go, men," Franz was shouting. "Wapiti takes the field."

"Okay, Pete," Thom said. "If I've got anything I better not throw it away here."

"You're all right. The only pitcher we've got."

"Thanks a lot!"

Ernst met them at home-plate. The team had practised several evenings and now Ernst just said, "Okay, let's go." They scattered to their positions, Pete pounding the one glove into shape while settling himself behind the plate.

Joseph Dueck stood by the pitcher's box to umpire the game, grinning at Thom as the latter approached. It was not Joseph's attendance at University that made him so odd: they had had teachers in Wapiti with a year of University before. Rather, despite his strong belief in the truth of the Bible, you could not depend on him to behave traditionally. He and Herman had gone fishing with Louis Moosomin seemingly without thinking about it. Herman had done what he had done, but the teacher?

Thom, wriggling his feet for the right set, felt Joseph lean over his shoulder and heard his quiet voice, with the smile in it, "I will not speak to you for two weeks if you lose this game. And I am not giving you two cents' worth of help."

"Okay. Just call Beaver the same way."

"Right! But a tie goes to them. You can take it, Herb can't."

Thom wheeled. "He started it this morning by the boats."

"And it bothers you. You can't fight him like that. I told you the other evening that antagonism won't do." Joseph was the only man in Wapiti tall enough to look Thom straight in the eye. The gentle smile spread over Joseph's strong, rather ugly, tanned face, up into the black-bushed eyebrows and hair. Thom did not smile.

"I got mad."

"Yes." Joseph's voice leaped, "Pla-a-y ba-a-all!"

Thom turned to face the plate. Herb Unger, the Beaver catcher, stood poised, his bat tracing a tight circle over his right shoulder. Pete's glove was just beyond Herb's belt buckle. Thom gripped the ball for his fastest pitch and, in the silence of the crowd, he hurled it. There was a crack, the ball shot past him in a streak as the crowd erupted; Herb lumbered around Louis at first and hit Franz hard to jar him off second as Jacq Moosomin threw the ball in swiftly from centre. Franz hung on and scrambled up as Herb gestured for third.

"Nice, Thomas." Herb's grin was cold as he stamped the wooden block that was second. Franz threw the ball in and Thom faced Jake Rempel. It would be tough.

And it was, though he gloried in the feel of the ball and the sting of the bat at contact. The bat always hefted as light as a straw, and each time his turn came the power in his limbs assured him he could knock the ball into the lake that gleamed beyond through a straggle of trees; but it was never so simple, and when Wapiti came up for its last inning, Beaver was ahead, 8 to 7. By then his whole arm and shoulder ached from the pitching, and he was despairing of the two runs that would win the game. But Jacq finally hit a good one along the first-base line into the shrubs and raced home before Moses Labashi could find it. The score tied, both Harry Razin and Jim Mackenzie popped out, but Pete lashed a screamer past Menno Giesbrecht at short and when the dust and shouts eased away, stood on second with a smile almost wider than his wide face. The winning run was in the balance as Thom came to bat.

He had often, as he worked long hours in the field, planned what he would do in various situations. In softball, concentration was what mattered. A single and the game was won, for Pete would be off with the pitch. As he stepped to the plate, he knew exactly what had to be done and, despite his shoulder, knew he could do it.

The Rempel twins had switched; John was now pitching, with Jake on first. John's pitch, he knew from long experience, had a weird up-shoot. Unless absolutely certain, it was best to let the first pitch go by, and he stared hard at John's motion, pushing all else from his mind, and saw the ball approach in swiftness, rising as it came. It was a good pitch, and Joseph barked "Strike!" as the crowd answered. Only then did Thom hear Herb, crouched behind him. It was as if the catcher had been muttering for a long time, not now chattering the ball-banter for all to hear. It was a phrase repeated over and over without pausing even for the throwing back of the ball. Thom would not allow his mind to hear as he fixed on John's deliberate motions, but for an instant he felt almost savagely that if Joseph were umpiring behind him, Herb would not dare mumble what made no sense. He would not allow his mind to think of it as the ball left John's hand. Then he knew it was the same pitch and he shifted his shoulders and swung straight and level, just a bit higher than usual to spike the ball between first and second, and even as he brought the bat around with the aimed swing of his body, he felt it glance up hard off the thick catcher's glove to top the ball in a dribbler that John had picked up before he broke from the swing.

It burst in Thom like an explosion: he made no futile gesture for first. All he knew was his flaming mind and his yelling "Interference! Interference! He hit my bat with his glove, the—" and he swung round to Herb, who stood back a few steps, a half-grin on his face, arms hanging easily, waiting. Thom felt the bat in his grip. He wished it was a steel club that he could crash across the grinning mockery still soundlessly framing the phrase, "Hide behind your Pa's pants," which he knew he had heard and comprehended from the very beginning. Wood would do. He could already sense the smash of the bat as he swung when Joseph's great hands clamped his wrists. "Thom! Drop it!"

It was gone as quickly. At Joseph's grip he dropped the bat like a brand. He stiffened, aghast at what he had already committed in his mind and the flashing joy of that committal. He could have sunk with gladness beyond earth into oblivion. But he had to stand there, before them all.

"Thom! What's wrong?" Ernst's concern was bare in his voice. Joseph opened his grip as the other players ran up. Herb stood, silent.

"Okay, men. A hot game and frayed tempers. Nothing serious. Now, what happened, Thom?" Joseph inquired calmly. Then, "Have you a complaint to make against Herb?"

Joseph was dependable. "No—no complaints."

Block came pushing between them, his big voice covering even the question in Ernst's eyes. "What's going on here? Get the game finished—we have to get home to the chores."

"The game is over, I believe, Mr Block," said Joseph, still calm. Miss Friesen came up, her score sheet fluttering. Joseph checked the paper and then announced clearly: "The ball-game is over. Final score: Wapiti 8, Beaver 8. We'll have to wait till next year to break the tie."

There was disappointed cheering and the crowd broke reluctantly. Block looked at Thom oddly for a moment where he stood, half turned from Herb, and then faced Pete coming slowly from third. Thom did not wish to think of their thoughts, for no one could have failed to see his exhibition. The other players slapped him on the back with varying remarks of "A good game, Thom," and moved away. Pete did not say anything. They were all going.

He looked back at Herb, bending over to pick up the two bats, and he said, "I'm sorry." Herb's eyes said nothing as he straightened up, bats on shoulder, and Thom turned finally, the hopeless inadequacy of words like a boulder in his stomach. Then Herb walked past him and said in a tone only he could hear, without any expression whatever, "Gutless."

Franz was shouting in High German from a bench, "Remember, all young people who possibly can are to stay here for a lunch and the young people's program after by the lakeshore. We have a good program planned. Mr Dueck will speak on non-resistance, a topic of very great importance to us today. Please stay if you can arrange for your parents to do the chores." Laughter sprang up from the scattered groups.

His mother touched his arm. "Thomas?"

"It's all right, Mom." He never could keep anything from her long, and she knew as well as he that it was by no means "all right." Some time, when they would be together alone and not saying anything, because their experience of each other was hardly ever a matter of spoken words, he would talk. He was suddenly conscious of a unique statement she had made once, her hands kneading bread dough, "Sometimes you have to do something just so you can finally master yourself doing it. You cannot avoid everything. Sometimes it is merely running away when you should stay to overcome." To master yourself!

Now she said only, "We want to go home with the Lepps so you and Margret and Annamarie can stay for the evening. But where's Hal?"

He recalled his small brother; that he had last seen him at the race where, to Hal's boundless chagrin, a little Russian girl from Beaver had struck the finish line just before him. "I haven't seen him—he wasn't hollering during the game," and then he thought of Two Poles and his son Hankey. "Maybe he's with that little Indian fella, like last year."

"Yes, and all the lice I dug out of his hair and clothes! If they've been in that tent again—" the distaste in her voice recalling all the vermin-plagued years of Russia, but her face lifted at the shout behind them.

"Mom! Thom!" Hal was running towards them through the trees, knocking with a peeled stick, a small ragged shape behind him. Explanations flew. "We've been watchin' beavers—we saw three biggest ones! Hankey took me—we lay right on the dam, under the bush—man!" He panted up, his happiness a beacon. "We just watched 'em. Sneaked right up an' then one came swimmin' with a log an' ate it against the dam an' another came —I think it came from the house 'cause there's a big pile o' logs an' mud an' Hankey said it was the beaver house. They live right up inside with the door under water."

"Why can't you stay here with the others? You always want Mr Dueck to take the school on a picnic, and when you do have one, you run off into the bush with—" and she glanced up at the tattered boy standing beyond the back-stop, awed by her whiteness, understanding her tone well, "—Hankey."

"Mom, aren't there any candies left at all?" Realization dawned pitifully in Hal's voice.

Thom felt a softness inside his shirt pocket; the chocolate bar, spongy from the heat of playing. He took the yellow package, walked to the back-stop post, and cut the bar in half against it with his pocket knife.

"They handed them out before—when you weren't here. We're driving home. Now come." Their mother turned to where the wagons were already coming one by one along the trail. Hal turned to wave with childhood's quick forgetfulness. "'Bye, Hankey," and then his eyes glazed with adoration as Thom gave him half the smudgy package. "Oh boy!" There was nothing to be added to the afternoon. "Oh boy!"

Thom turned and stepped toward the Indian boy. "Come on, Hankey, have a piece of chocolate bar." But the straggle-haired child sidled away at the motion. Hankey did not look up; he looked as if he were staring into the bush and had a great deal to do there; as if it were quite accidental that the distance between them remained the same. He had not looked up since longingly watching Thom cut the bar in two against the post. Thom could hear the shouts of people behind him in the trees, the rattle of harness, the creak of wagons. They were alone in the clearing. How can I give it to him, he thought. I should be helping with the program—that's the least I can do after all my stupidity. Suddenly he placed the bar on a stump sticking up before him. "It's for you, Hankey." There was no motion or sound from the small figure looking steadily away as if no grown-up existed. Thom turned to where the others had disappeared, and then he saw the straight outline of Two Poles standing in worn blue denims, tall, with arms folded across the leather shirt, just beyond the dusty diamond. It was startling to see him there with the falling sunlight on half his face, without a stir of his coming, like a spirit materializing. Thom hesitated, no speakable word forming in his mind, yet, having seen Two Poles, to just walk away— He gestured. "It's for Hankey." That seemed worse than nothing at all. He wheeled and strode across the clearing, the straight look still in his mind, finding the strangest thought forming in his head. At the edge of the trees he glanced back.

He could see the yellow wrapper of the bar on the stump, and beyond, the figure of Hankey, dwarfed by the bush he was still peering into. On the other side, the arrow-like figure of Two Poles, gazing at him, motionless in the fading sunlight against the shivering poplars. It was the strangest thought Thom could imagine. Perhaps it would be better living in a community with a man named Two Poles than with a man named Unger.

CHAPTER THREE

The two horses had reluctantly passed the corner where Wapiti School looked south, its front windows glazed in the first light of the moon, when the strangeness of what they were doing edged into understanding in Thom. The day, long anticipated, had reeled past, soaking him in weariness. They had dropped Pete where the Block driveway wound stark into the trees, his "'Night!" fading after them to the "last-mile" trot of Star and Duster. The horses snuffed deeply in the spruce air where the roadway skirted the muskeg just before home. When the team halted at the home-gate, both he and the girls, whose murmured talk had never hesitated, abruptly realized he should have turned north at the store-corner to take Annamarie home first. He sat in his haziness, but Margret clambered over the wheel, "Never mind— I'll walk to the house. You take Annamarie home."

So he sawed the horses, their heads and bodies heavy in protest, round to the north. Lax, he watched the spokes twirl against the road-sand in the last spray of sunlight over the north-west cloud-fringe.

That hovering sun was gone now. They were beyond the Mennonite farms, beyond even the trail to the Razin homestead, and only a mile from the crest of the valley where the bow of the Wapiti River could be seen. It seemed an eon ago that she had raised her head as they neared her driveway and asked, in her quiet voice, "Are you tired, Thom?" and his unthinking answer, "No, not a bit."

It was the first word they had spoken, alone. She had laughed,

"I'll believe you." Then she added, as if they had driven like this every day of their lives, "Have you seen the Wapiti at night? It's just three miles—let's go!"

His "Okay" had been the instinctive agreement he always proffered when he could not lever his mind to reason, but now he grew aware of the world. Though they were on a road-allowance, the road, wound within its limits to avoid swamps and dry mud-holes, twisted tightly through the canyon of poplars, moonlight a burnished roof above. The harness squeaked on the hanging air, the buggy-dash was damp to his touch. Suddenly it struck him, though he had never driven like this with a girl, that silence was not always necessary. Joseph would have known a story to fit this evening. Thinking of Joseph riding to the picnic, he asked, happy to anticipate her voice again, "Does Joseph drive with you ever besides going to church?"

"He says he likes to be independent. Father had quite an argument when he came last fall about his riding to church alone. He finally gave in there, but otherwise he never has. Grey's smooth as a rocker, he says. It must be nice to ride wherever you like, when you please. Sometimes on Saturdays he takes his binoculars and a sandwich and stays away all day. Just watching animals."

It was when she drew in her whole family with the word "father" that he realized that his bare-faced question could have been answered quite differently. As this ran through his mind in embarrassment, he could not but believe that unconsciously he had asked the other question also, though he could never have asked it now, having once thought of it.

She added, after a pause, "Joseph told me once that if I ever wanted to see a beautful sight, I should go see the Wapiti under the moon. But you know how far a girl can go."

He had not thought about it. Once past fifteen and grade eight, girls stayed home with their mothers and took care of the farmyard. They visited their friends on Sunday, when there were fathers or brothers to drive them. When, rarely, work was done, he himself rode around where he wished, but women were always at home, working, there to return to when one was hungry and cold. Perhaps they too liked the creek ranting its brief spring life away in the hay-meadow—or moonlight on the Wapiti.

"I suppose girls—women—" his confusion bogged him, "you—don't get much chance to get to see things, if you want. The horses are always used—it's no fun—" He sounded like a five-year-old to himself.

"Who has time? Mennonite women belong in the home, so they say. And I rather think that that's a better place than many others one reads about, or hears about on the radio. Ten years from now, it will probably be changed with us too. Now, even men aren't so free. When do you ever get away from Wapiti? Others—they're waiting for the call-up or have been hauled into bush camps that they can't leave. Cornie writes that it gets pretty bad, sometimes. But not as bad as Normandy, I should think."

"Did you hear it too?"

"Yes."

The horses jerked the buggy up a short ditch into the open moonlight of the federal forestry road drawn like a knife-slit across the bush between the highway to the east and Poplar Lake to the west. On the rise beyond Poplar Creek, a finger against the sky, was the fire lookout. The trail to the bluff yawned before. Then they were over: the tree-gloom swallowed them again.

Her "yes" echoed his remembrance. He had been picking stones last Tuesday and at supper, before they milked, the news had come. It had been in the air all day, but they had heard reports that evening as supper grew cold: "The time of waiting is over; the invasion of France is taking place before my eyes here on the Normandy coast. The War is at last crossing the English Channel to the Germans. As I speak . . ." The reporter spoke almost calmly, for behind the thin film of his voice blared the sounds of war, the whining, the roars, the explosions, the splashing, the staccatos, the drones, and sometimes, far away, a scream. There was no need for dramatic speech. Occasionally, when the sounds drowned all, the reporter could say nothing. It seemed beyond comprehension to sit at supper in a log farmhouse in Canada and listen while men, at that very moment, tore each other for reasons none really knew; to listen while a landing craft exploded, and the voice of the announcer choked, "—out of the sky—parts of bodies falling—masses of water . . ." Then the report had been cut abruptly and he had gone out, his mind clogged, the white faces of the family staring soundlessly after him. She had listened too. A whole world listening to men killing themselves savagely.

A marvellous invention, radio.

They were almost there, and he stopped the team by the scarred poplar. "We'll walk from here: can't drive farther." As he slid over the wheel she said quickly,

"You've been here before."

"Yes." Star nuzzled him like a question as he tied the halter shank about the ribbed tree, and he murmured, rubbing the grey forehead, "Home soon, we'll be home soon." He wondered as he stood there if Joseph would have talked as he did about non-resistance, before the invasion. Undoubtedly.

"Listen!" She was at Duster's head. "The frogs!" The night was full of them, like the stars in the narrow rift above them in the trees.

"Come," he said, and led the way down what was now only a footpath, her quick steps padding behind him. The tangle grew flush to the valley rim and he stood aside at the last turn under the jack-pine. "You go ahead. Just four steps around this bush. No more."

Her narrow face looked up at him, grin roguish, but then she stepped by, her paces exaggerated, tolling her unbelief. "One—two—three—fo—" He was directly behind her as she gasped.

It was best by moonlight. For miles the trees hemmed like walls, only the narrow road over the rock-rumped earth and the wriggling path of the sky above. Then, as if wiped by a cosmic hand, the brush was gone, the ground plunged away to the valley floor, the sky stretched beyond seeing, and the earth spread hugely below. Beyond a line of trees, like shrubbery in the depth, lay the immense wanness of the muddy river, emerging from nowhere under the thin north-west moon to enfold an island prickly with spruce and fade to the north-east in the half-light as if it had never been. Across the Wapiti, rising ever-rising hills of the Cree Reservation were sketched against the stars. Though at their very feet, all was unreal as a misty picture.

"It's unbelievable."

They had been standing he did not know how long. Her voice was awed. A breeze stirred the poplars and the branches of the pine like an organ.

"Fifteen years—and never saw it."

"What?" he said, not understanding.

"Oh, I've seen the valley—from the road down Poplar Creek and below at the ford. Never here, under the moon."

To live three miles away for fifteen years and not to see this! It was incomprehensible to them both.

"Anyway," she said, "you never know what you've missed." The river below them, a vista opened in their minds: what else had they missed and were they missing at this moment?

Abruptly she said, "Where are the frogs?"

"Probably the old gravel-pit they used for the cut-line—just back a bit through the trees."

"Let's go there."

"There's nothing to see, really."

"We can hear them, close."

"Okay. It's best along the edge." He led to the east, walking along the fringe of the valley. The brush flexed, tense to push them off. "Watch," he said, holding back a branch, and she came close to him, breathing quickly, holding her long skirt narrow about her. Her brown hair shadowed the happiness on her face. "We better go through the bush—it's scratchy, but we can't fall two hundred feet." The branch swished back over her head. "It thins soon."

She laughed behind him in the trees. "What would you say to Dad and Mom if I got pushed into the valley?"

"I guess then we better stay away from it." Her banter at his shyness made him forget it.

Then the bush faded to scrawny trees and they could walk side by side. He could think of nothing except the beauty of the evening and the wonder of her presence. The world was alight with it. There was even enough breeze to chasten the mosquitoes. Abruptly they encountered a truck-road, once used, now brush-grown like the ancient rocks. Its ruts sloped into the earth, and soon they emerged in the abandoned pit, shallow but huge, a gnarled pine pointing over the rim here and there, the gravel gouged beneath their feet. Walking carefully, he led her over a small ridge in the pit, and before them gleamed a flat level of water. The only sound was their breathing, the wind-sigh, and the frogs.

After a moment, he said, "If you throw a stone into the water, they'll stop right away."

"Huh-uh," her voice doubted him.

"Sure. Watch!" and before her "Oh, don't!" could deter, he stooped and in the motion flipped a fist-sized stone into the inlet at their feet. Only a deep croak near them ceased; the rest went on as though no sound had splashed on the night.

"Can't even depend on the frogs, eh?" she laughed past him, peering at the half-hidden pool. "But you spoiled the nicest one. Such a lovely bass. He sounded like the one in the quartet in church with Reverend Goertzen in April."

He laughed. "But they should all have stopped—"

"Please don't again," her voice was quick. "We want to hear them."

"Yes." He hunkered down on the gravel, the mention of the visiting minister busying his mind. She sat down farther, her white dress pale against the grey rocks, clasping her knees, eyes intent on the rippled water. She echoed his thoughts.

"Do you think Joseph was right about what he said?"

He had not thought clearly all evening, but now he was awake as if he would never again need sleep. Struggling, he voiced the one point he recalled having pondered.

"If he speaks from history, I guess he's right when he says non-resistance is possible only for a small group. But what does that say? Does what has happened in the world show us what a Christian should do? Or does the Bible?"

"But if you agree, you have to go the next step. If only the minority can say, 'It is against our conscience to fight because we must love enemies as well as friends,' and the majority must say, 'We must fight to protect pacifists so that they may have the right to think as they do,' then the majority, the non-believers, die so that the minority, the believers, may live. Who, then is the martyr for the faith?"

As she spoke, his remembrance of the talk by the rippled lake grew, to his discomfort. There was, somewhere, a great deal wrong with what she and Joseph said. He had always heard it explained from another angle.

"Look, do you think a soldier thinks of all this when he comes round a corner and there's a German? He doesn't think. He either shoots on the spot or he's dead. That's all. War isn't one country against another. It's only, and always will be, one man killing one or more other men."

"But the principle still holds, doesn't it? In Germany no one can say, 'I refuse to join the Army.' They either join or are shot, which ends their earthly usefulness as witnesses to Christianity. If Allied soldiers did not stop the German advance, we could not live to hold our belief in Canada because Hitler would soon control us too. As the Russians are doing to the Mennonites that still remain there. One reason our parents fled to Canada—why our fathers left Holland and Prussia—was to be protected from serving in war, wasn't it? What will you and I do, now that we, in our turn, have no country to fly to for protection?"

He had a feeling that he was discovering some new planet. "Look," he fumbled, not knowing what to counter, but her passion relieved him.

"Oh, I'm not—really, I couldn't accuse anyone. So many did die in Russia. Of the thousands who streamed to Moscow with us, only a few hundred left for freedom. That our families escaped is only God's mercy and we can be eternally thankful. But the world is only so big; there comes a time when you must make a stand." Her voice-timbre deepened as he remembered his mother's words about "overcoming." "I don't know—now. It seemed so clear when Cornie and then Sam went to CO camp. But Joseph keeps questioning: can a Christian cast off responsibility by mere refusal—by mere avoidance? And I wanted to ask you. You're always so sure of yourself."

Her trust ground chagrin into his inadequacy. He was certain of only one thing. "Annamarie, can't the teachings of Christ lead us? He doesn't ask something reasonable—as the *right* to return a blow—but He expects holiness, a denial of all force. It was not reasonable for Menno Simons to give up a fat priesthood to become a hounded minister."

The bass of the frog near them had begun. Her face was still intent on the water as she said, "I wonder if we understand all Christ taught. We've got it sewed up into such neat dry packages. There is a sure-fire traditional way of acting for almost every situation you can imagine. But in some ways—in some situations—Menno Simons helps little. It was fine to say, 'We can have nothing to do with war' when—remember how Joseph put it?—wars were skirmishes on the next quarter and the king who led his troops to a day's victory won. Then it was possible—"

That had been Joseph's trend and Thom pushed in now, as he could not at the lake, "What difference does it make at whose command you kill: a king who hollers as he leads you, or a general who sits behind and tells you by radio? You're killing both times."

"The result is the same, yes, but the circumstances are more involved. The whole world is now in it. We can't avoid it. Father raises pigs because the price is high: some men charged up the Normandy beaches last Tuesday with our bacon in their stomachs. Pete Block can stay home because Mr Block's farm is big enough to be called an essential industry. Sam works in one now too. He wrote last week he was being shifted to Ontario to work in a boot factory. Alternative service is necessary to winning the War. Wars can only be won with some fighting, so we divide the job: I supply you with bacon to eat and boots to wear and you go kill the Germans—for the good of both of us."

Thom shuddered. After a moment, she went on. "Only, we have the better part. We don't take any risks—and grow rich besides."

He arose slowly and, using his entire body in a flare of viciousness that spurted and died, flung a stone against the pool. But it did not splash. It skipped beautifully in its flatness, dropping gently with a final plop into a far gleam of water. His shoulder ached. A few frogs ceased, the rest croaked on. You'd have to throw a lot of stones, he thought idly, and even then they soon start again. Must these things be thought of? There was always the bush between them and the world. With the invasion, the War might soon be over. Perhaps his call would never come. He knew that tomorrow, when he remembered, these thoughts would rankle like poison: having once seen the problem, he could never forget it. That was what made thought so frightening.

He said: "So you believe with Joseph that if you have a war anyway, you are not acting as a Christian just because you refuse to go and do the killing?" Articulated, shared by other human beings, the thoughts he himself had skirted reared as crassest heresy. His conscience balked.

"I think that's true." She paused, sad.

A verse arose in his mind with startling clarity: "But Jesus Christ said, 'Love your enemies, bless them that curse you, do good to them that hate you, and pray for them which despitefully use you and persecute you. For if you love them which love you, what reward have you? Do not even the publicans so?' "

"Yes, He said that," she returned, and silence lengthened between them. Four hundred years before, that verse had been the guiding star of their fathers, but somehow, through the centuries, they had worked it into an impasse. He wondered, thinking of Wapiti's isolation, whether now they could even be termed as loving their friends.

"We should go," she murmured.

"Yes."

They both looked at the pool and heard the frogs again, without thought, and then she rose and they returned as they had come, feet unsteady on the round rocks. "Let's just look at the river," he said, and pushed ahead through the tangle until they emerged on the lookout. She stood beside him, smoothing back her simply coiled hair. The clean curve of the moon hung naked at its height in the north. The long river lay dully silver, holding the island as in its arms. The wind flickered the poplars and murmured to the pine; there was no cry of a bird to nag. He knew that in this moment behind the hedges of France men lay silent under the shriek of shells, lurking; here, peace—as when only two people, and God, were on earth. But to stay here.

They looked at each other. He could not have touched her if he had thought of it. Then they, too, had to leave and he led the way back to the horses and buggy, and the glances that had met and the sound of their footsteps on the trail were a covenant between them.

CHAPTER FOUR

A church meeting, abruptly called on Sunday for the immediate Monday night, was beginning.

In the warmth of the June evening, they were singing the opening hymn, voices about Thom swelling harmony, craggy faces intense. The women's voices across the aisle lifted high the melody. The hymn strong in his chest, Thom, as always when in church, was raised beyond the waver of his doubt into confident worship. Only at such moments could he lose what appeared to him then to be his petty personal problems. Singing

When life's billows roar about me
. . . He will hide me
In the shadow of His hand,

he felt that everyone in the building stood separate yet united, one body crying with one voice to the one great known worthy of worship.

Several days before the picnic, while picking rocks from a field hesitant to sprout in the dryness, Thom had mulled over the meaning of the church. To him it was something quite beyond a building or a focal point of community activities or a group of people with similar interests. The church stood, starkly remembered, where his faintest memories merged into the void of early childhood. The first summer in Wapiti lived for him only in blurred scraps, when, as his mother told him later, they held Sunday services at one unfinished house or the next; but the building of the church, though he had been only six, had caught in his memory. In late Indian summer, despite a very disappointing first harvest, the men had begun scrubbing the hillock on

Block's quarter that fronted the road in the centre of the settlement. There were not enough clothes for Thom in the Wiens' cabin to allow him to leave the house on cold days, but once, when the sun shone wanly, his father and David had at last taken him along to the church site. At that point what seemed to him a huge hole for the basement had already been lined with logs and the floor and walls were being erected above it. Everywhere men trimmed and heaved logs; everywhere Mr Block was directing and planning; the best small Thom could do was to avoid tripping the labouring men. Numb in his thin clothes, he wandered around a corner and saw a small forge blazing in the lee of a wagon-box. Fascinated, he inched nearer, half intimidated by Aaron Martens' thunderous hammering on a partially opened discarded gas drum. The man's grime-faced grin beckoned him.

"Ho, Thomas—you're shivering so loud even I can hear you! Come close and warm here. And you can maybe turn the blower. Sure—but careful." The blacksmith's tiny voice seemed to issue from some lost fissure in his immense body, one ham-like hand hefting the hammer, the other almost losing a chisel in its grip. "That's the door I'm heating there—the door for this barrel that's going to be our church heater. Just turn steady—see how the coal fires," and Thom, glowing already with pride, exertion and heat, laboured mightily. "That's not a forge like I had in Russia—oh no! but it will come, never you fear, Thomas. We're building a church now," words clipped between series of hammer-blows, "a solid church. It'll stand when you, small one, are as old as I; when your children are as old as I." He paused in his cutting and pointed to several iron rods half-hidden in the dead leaves of the tree-copse behind them, "See those rods there? They cost plenty—money none of us has. They came all the way from Hainy." He began his thunderous assault again. "But we need them for the church; to hold the walls solid and upright. Log churches built right hold out long. Ours'll last because its built on the Rock," and broad sweat furrows pushed through the grime on the blacksmith's face.

Now in the church fourteen years later, glancing up momentarily between verses, Thom considered those iron rods above his head, forged together, holding the walls immovable. Aaron Martens' words came to Thom as he concluded the hymn unconsciously. Already on that day, when he had seared his fingers leaning too ardently at the forge and had to be taken home by an irate young David, he had known the church to be something beyond trimmed logs and mud chinking and iron rods. And this vaguely perceived knowledge grew into definite dimensions with the years: when the farm proved so prostratingly disappointing and his father would hitch the bony horses and drive to church completely discouraged and return home to lead their evening devotions in calm thankfulness; when at that first barren Christmas two huge parcels containing clothing and candy and even a tiny toy truck arrived from Eaton's, ordered and paid for by no one knew whom; when he, poised with other small boys on the front church benches under watchful parent eyes, comprehended the preaching of Pastor Lepp. They as a community had built this church, but the church was a House built on the solid Rock.

And Joseph's razor-edged analysis cut in again. "Thom, you cannot, as it were, retreat from reality into worship. You can never really worship without the proper ethics." Thom abruptly pushed the thought from him as he slid the hymn-book into its bracket. Joseph was not necessarily right at every point.

Pastor Lepp was reading, in his precise German, about "being at peace among yourselves." Hearing that solemn warning, Thom could hardly doubt what the sudden reason for the church meeting might be, but the serene brotherliness about him was reassuring. Their church did not have quarrels: the problem would be solved and the matter concluded. Thankful, he rose with the others, to echo in his thoughts the Pastor's prayer. Annamarie's father. Back beyond memory Thom had heard that gentle voice in prayer. He could not imagine a church without that gentleness, as he could not imagine Christ without the blessing of the children.

The congregation sat with a straining of benches, and Wiens, as church secretary, took his seat at a front table. Franz Reimer was immediately acclaimed chairman, as was usual; his impartiality had never faltered on any matter during the years that

Wapiti Mennonite Church had existed. Domed head bending over the agenda, the burn of the sun a line creased across his forehead, the old man read the first item: "Election of delegates to the Canadian Conference." To Thom, the Conference was a sort of omnipotent power where the Mennonites of Canada convened for doctrinal and general policy decision. Though its fifteen thousand members were almost lost across the sweep of five provinces, to him, who could not recall seeing over one hundred people at one time, their united belief was solidarity itself. Not that he had ever been to a Conference. He was, with two exceptions, the youngest of fifty-six members. Block, Reimer and Pastor Lepp were usually the delegates: they had had the experience.

As the church went through the formality of election, Thom's mind slid into hazy reminiscence; the evening in the log building seemed the final steam of a boiling day. Despite Joseph's hard analysis, the events Thom had experienced in this building were sacred to him. David's ordination for mission work in India: when old Brother Janz, conference moderator, had come from the south and David and Nettie had knelt on a grey blanket beside the shiplap pulpit after they had pledged themselves to God's service. He remembered how David had risen, hair rumpled by the Reverend Janz's unsteady hand, and prayed with the triumphant intensity of absolute dedication until Thom could only breathe to himself, overcome, "Holy, holy is the Lord." Two years later, he and Pete and Frieda Martens had been baptized: the entire congregation, except for the oldest women riding in the bennett-wagon, had climbed up from the creek below the church where the baptism had taken place, singing in sombre harmony, "My God, I am persuaded, forever I am thine." Pastor Lepp had led them in, they three had knelt to be accepted into the church, then Frieda had sat down on the women's side, Pete and he on the men's, to receive the Lord's Supper for the first time. Finally, he had bent his head at Franz Reimer's hand-clasp, received on his cheek the rough kiss, and heard the old man say, "Welcome, my son. God bless you!"

A silence lengthened about him, and he looked up to find Reimer gazing thoughtfully at the slip of paper. The issue for the hasty meeting was about to be broached. He could sense everyone with him sitting coiled with curiosity, almost knowing. Abruptly, Thom felt cheap for them. The church was meant for greater things! He saw Pastor Lepp rise and face them. When the Pastor spoke, Thom could understand why he was re-elected year after year.

"Certain younger and older members of the church have expressed concern about the young people's meeting held last Friday at Poplar Lake. An outdoor gathering for the young people alone like this has never been held before, but the Church Board felt, when the Youth Committee presented the suggestion, that no harm would be done. Now no one has felt that the meeting itself was actually wrong, but several brethren have mentioned that certain aspects of it were not in the best Christian traditions of our church. This matter must be clarified. There is no need for ungodly gossip to develop. The Church Board has asked Brother Franz Reimer, Junior, as leader of the Youth Committee, to explain what happened. If there are any questions, they can then be asked."

The exact objections would come shortly, Thom knew, but who could possibly have complained? Everyone had been so moved. Young Franz, slender face peaked in seriousness, rose near the front; Thom glanced at Block whose handsome face with its crest of iron hair concentrated, expressionless as granite, on the speaker.

As Franz spoke with gradual fluency, Thom remembered. Scalding coffee in enameled cups; jam sandwiches eaten squatting; high laughter of the girls under half-hushed pines; still-hot sand by the lap of the lake with the sun blazing down to the tree-line; songs sung to the lost echo of the wilderness: nothing could deface that evening. Not having books, they had sung German songs learned at home when the winter night lengthened to the bulging redness of the heater, or learned in the moving harmony of young voices in the choir on Saturday evening. Joseph had followed with his reasoned questions on pacifism, probing questions, and finally, when the sun was only a burnished path across the lake, the closing prayer by Mr Rempel.

Mr Rempel. He had forgotten the older member of the

Youth Committee who had hovered on the edge of the gathering. He turned slightly to see the grey mustached face of the twins' father flick a glance at Block. Thom could not doubt who had raised the matter. Two definite issues were shaping in his mind as, with the first question, Block took over the meeting. Across the aisle from him, Thom could barely see the back of Annamarie's glossy hair. Her questions—and his own—would be answered; he felt a faint uneasiness for Joseph, but also vast relief, for what he himself had so long hesitated to mention would now be bared to all.

"In what language was the evening program carried out?"

"The singing was in German, but Brother Dueck spoke in English."

"Was this by decision of the Youth Committee?"

"Well," Franz's discomfort was evident, "actually no one spoke about it one way or another—obviously it was to be German. But at the lake Brother Dueck pointed out that there were some people there from both districts who were not Mennonites and could not understand German. Also, we noticed some Indians within hearing distance, and so he suggested he speak in English."

"Did only you and Brother Dueck decide this?"

"Well yes, because Brother Ernst was leading the singing and Brother Rempel was not there at the moment. It was done so that all might understand—"

"Could I say a word, Brother Chairman?" Joseph's voice cut cleanly from the back of the church. Everyone stirred expectantly. "Could I ask why it is so important that the church know I spoke in English?"

Thom could feel all eyes turn with his towards Block. The Deacon rose, his voice almost puzzled, "I think that must be clear to anyone. We as a Mennonite Church hold our services, whether for young or old, in German. Why was that changed?" A slight loudness crept in now. "When this 'outdoor' meeting came before the Council, the brethren will bear me out that I questioned the wisdom of such a procedure. Church services, of whatever nature, belong in the House of God. However, I gave in on that point, but I said I hoped we would have nothing to regret later. What has happened makes us very sorry that we agreed to the suggestion of, as we were given to understand, the younger members of the Committee."

"I'm sorry, but I still do not understand," Joseph's voice insisted as Block made a gesture to sit down. For a moment Thom had the impression they were all merely bodies separating these two giants talking over them. Even Mr Reimer did not call them to order. "Is the church as a whole objecting that we had a service at a lake-shore in English? Agreed, this is new in Wapiti, but is there something *wrong* with it? It seems to me that Christ held several services by a lakeside and he did not even use English—he spoke in Aramaic."

A wave of air swept the church, like tension cracking. The Rempel twins, beyond Pete on the bench with Thom, snorted uncontrollably, and quickly ducked their heads below the bench-back. Block's face, now confronting the chairman, snapped the chuckle surprised from Thom.

Reimer's voice cut across the sprinkling of overt laughter, "I must ask the brother to speak with Christian respect."

Beyond the window, the sunken sun etched the black roof-line of the stables. The hissing light of the mantle-lamp burst through the door at that moment and John, the caretaker, shuffled up the aisle. In the hush of waiting for the grizzled old man to hang the lamp from its hook beside the pulpit, Thom thought, Not that way, Joseph. Joking is the worst. As the crooked figure straightened in its stretch for the hook, pushing the light up, Thom remembered a line he had read: "We have nothing to offer but broken gargoyles." Nothing else remained in his mind, not who "we" were or to whom the offering was being made. When the hook caught at last, the shudder he had known on finding the word in the dictionary gripped him again. Why should he think of that in this connection? Rempel arose.

"Brethren, levity has no place here." There was a murmur of agreement. "It is correct as Brother Franz has said. During the singing I heard a disturbance among the horses in the bush—when I returned Brother Dueck was already speaking—in English. I was surprised, since there did not seem to be any need to depart completely from our usual manner of service."

From the nods of the older men, Thom knew that this was damaging to the two younger members of the Committee. True, Ernst and Franz were both married, but neither was yet thirty. Joseph's voice was slightly stiffer now:

"I apologize if I spoke disrespectfully before. But I still do not understand. When we hold a service where some are present who cannot understand German, but all can follow English, why—"

"You are wrong," Block's voice was cold. "Brother Rempel tells me he understood nothing of what you said. Only later was it explained to him."

"Why, yes—," it was the first time that Joseph had stumbled, even slightly, for everyone knew that Rempel understood very little English. Joseph paused, as if understanding the gravity of the situation for the first time. Of the older people, only Block knew English to speak it with comprehension. Wiens had explained to Thom years before, "If one man knows the English, that is enough. He can handle matters with the government. You children learn English if you must, but we will remain German here anyway, so why should we bother? That's the way they did it in Russia." Everyone understood a little, but only the younger people spoke to the breeds at length; when they whipped their jaded horses into a Mennonite yard to buy eggs or a few sacks of seed grain, there were always youngsters to interpret. Old Lamont stumbled through Low German and all his store wares were labelled by a half Low-German, half English jargon anyway. Now, with all the older people gone except Rempel, and he the man who, of them all, understood English the least, to hold a meeting in English for the young people could easily appear a well-planned accident. And what Joseph had said could, depending on the reporter, have various meanings. Or perhaps any meaning! Tension tightened over the church: "Just give the young people an inch!" Despite his concern, Thom found himself strangely elated when the peering suspicion about him retreated to the defensive as Joseph spoke:

"I addressed the *young* people in English for only one reason: at least four in the group could understand no word of German. Since I was speaking on non-resistance and believe it to be based on the love the Christian has received from God, Franz was persuaded that my using English would benefit them also. How can we dare keep the gospel to ourselves? This church has sent David Wiens and his wife as mission workers to India, but if we are concerned that those half-way around the world hear the gospel yet allow no syllable to escape to unbelievers living beside us, then I wonder if Wapiti Church is concerned with spreading God's Word or having the record in the conference yearbook of being the smallest church in Canada to support a missionary couple."

For an instant there was no stir. Then, as if compelled by unbelief, one by one the congregation turned to look back at Joseph. Even from the teacher, Thom could not quite believe it. He had moved his head only slightly when his glance crossed with Rempel. Beyond the surprised indignity of the older man's gaze there stirred pain. One could not doubt his sincerity. Thom twisted to stare at the pulpit, torn.

The chairman spoke into the silence, discomfort edging his voice, "Well, brethren? Time is passing."

The rustle of turning to study the clock on the wall eased the hush. Then the Deacon rose to face them, grimly handsome, his body pushing broad against the shiny suit. Thom glanced sideways at Pete; his face was set like his father's, but staring at the bench-back. As, in the years of their growing up together, Thom had comprehended the difference between their fathers, how he had envied Pete. Prompt, accurate decisions, always perfectly confident of direction and purpose: small wonder Pete could be so rock-like in his belief; there would be only one way for Joseph when the Deacon was through. Yet now, for the first time in the three years he had been a church member, Thom was not certain he was about to agree with all.

"When, by the grace of God alone, we were able to escape the terror of Russia and come to Canada, we were as destitute as it is possible to be. We had nothing—only debts. Yet despite the Depression years, I know no one doubted but God would see us through. We all believed that the faith of our fathers which had carried them across lands and seas was with us still. There is not one here whom the Lord has not prospered. Our travel debt has been paid to the CPR; we own our land; we have enough to eat. And all of us agree that our children know the Bible and the traditions of our fathers because we have been separated from the worldly influences which bother many other Mennonite churches. We also know that much of this separation has been brought about because we have held to the German language in both church and home. Our church depends upon these young people; if we who remember the old home in Russia grow lax, we will quickly find that we no longer care to come to church. 'We can stay at home and listen to the radio as well.' Soon the young people, tired of our simple ways, will want to go work in the towns where there are no Mennonite churches. Then, 'The English churches are just as good—I can just as well go there. And besides, I can do anything I want and still remain a good member in their records.' Only too well do we remember with an aching heart those young men who once confessed Christ in this church and who have since gone the way of sin because the world offered new enticing things. If their example teaches us anything, it is that we *must* hold to *everything* we have ever believed! We can drop no iota! Especially in these days when the war madness grips this good country that has given us shelter. *If we are to have a witness in the land we must remain firm in the ways of our fathers!* You young people will ruin the work that God has given us if you neglect the teachings of your elders."

From Reimer's glance, Thom knew that Joseph must have raised his hand, but the Deacon remained standing. They had all heard the decisive summing up in other situations, but more than ever Thom felt the uneasiness. As Block continued, he found, surprised, that now he felt it for the Deacon.

"The brother tells us that he spoke in English that all might understand. We want to believe his good motives. Would he tell us what he said?"

"Gladly. I have my notes here—I worked them out in German anyway—and the young people can bear me out. Being of military age myself, my attitude towards war has caused me a great deal of thought. I outlined my ideas in the form of questions. First: what is the basic force in the Christian's life?

Using Scripture, I tried to give the answer as Love—Love given us by God to reveal itself towards Him and towards all our fellow men. Second: how has this Love been expressed in the past? Its followers have not asserted their own rights; they have always been ready to give up what they possess, even their life, for the sake of their faith or their neighbours. History shows that Mennonites have not hesitated to back their faith with their lives.

"Then the final question: how are we today expressing this Love in the comfort of Canada? We can in no way assert our rights against our neighbours by any means, violent or otherwise, yet what if our neighbours molest our country? Can a country then continue to exist, a majority of its people being non-participants in war? If we have followed the War that is ripping the world now, I think we know the answer. Given a war situation, we Mennonites can practise our belief in Canada only because other Canadians are kind enough to fight for our right to our belief. The godless man then dies for the belief of the Christian! Further, is it even possible for us *not* to participate today? Ultimately, even the farmer works for the War because he produces the food that makes fighting possible. Mere refusal will not do: positive action alone is possible. But we as a church have gone on in the traditional ways of reacting to war, not considering that the world has changed, even since World War One. Our church—"

"Brother Dueck!" The Deacon's voice overwhelmed all, steel eyes flaming. Joseph's voice was snuffed; the sound and the look a bolt to blast everyone.

"You criticized the church before *that* group? You took pains to speak a language they could all understand to slander our church?"

The silence was deafening. Only the hiss of the lamp—and that seemed part of the waiting. No one could plunge into the abyss of speech after that thunderous question. Stupidly, Thom noticed a moth frantically circling the glowing mantles, fiercely attracted by the light and as fiercely repelled by the heat.

"I was not concerned if what I said made the church look fine or not. I wanted everyone to know our only concern is to find the Truth. If the Truth is unflattering, then we know what to do." Joseph's voice washed gently against the rage still twitching the Deacon's face. Block's voice hit like a hammer.

"Can one even grasp how unbelievable it is that anyone in this church should make such accusations before—Indians?" In his pause, Thom sat numb. At the lake, these ideas had gripped them all, yet now Joseph alone bore the brunt, as if, having been told formally that these ideas were wrong, they could all wash their hands in silence. The older faces before him were set in rigid rightness. "How could you so tear the unity of the church—"

"Was it so wrong," Joseph cut in, "to tell those 'half-breeds and Indians,' as you call them, what they already know for themselves? They know that when war was declared, we all, on the instant, professed a love for our fellow men, men thousands of miles away whom we had never seen, a love which they, living beside us for fourteen years, had never felt. How can they believe us? Was it wrong to tell them we realized our failure—"

"You," charged the Deacon, the scar at his right temple a dull red, "having lived here nine months—"

Thom surged to his feet. "He is a member of this church and can speak! Every person who heard at the lake was convinced that we should do—"

"Brother Wiens," Block slit Thom's speech, "after your tantrum at the ball game, it were best you remained inconspicuous."

"Brethren, brethren!" Reimer interjected.

"What are we trying to do here?" a new voice sounded. Thom, sagging stunned, dazedly recognized the high voice of Aaron Martens. "Point fingers at personal failings? Then few of us could do the pointing. And there is some truth in what Brother Dueck has said. We need some self-examination, not accusations."

"I agree," Herman Paetkau's voice was strong. "What have we done for them?"

"Brethren," the Pastor rose in calmness, but the lines of his face seemed more deeply scored, "such shouting and personal reprimands are most unbecoming to a church meeting held among Christians. We wish to discuss this most serious matter, true; but in love, as Christ behooves us. We all, old as well as young, want to believe our brother that what he said at the lake he believed to be the truth. He acted impulsively, but who is perfect. I am sure that many good things were said at that meeting. If the brother will apologize for some of the unwise statements he made that night, and heed himself to be more judicious in the future, I'm sure we are all ready to forgive and forget."

Block was firm: "I ask pardon for my impulsive words. And I gladly and wholly agree with Brother Lepp. It is getting late. What harm has been done cannot be helped now."

There was a rustle as Joseph arose for the last time. Beyond his own numbed incapacity, there welled in Thom the overwhelming feeling that something of immense value was being abused here. As if Joseph's beliefs were being used to coerce him into the virtue of asking forgiveness where there was nothing to forgive. Only two, from the back benches, had supported the teacher; there was no further sound now. The leading men Thom could see before him, erect and half-turned to Joseph, waiting: Rempel's face ham-like, Block's sharp and clean as a knife, Reimer's gleaming head, Pa hopeful, pen poised; the younger men, Ernst, young Franz, Pete, the Rempel twins beyond, had their eyes hard on their shoes. Across the aisle only Annamarie's head was erect among the girls. Despite his personal shame, Thom stared fiercely at the front of the pulpit as Joseph spoke:

"How can I think that my saying two words, words I could not ever mean, would make all well? How can two words of mine erase all that has been done in Wapiti for fourteen years? How can man's *words* ever change anything?

"This year has meant a great deal to me. Personally, the warmth of your welcome—all of you—could not have been more Christ-like. But we Mennonites, every one of us, are not better than other men. There can be no other reason for our being spared war duty and possible death on the battlefield than that we are to be so much better witnesses to Christ here at home. Understanding the truth only brings with it greater responsibility of action.

"I had not planned to say any more, but since we are apparently at the point where we must separate, let me clarify my position. I hope someone will be willing to carry on the Sunday afternoon Bible class that I began with the non-Mennonite children in school, for my army call, which was postponed during last winter because of teaching—as was explained to the School Board when I came, I was really only 'on loan' from the draft—my call has come again and I must leave on June 30. I will go into training in the Restricted Medical Corps. As a Christian I must *do* something about the misery in the world, even though there are aspects about the Medical Corps none of us like. I find I cannot—lose myself behind bush and pretend the misery is not here. I cannot talk of giving a bit of my time when others are giving so much more. I am sorry if I have appeared ungrateful after all your kindness."

Joseph had told no one. The furore this calm statement roused ebbed about Thom. He cared nothing for the concluding efforts of the Pastor and the chairman, or Block's heavy silence. Everyone in Wapiti knew and agreed with the Deacon's strong stand against the medical corps service, but it had been ratified by the Canadian Conference despite the opposition. But now Thom cared nothing for what amounted to Joseph's final drastic break with Block's concepts. It seemed to Thom he staggered alone where guide-posts bearing the same legend pointed over horizonless dunes in opposing directions. Where could one go?

He arose, obedient to Reimer's gesture for closing prayer, but he heard no word. Quite irrelevantly, he noticed the duller glow of the left mantle above the pulpit. The moth was gone now. From the blue flame spurting from the mantle he knew it had finally dared all for the light that drew it and now lay, a tiny cinder, on the bottom of the ruptured sack of ashes that that still hung, giving less light now, but more heat.

As the deep voices about him echoed "Amen," his mind could only dully comprehend that in all the talking that evening, no one had disposed of any of Joseph's questions. They had not even been considered.

Summer 1944

PRELUDE

They lay in the gloom stuffed beneath the rafters and waited for the thunder. Under the sheet, the long shape lay motionless in the twisted-wire bed, but the small curled one, in the bunched darkness where the rafters closed their jaw, squeaked the straw-tick. A long-avoided touch was clammy. Somewhere, a calf bawled, lonely as the night, and then in a stir the two felt coolness and the mutter of myriad spruce beyond the screened open window. The ribbed roof reached up to the peak where holes like distant stars filtered through the darkness. Mosquitoes probed in high song.

Abruptly, without a sound, the lightning reached in and tore the darkness wide before their eyes. As a revelation they saw all about them to the hole ripped and hanging folded in the curtain partition and the leaning joints of the stove-pipe edging up, before the night rallied to enclose.

Then thunder. Like long walls breaking.

Under the rafters, "M-mom says that thunder is God speaking."

No stir from the long figure. The shorter squirmed close to what seemed a bodiless sound. "Haven't you learned in school what it is?"

"The Indians say so too."

"In the hot day one cloud gathers more electricity than another. When the wind blows them close together one discharges to the other. The flash of the discharge moves very quickly—that's the lightning. But the boom moves more slowly. That's the thunder."

Without a sight came the thunder over and over the bent world rolling. Like righteousness.

Under the thunder, "It s-sounds like—God."

Long after, as if no longer awake:

"Yes."

CHAPTER FIVE

On the fringe of day balanced the sun. The July world lounged clean as a washed cat. Then Nance, flirting her tail to the morning flies, rocked Thom off the bare ridge into the bending trees along the cow-trail. Just to live, following the sound of Boss's bell, Carlo charging into the hollowed path from a raucous rabbit-chase! He could not even feel selfish at his thoughts.

Abruptly, when the path emerged to skirt the fence along the oatfield, he saw cattle where they had no right to be. As he kicked Nance into a gallop, thinking they were the milk-cows, he saw the crook-horned brindle cow lift her head from the oats, her dull bell drumming. Herb's stock! Again.

He reined close at the barbed-wire gate and, with a wrench, sprawled it open. Nance stepped over carefully, and then they were racing around the edge to the gate that opened into Herb's pasture on the adjacent quarter. After two weeks of intermittent rain in June, the hock-deep oats quivered like a living carpet. He had to dismount to get the gate open, then he was away. All seventeen head of Herb's scrubby stock stood bulge-bellied now, among trampled trails, squashed patches, splattered dung, staring at his gallop. In a whirlwind he rounded them up, Carlo glorying slaver-mouthed at the uninhibited chase. Thom's mind was black as he crowded them hard down the edge of the field, not caring about their laboured breathing.

He did not milk that morning. After driving their own cows home, he returned to the field and easily discovered the break. He strung a double wire across the gap in the rails.

"It was the bottom rail again," he said to his father, who questioned him at breakfast, face moving in the motions of eating. "If they rub on the rail long enough, it finally breaks and then they scrape through, getting a good back-rub for their warbles from the wire."

"Uh-huh. I told Herb last year he should put a wire on too." Wiens stared into his porridge-bowl, afloat with milk.

"Sure you told him! And what does that help? Last year they got in earlier; at least the barley came back; but it's late now. Wrecked at least six acres. You've got to do something with him about that fence, not just tell him and have him laugh in your face again." Thom's voice lifted as he leaned back on the bench, against the plastered wall, staring at his calm father slurping the thinned porridge. Mrs Wiens, standing by the stove where pork spat in a pan, turned.

"Thom, remember he's not a Christian and we have to be especially careful not to annoy him. Perhaps, if we're lenient enough—"

"Mom, we *have* been lenient and I know he's not a Christian, but it's common decency to do your share of fencing. Everyone made the rules. If Pa wasn't always so apologetic when talking for himself. He doesn't have to excuse himself for having a good oat-field—just tell Herb to get that bottom wire on like—"

"Thom!" from his mother. He saw Hal, sitting beside him on the bench, gawking. He said to Hal, in English,

"If you're through breakfast, why don't you scram? It's nice out."

"Sure!" Leaping up, Hal slid along the bench from behind the table and, scrambling over Thom, charged out the screen door. In massive silence the family continued eating.

Margret said, the boy's shouts fading to the corral in the flurry of Carlo's barking, "Why don't *you* go tell him to fix it?"

Thom shook his head quickly, looking away from her work-lined hand that was reaching for a piece of bread. "That's not my business."

"Stop talking about it!" Wiens' voice broke in. "I'll get it done and that's the end of the matter. Since when do the two kids have to run the whole farm?"

Neither said more. Thom did not know about his sister, but

since the church meeting, for him many unconsidered circumstances meshed into place. Beyond his boyish need for solidarity, he now comprehended more fundamental weaknesses in his father. David and Ernst managing the farm; Pa as church secretary, though he occasionally murmured mild objections at home, at church meetings always agreeing with church policy —policy originated almost exclusively with Block; Pa ever agreeable: let it affect his own family as it would, as long as the next man held him in good reputation. To be a true Christian, must one always agree? Until now, to consider what he suspected to be the inadequacy of his father had seemed to Thom like the wavering of his own faith. But all the leading men had wavered and said nothing in the face of Joseph's ranged facts.

He remembered Joseph's departure the week before. A leather suitcase strapped behind his saddle, the teacher had ridden up in the early morning. Gray fidgeted as Joseph swung awkwardly down.

"Poor boy!" Thom ran his hand down the silken neck. "Why don't you ride with Block's truck on his cream haul? You catch the same train."

"No need to bother anyone. I have to sell Gray anyway."

"The livery in Calder?"

"Yes. Wish you could buy him."

"I do too." They looked steadily at each other, the horse nuzzling Joseph's pocket. Neither spoke.

"Is that all you've got?"

"Mr Lepp will send the trunk to the folks sometime when he goes to Calder. I don't need it now."

They stood, hearing Margret heave the corral-gate open and the cows amble across the yard to the pasture. She came by them then, milking skirts heavy in the level sun-rays.

"So you're deserting us," she paused, her pails foam-topped. "Come in and say good-bye to Mom."

"Yes. In a minute, Margret."

The slab house-gate squeaked.

"There's no chance of you visiting your relatives in the south a bit?"

"Huh-uh. My call could come. And we've no money for that."

"You live so differently here from most Mennonites. If you could get out to see for yourself. At least you use modern machinery and wear ordinary clothes: you haven't fallen into the pitfalls of some Mennonites who almost equate Christianity with a certain cut and colour of clothes, prayer caps and beards, but if you keep on insisting on the German language and tie your belief to cultural expressions, I wonder. In some ways you're so progressive here, and in others you're still so like a colony, so much under one man's—Thom, you personally are hemmed in—physically—you lose all perspective. There are Mennonites in the south—too many—who live in settlements as you people do here, but others are getting away from this 'physical separation' idea. They are living out our common faith. And they do it better, I believe, than you are here, because it reacts and comes alive in contact with people who do not have it. Of course there are big problems too, but those spring up everywhere. If you could only come and see—" Both stared at the ground beneath their feet, in the familiar, useless, circle of their talk.

"A person can't ignore all he's ever done, Joseph, what he's grown up with."

"And you shouldn't. There is much good here in Wapiti, and you should hold to that completely. But that only. Don't be afraid of your mind." The screen-door banged in their silence. "I'm convinced you'll do very well with the Bible class, Thom. Remember to watch Jackie Labret—the others always take their cue from him. I tried to sound out Pastor Lepp again, just last night. I'm certain if you talked to him, say some day at work, man to man, he would give you some help with the lessons, unofficially, of course, but he'll help. And I'll write to you from camp, tell you what it's like."

Get Pastor Lepp's assistance. Hold only to that which is good. Thom drained his coffee-mug, looking at his father's grey face as he wiped grease from his plate with brown bread.

"You go ahead with the fencing on the south line," Wiens said as his son slid down the bench and got up. "I'll drive and see Herb later in the morning." Thom silently tipped his sweat-moulded cap off the nail by the stair-steps and strode into the blazing sunshine.

It being Friday morning, Block had just returned from Calder. The Deacon was a striking man, pale scar across his temple, steel-like hair bare to the sky. He wore, instead of the usual overalls, denim trousers and a tan-checked shirt. As Old Lamont shuffled out to take the weekly mail bag, streaming ignored chatter about the Indians bringing in a fresh load of seneca roots, the Deacon pulled empty cans from the ton-truck and stacked them on the store-porch. He was not occupied with usual business thoughts; last week's encounter on the railroad platform in Calder intruded. Since they had not spoken together after the stiffly formal school-board meeting, he had not expected the teacher to ride with him to Calder, yet he had felt sorrow at the man's departure. As they nodded to each other, the length of the platform between them, the Deacon mentally reframed his great hope. He did not want his community to remain in ignorance of the outside world. He himself had been the first to buy a radio and mechanized farm equipment for after a few years he had realized it was impossible that they cut themselves off entirely from Canada. If the children could be taught just enough to know about the world's evil, they would be happy to remain in their seclusion. Some, like the Unger boys, missed the way, but the others were the more solid for such knowledge. Like young David Wiens. A teacher was needed who knew the way of the world and yet adhered strictly to the Christian principles of the fathers. Old Miss Friesen would remain in Beaver, but for Wapiti Joseph had been perfect; until his glacial logic hardened him beyond all usefulness. After ten short months in Wapiti, Joseph waited for the train. For an instant Block felt a half-formed fear that had pricked him at the church meeting. Were the young people already nipped? At the church meeting —but Pete and Elizabeth had not seemed affected.

Three men idled from the town to stand near the unused railroad shack, chatting. Block waited by the cream cans. As the train puffed into view round a cut, Joseph suddenly strode the short length of the platform. "I'm sorry that I have disappointed you, Mr Block. A man has to follow what he cannot but see as the truth. You have to—even though you seem to be tearing someone else apart."

The Deacon looked up at the rough face, and for a moment he could have wished him his son. He said, the train halting in myriad screeches, "Good-bye Joseph. You could have done something for us at Wapiti. I pray God that He will show you where you have gone wrong."

Joseph, turning after the handclasp and clambering into the one passenger car, knew he could not doubt the sincerity of that voice. He wondered, as he bumped his suitcase into the dusty car, what would have to happen in Wapiti to move that titan. When he thought of it, Joseph felt a pang, almost of happiness that he was going out. Ha! he was thinking like them already: of going outside. Outside what? Stooping, he stared through the grimed window. The bush beyond the fence blocked his view.

For Block, ignorant of the thoughts he aroused, stacking the last of the empty cans on his store-porch a week later, the remembrance of the bent figure disappearing into the train worked oddly. The recalled ringing of the train bell tolled him back to his early boyhood in Russia. He leaned against the truck-box, his right hand fingering the welt of the scar.

The iron monster had rested on the tracks, panting to carry their whole village from the crowded Ukraine a thousand miles to the plains before the Ural Mountains. He had never seen a locomotive. Heedless of the crowding villagers, he deserted his parents and went around the front, beyond the other admirers. Alone, he ventured close, touching the great wheels and the gleaming piston-rod, overpowered by the immensity of the chained force before him. Suddenly, in a shrill scream, a blast of steam blanketed him. Terrified, he ran he did not know where, stumbling over rails and cinders. As swiftly the steam was behind him and a Russian voice cursed above his head, "Get in your car, brat! We're going!" Where? The doors shut above his head, the freight cars stretching endlessly out of sight, the steam nozzle threatening behind him.

"Around the front to the other side, stupid! Move!" He glanced up and saw the heavy bearded Russian face, and he knew that this man who controlled the monstrous machine was only a Russian, like all the rest. Without another look or the slightest flinch, he turned rigidly and walked past the nozzle, which dripped hissing water on the tracks, and round the front to the other side.

After nine days they arrived at the Volga River. The migrants crowded to the doors of the freight cars, gawking in dumb wonder at the skeleton of steel that leaped the mud-swollen river. After a pause, the train crawled on to the bridge, and slowly the shadows of the girders passed over his face. It was unbelievable that such things could be in the world!

"Hello, Block!" In a swirl of dusty buggy-wheels Wiens pulled up beside the truck. "One doesn't see you dream very much. Business no good?"

Under the bronze of his face, Block felt the skin tighten in embarrassment. He slammed up the tail-gate. "Morning, Wiens. One has to stop and think now and then."

"I know, but everyone says you do yours in bed when the rest of us have to sleep. That's why you get so much done." Wiens had wheeled Nance over to the hitching-rail and was tethering her. Block was about to slide into the truck-seat when the other came, almost hesitantly, around the vehicle. "Very busy now?"

Block was thinking of the mower-blade that needed sharpening for the haying, but he said, as he always did, "Not if it's important."

"Well, Herb's stock was in our oats this morning." Wiens spat it out, quickly.

Block looked down through the open window, one foot still on the running board. "You haven't had trouble with his fences before, have you?"

"Well, yes. Last spring his stock got in that same field on the west quarter. We had barley then, and it came back. It happened quite early—better if you can settle between two."

"Yes, and we both know Herb. What's the fence between you?"

"One wire, and a rail at the bottom."

"You know we decided only double wire would do around crop-lands. Herb's rail?"

"Yes. He says one rail and one wire around a pasture is enough. After all, he said, on his side it's pasture."

"Stupidity." Block thought sharply: We must go carefully with him. He's far from the church. To Wiens he said, "Much damage?"

"All seventeen head were in there, Thom said. At least four-five acres tramped."

Block shook his head. "You should have—well, get in." He pulled in his leg and slammed the door. "We'll go see the old Unger."

They bumped south on the main road away from Herb's quarter. Wiens, relieved of initiative, mused, "It's odd how some boys turn out decently and others—always against grain."

"Depends on the home," Block said curtly.

"I suppose." After a pause, Wiens ventured, "Yet look at Unger's youngest boys. Probably apply for baptism this summer—fine boys. And the two oldest—"

"That's true." Block offered a rare insight into his knowledge of the community. "When Unger first came to Wapiti, if his boys fought with anyone in school, Unger would whip them for it that very evening when they came home."

"Fight?" Wiens was astonished. "My boys never fought in school!"

Block smiled faintly. "Ask Helmut—or better yet, Jackie Labret." He continued, thoughtful, "After a certain age you can't very well whip a boy. They have to know who's who before you reach for the whip."

Wiens sat, immersed in thought.

The rolling field to their right belonged to Block, and a flock of gulls circled over a distant outline of horses and disc. Block estimated the width of the green strip of unturned summer-fallow. They could start haying Monday. The scar glowed faintly at his temple: that Louis! to leave them just before haying. Weins, sitting erect abruptly and looking at the field, asked "When's Louis coming back? There's a lot of work there for Pete."

"That's Elizabeth with the horses. Pete's on the home quarter with the tractor. Jim Hannigan in the Calder Post Office told me today he'd heard Louis was caught by the police in a drinking brawl in 'Battleford; he's in Prince Albert pen for six months. The fool wanted three days off—promised me he'd stay away from drink. I only gave him ten dollars of his wages. But you can't change a breed." Block steered viciously to avoid a puddle.

"Once a pig, always a pig."

"So now I'm behind in my work. Elizabeth will have to work all this summer again."

"I'm sorry that I bothered you with—"

"Oh, this matter has to be cleared. We can't have cattle ruining crops. Feed will be high this fall; the drought isn't over in the south."

They were between two fields now: Wolfe's on one side and Hiebert's on the other. As they drove, the glimpses through the trees that pushed between the rock-ridges edging the fields showed dust-clouds and reels of gulls as both farmers rushed the fallowing before the haying season. Patches of crop stretched solidly green. Then they were opposite the quarter Unger farmed with his teen-age sons and in a moment wheeled into the yard. The house was shabby and the barn, covered with blooming sods, leaned crazily against the rump of a haystack. As Block stopped the truck to the barking of a black mongrel and a scattering squall of chickens, Unger himself came from a slab granary.

Block said, getting out, "I'll talk to him alone." Wiens, relieved, stayed where he was, scanning the yard. Herbert Unger had made a good start too: been elected Deacon in the early days. He wondered.

"Hello!" Unger was cheery. "Not often that we see you on a work-day, Peter." He was the only man who called Block by his first name; they had met during the First War in the "Forstei" bush camps of Russia where the Mennonites had worked in lieu of military service.

"Morning. We've all got our work measured out for us this time of year. Soon ready for haying?"

"Jake should be through with the summer-fallow next week for sure—seems we'll be a bit behind this year again—"

Block interrupted, "Herbert, there's some trouble with your Herb." The farmer's face dropped into the pathetic despondency it held whenever his two eldest sons were mentioned. The irony of once having envied this man his *two* sons flicked across Block's mind. "I think we can fix it. It's about the fence between him and Wiens. His cows broke through the rail he has into Wiens' oats this morning."

"I've told him and told him! But what can I do?" with a futile gesture.

"Now look. I lent you that money to get Herb started on the old Green place because while he's here among us he may become a Christian—maybe even a decent girl will marry him. He can wait another year with that first payment, but we can't have him bothering others with his sloppiness. He's twenty-five years old."

Unger stood shaking his head, sorrow graven on his face. "He has a good crop this year so far—but what can I do? He hasn't listened to me for so many years—"

Unger's weakness never failed to stir the ire in Block. He said, hard across the pity that welled to tinge his impatience, "Children have to know who the father is. It's late now. Come along—we'll drive to talk to him."

Fifteen minutes later the truck rolled to a stop and the three men scrambled down. In one swift glance, Block knew that the Green place was worse. Weeds rioted everywhere. Crouched against a scrawny poplar, the log shack appeared to have been used for a century and then hastily vacated before the filth devoured the inhabitants, its litter sprawling out after them. A hen clucked her brood across the yard. Tied to a tree near the barn, a ribbed calf bawled forlornly at them, once.

"Well, where is he?" asked Block. The two with him stopped, Wiens staring in astonishment. He had never seen a Mennonite yard that looked like this. Unger said nothing. There was a stamping splash in the barn. Block stepped carefully towards it, and then hesitated at the edge of the black puddle before the door. Leaning over to look inside, he supported himself on the axed door-jamb. Three horses stood unhaltered, gazing curiously, swishing at steel-blue flies. Sunlight filtered in through the rotten-straw roof, gleaming on the backs of the horses and the hock-deep slime in which they stood. With a kind of horror Block recalled that it had not rained in three days. He pushed himself back and, wiping his boots on a rank of weeds, called, "Three horses here—can't be working on the field."

Unger called, "He has four—he's probably riding—" and even as the two came towards Block, they heard the running hoof-beats behind the barn. Block sighted a brood sow emerging from behind the house, rooting around the tree with her nosy following; then Herb galloped out of the poplars and strained his horse to a slithering stop at the pasture-gate. Glancing at the three men, the bachelor left his mount ground-tied, ducked through the gate, caught his shirt, tore it loose with a suppressed curse, and strode towards them, his face betraying no reaction at their visit.

The older men greeted him civilly. He merely said, "I was out in the pasture and heard the truck stop, so—" There was no mention what he had been doing. The Deacon, pondering, slid his glance past the streak of egg-yellow on Herb's week-old whiskers to the horse, heaving in the shade. A rifle-butt protruded from the slung scabbard. A man didn't go idly about shooting in weather like this! He turned to look at Unger.

The father said, "It's about your fences, Herb. Your cows were in Wiens's oats this morning—broke through on that bottom rail. They ruined about five acres."

Herb's face hardened swiftly, glance flicking from Block to Wiens. "Oh—you two come to talk to me in the good old Mennonite way, eh?" His mouth twisted in High German. " 'If there be a division between two of you, discuss it calmly in the presence of a third party.' " He slumped back into Low German, "And since you still think I'm a boy, you had to bring Pa along. Now just you—"

"Wait," Block broke in calmly, across Unger's obvious defeat, "think before you holler. We came to straighten this out decently like any other—"

"You came to talk to me like I was a kid! I'm old enough to run my own place and nobody's telling me—"

"Are you going to listen?" Herb glared at the Deacon for an

instant, then dropped his glance. "If you're old enough to run your own place, you obey the rules of the community. We all decided to have at least two strands of wire around every crop-field. Wiens has put up his strand—and all the posts besides, right?" Wiens nodded. "Then the least you can do is put up your wire."

Flies buzzed on the hot metal of the truck. Herb muttered, sullen, "It'll come back. Can't have wrecked that much. And I haven't got any money to get wire, so—" and he shrugged his shoulders.

Block felt rage rippling through him. No consideration for anyone: just chase his horses uselessly to death; just lie in the shade and uselessly shoot every cent away. The Deacon half-heard Unger's pleading voice, saw the sullenness shift to stubborn anger, and he turned quickly to Wiens, who had not yet opened his mouth. "How much wire for that field?"

"About a hundred rods."

"Herb, I'll give you that wire on account right now. You pay this when you clean up your other bills at the store with those hogs you told me the other day were soon ready for shipping. About two weeks?"

"There's all sorts of things I have to do with that money. I can't—" Much as it maddened him, Herb never could argue at length with the Deacon. The scathing replies would come, later, when he lay fuming on his blankets.

"You have to have this *now*. And get it done before the haying starts next week." Even as he spoke, the Deacon realized that Herb, if always proven completely wrong in his actions towards others, could only harden in his antipathy towards those who levelled accusing fingers. The man needed help. Yet Block found himself strangely at a loss: he hesitated, then tried for reasonableness, "No one can do anything without other people's co-operation. And we all want to live at peace together. That is best." Herb stared at the ground. Block turned to the truck.

Herb said abruptly, "That was the trouble with the cows this morning! I heard the bell running like mad—was that Thom running them off the field? Wiens, doesn't that kid of yours know how to chase stock—winding 'em with a full belly of green oats? The old brindle was sick at milking." Herb worked himself up quickly as he saw them about to leave. Foot on the running-board, Block paused, scar darkening.

"You keep your stock where it belongs and it won't get winded." He hesitated, as the two others climbed into the cab. "Get a sod roof on that hole of a barn. And drain it. You're ruining your horses' feet."

Herb watched the truck vanish, cursing silently. In his thinking Thom appeared the culprit. He had egged Wiens on—last year the old man had been pliable enough. And once the Deacon was involved— That he'd mention those hogs! There wouldn't be a cent left.

He kicked viciously at a soft cow-dropping near his feet, and walked towards the house. The litter of pigs grunted away as he neared. Before he entered, he slammed his filthy boot against the single gate-post that had no fence to support.

CHAPTER SIX

Grosser Gott, wir loben Dich!
Herr, wir preisen Deine Staerke!

Morning sunlight sprayed through the reaching branches of the trees, hung wispy with hay clawed from homeward passing racks. New day triumphed in Thom like the song in his throat:

Vor Dir neigt die Erde sich
Und bewundert Deine Werke.

He looked back, balancing on the jolting rack, hands loose on the reins. Pa and Hal would not be coming for an hour. He liked the next line, both for the words and for the music which went up and up to the peak of exaltation; there was no one but the pricked-eared horses and the wilderness and Almighty God to hear:

Wie Du warst vor aller Zeit,
So—

and he held it, like a trumpet, his chest in the cool morning steel-bound, feeling the song reach beyond the raucous banging of wheels on rocks into each body cell-tip,

—bleibst Du-u in Ewigkeit!

"Come on, let's go. Hey!" and he chirruped with a laugh and a flip of the reins; the horses caught the trot with three shakes of their heads and ran with amazing silence through the muffling sand up a ridge-side. Without thinking he cried, "Let the mountains *shout* for joy!" because the morning said it to him. But there were no mountains here, rather great clothed ridges from which, over the poplar-tips that faded to willows below him, he could see the open of the hay meadow where stacks sprawled like stubby caterpillars. He had never seen mountains that he could remember, though his father said he had seen the Urals from their village in Russia. Somewhere in Isaiah it spoke of valleys shouting for joy, but mountains seemed better: the picture arose in his mind of a monstrous mass opening its craw in an abysmal bellow of recognition to its Conceiver. He grinned, thinking of yesterday afternoon's Bible lesson, one that had even impressed Marie Moosomin and Jackie Labret, concerning Elijah shivering in his cave. The meadowlark tipping the post was best of all. Its song floated as he passed.

The Wiens' farm being nearest the haymeadow, Thom knew he should have been out first, but he was not; Pete had rattled by while he was coming out to hook up. Star and Duster now trotted in the wagon-tracks across the Block lease to the next quarter north, which Wiens had leased for the past ten years. Farther north and south other Mennonite families had land for haying, so that in the middle of summer half the people of Wapiti and Beaver districts laboured the length of Eight Mile Lake putting up their winter feed. Thom could hear the clatter of Pete's mower cutting into the last strip of hay bordering the rushes of the swampy water that stretched in a wriggling line down the middle of the once-huge lake. The long stacks settled here and there, waiting for the winter that would whittle them down one by one. Thom thought of Pete and himself hauling hay each day, of the cold, and of the hoar-breathing horses. Would he be there to haul? Passing a stack, he saw Pete had halted; he aimed his team across the meadow towards the bending figure.

The rhythm of the horses' hoofs on the stubble was like dry bread under a rolling-pin. Stems popped, dew flashing in sun-flung crescents before the running feet. It was too wet for anything except cutting. At the hay-edge he pulled up, swung over the rack-rail, and crunched along the cleared border of the single swath.

"Hi, Pete."

"Hi, Thom. Thought you'd never make it." Pete finished kicking the great jumble of jammed hay over the bar into the swath. His blue-denim trousers were black to the knee.

"Some of us have work to do at home too. Pretty wet, isn't it?"

"Almost too." Pete brushed a long series of spring-green insects from the cutter-bar. "Think I'll walk ahead and see how far we can go. Papa said go as far as possible."

The youths passed the horses who, swishing their tails idly, dreamed belly-deep in the slough-hay. Thom, each step into taller grass, could feel the wet coming through his trouser leg. He paused, looking at the cut in the trees across the marsh before them, then back at the slash half a mile behind them. "Seems to me you're edging over, Pete. Want our hay too?"

"Never know—those extra two fork-fulls may see us through the winter." The yellow-throated blackbirds leaped hoarsely as they neared the rushes. Even while treading on the knife-like grass, which they knocked down in showers of dew, the ground began to ease away under the men's feet. When they looked back, water seeped into the footprints while grass-blades bent ponderously erect, one by one.

"No good. The horses would go out of sight. Besides, it would never dry."

"I guess we can go about as far as here, but it angles east sharply just in a ways. Our chunk is big yet."

"Papa says there's about as much hay on your one quarter as our two."

"This year maybe. Last year the water was higher—that big stretch of ours is low. You'll be done before us."

"Even without Louis, it's gone better than Papa hoped at first."

"Elizabeth really worked." For a moment Thom thought of her, tramping and setting stacks like a man for weeks. He ventured, "Isn't it a bit hard—?"

Pete nodded his head slowly. "In a way, I guess. But Papa says that women in Russia worked like that all the time. She and Ma did when we first came to Wapiti too. If you've got stock, you've got to feed it." Thom could not deny that. If it was true that there was nothing to the Mennonite life beyond hard work as the English mentioned now and then, it was especially true in the Block family. He thought fleetingly of worn Mrs Block. And of his own mother. Hacking a farm out of the wilderness demanded women strong as men, but once comparative security was reached—in work where did virtue end and cupidity begin? He could not remember anyone ever having shown him the line: it was never even mentioned.

He glanced at Pete, who stood looking south, absorbed in gauging the contour of the marsh and how far he should stay away from the seeping water. After a moment they pushed back, their teams waiting, the still-cool day seeming to hesitate over the ancient lake-bottom to see what they would do with it. Thom stumbled suddenly, feeling something abrupt against his boot. He bent to see. Pete, peering with interest, said,

"Shouldn't be any rocks here in the swamp," as Thom felt the broad turn of the horn. He tugged hard and it came up with moss and roots dangling. The lower nose had rotted away; the roll of bone at the skull-top and the thick jutting horns were all that remained.

"Must have been a wood-buffalo. Man, look at that, eh!" he held what was left of the skull at arm's length, a finger on each horn-tip. They looked. The top was a perfect bow-line turning almost back on itself. One horn was clean, the other mud-grained, but both were scarred with rot. Below the gnarled horn only a broken suggestion of the great blade of the skull remained. Thom gripped the clean horn at the base with his hand and, huge as they were, his fingers did not go half-way round. He wished he had seen that horn when it gleamed in ponderous dignity below the massive shoulder.

"How long has it been lying here, you think, Pete?"

"Don't know. Not too long here—the water would have rotted it quick."

"These haven't been around for at least fifty years. Must have worked its way in with the spring run-off, year by year. Odd you haven't hit it with the mower." Staring at the broken skull, its heft heavy in his hands, a vista opened for Thom. Why was Canada called a "young" country? White men reckoned places young or old as they had had time to re-mould them to their own satisfaction. As often, to ruin. The memory of the half-Indian woman he had met last winter in a house where he would never have dreamt to find her forced itself upon him. As he thought unwillingly, the aura of impenetrable consciousness of her own being that she carried like a garment somehow enveloped him, now as then. His enforced habit of avoiding that scene asserted itself and, still holding the skull, he welcomed the thought of Two Poles at the picnic. Perhaps some lone ancestor of his had lain all day under the willows with the insects and bugs, spear or gun in hand, waiting for this buffalo to graze closer.

Pete moved forward and Thom followed. The horses were shaking their heads as the sun tipped higher over the meadow.

"You know, Pete, it's funny. There are stacks of European history books to read, yet the Indians—a people living in nearly half the world—lived here for thousands of years, and we don't know a single thing that happened to them except some old legend muddled in the memory of an old crone. A whole world lost. Not one remembered word of how generations upon generations lived and died."

"If you look at what's left on the reserve, we haven't missed much. A couple o' them came to buy eggs yesterday. Told Papa they were out digging seneca roots. This morning we were missing five chickens. Just a bunch of thieves now. Until the law came West, Papa says they were nothing but packs of cutthroats: whoever killed most was greatest. They would kill now too, only they're scared of the Mounties."

They were beside Pete's mower then. Abruptly, Thom hurled the skull as far as he could into their own quarter where the hay quivered untouched.

Pete said, "You'll run into it with your mower now. Why did you do that?"

"That's okay." He strode to his waiting team. "I better get cutting."

The sun blazed towards its zenith. On the clattering mower, Thom squinted through the shimmering heat that rippled the distant walls of trees. Wherever his eye probed over the meadow, blotches of figures moved: cutting, raking or pitching hay, bucking it towards their stacks, setting stacks, beginning others. He was part of the world of work that eddied all about him, a world he could comprehend by instinct. A hawk soared in lurking majesty.

Relax as he would, Pete's callosity crept ever back into consciousness. For a deep look into a uniqueness of the Canadian world to be blacked out by conventional triviality! So they were missing five chickens! Any silly hen could repair that. It seemed to Thom he had offered a wide new world that they could explore together and his friend had worse than ignored it. They had once had such times! They had spent every Sunday last summer together. His mind reverted inevitably to the early fall, almost a year ago now, when they had spent the Sunday afternoon inspecting Block's new steel-lug tractor. Though he was conscious that he could somehow never return to such a Sunday afternoon, in his memories it remained a delight. Even when Pete, having rallied his courage to advance on the house and ask, had been refused permission to start the tractor, yet the pleasure had grown as, in the shelter of the granary, they had cranked to test the "kick," muscled the heavy steel steering wheel around, and in every imaginable way edged to the very point of starting it. When Mrs Block halloed from the house, the signal for changing and getting the cows, they had paused, their only white shirts grease-streaked and Pete's forehead slightly gashed where he had stumbled against a lug, and grinned at each other. Where now was that friendship?

Sharply, he recalled that Joseph had arrived in Wapiti a week later. And that now, with the Bible class at school, he no longer had time to visit on Sunday. The mower-clamour called him back. He had to acknowledge that now his own lightning annoyance which, in the moment of throwing the skull he had scorned to disguise, concerned him more than Pete's dullness. Anger: in any slightly rousing situation it clawed at him. He looked up at the circling hawk. Anger like the eagle that descended daily on—he could not recall the name of the Greek giant. Memories flooded him of his school days when, ransacking the scrawny library for books, he had dug into some pale-blue booklets buried on the bottom shelf and discovered Greek mythology. He remembered reading, crouched in the awkward desk as the sun flashed on the snow outside, repelled yet unable to leave those blue books. There were only three, and the stories, in their gruesome fascination, made no sense to him. But now one opened into meaning. The giant, defying all Omnipotence and stealing divine fire to bring to man, still meant nothing, but the punishment: the robber crossed gigantically upon a mountain's scraggy finger and the eagle's daily ravaging of the writhing body, seemed to him suddenly like his anger forever tearing his own Christianity that was chained at its mercy.

He shook his head dizzily on the bumpy mower. The image horrified him, yet it fitted with fearsome perfection. Perhaps that was what a myth was for: to show man to himself; if he knew enough about himself, could he comprehend the whole story? Lifting his cap, he rumpled his sweat-soaked hair. A man might go crazy in this sun: it seemed he was already, trying to fit heathen stories into Christianity. He shuddered in his sweat.

The mower staggered and balked abruptly in the tall hay, the cutter-bar wedging back hard. As he jerked quickly on the reins, he heard a crack.

"Whoa, whoa there! Back Star! Back!"

He slipped the machine out of gear, slid off and kicked the hay aside. His foot hit hard, and he cleared the shrouding hay with his hand. A gnarled tree-root stuck up, jammed between knife-tooth and finger. It had snapped the latter off at the base.

In the silence of his mower, he could hear the nearing clatter of another. He looked up to see Pastor Lepp cutting towards him some distance away on the Lepps' quarter. As he unhooked the traces so that some inadvertent jerk of the horses would not injure him, he heard the other machine stop. He was loosening the pitman when the preacher crunched up, smiling.

"Good morning, Thom. Troubles?"

"Morning. I don't know how that root got so far into the slough, but it broke off a finger. Seems like it didn't bother the knife."

"A person never knows how trouble gets around the way it does, but it manages to keep most people occupied." Thom had the pitman unbolted and the Pastor hunched down beside him. With a heave, they jerked the knife a great length out of its groove. Thom said,

"That's enough. The break is near the top. Thanks. It would have been hard, alone."

"Yes." The Pastor stood erect, watching Thom scrabble in his kit for a spare finger. "Everything's easier, done together. Maybe your knife's bent."

"Could be. Do you think we should draw it out altogether?"

"Yes. And it would be easier to work on that finger if you had the bar upright."

They heaved in unison again. The older man said, "You go ahead with the finger—I'll check this."

"Okay." Thom went around and lifted the bar erect. They worked.

The Pastor said, "There's just a bit of a kink. Odd: the finger must have snapped very easily. The hammer should fix this." Having laid the viciously gleaming mower-knife on the pole, he rapped strongly, then sighted again. "Should do." He leaned it there and went round to where Thom, a knuckle barked from a slipped wrench, was tightening the dull finger into its shining phalanx.

Without warning, without looking up, Thom said, "Pastor, what are the traditions of the fathers?"

Startled, the older man said nothing, then, "Why do you ask? Surely you, having grown up here, know about—"

The short and almost chilly question brought Thom to himself. The Pastor's friendly assistance and workday clothes had not invited rudeness.

"I'm sorry, sir, I just asked the question out of the blue like that. It was rather rude of me. But living here all my life is just the problem. I've grown up here and readily talk about acting in the traditions of the fathers, but when I think about it, I don't know really what that means. For instance, our fathers never knew Indians so they could not tell us how to behave towards them. How do we act according to the fathers in many things of which they knew nothing?"

Lepp looked thoughtfully across the bird-haunted marsh. "Odd you should ask me now, Thom. I've thought about this a great deal, sitting on the plow, the mower. It seems to me we have to organize our ideas a little." In the sunlight, the wide hat-brim shadowed the long jaw. Thom rapped the bolt, listening. "The fundamental teaching our fathers followed was that the

Bible is God's recorded revelation to man. Whatever commands the believer reads in it are sacred to him. If Christ in its pages commanded them to turn the other cheek, then they did so."

Thom asked, mind aroused, "Does the Bible make Christ sacred or does Christ make the Bible sacred?"

Lepp said slowly, but warmly, "I don't know if that question can rightly be asked. Without Christ the Bible loses all uniqueness, for everything it speaks of centres in Christ. In the sense that Christ is God's complete revelation and that Christ's words are recorded in the Bible, in that sense Christ makes the Bible a divine book. So to get back: if Christ says we are to love our enemies if we wish to follow Him, then we cannot but do that. This is the basic teaching of our people: always we must be followers of Christ. The teachings of Christ, rightly applied, are the solution to every possible problem we can encounter on earth. Since He is the Son of God, it can be no otherwise."

"Yes." Thom knocked the finger with the back of his wrench, testing.

"From this foundation, they went the next step. Christ's followers are peculiar in this world. As His disciples, our fathers believed they could not participate in worldly affairs, whether of government, business or amusement. The Christian is called to do higher things. They withdrew themselves from the sinful pursuits of the world, and we are doing that here in Wapiti also. We avoid worldly practices. Over the years, our fathers developed simple customs which in themselves may not be particularly right, but are time-tested to be harmless and therefore worth our maintaining them. Those are the traditions of the fathers: obedience to Christ's commandment of Love, and simplicity of life."

Thom said, thinking hard, "The first step is obedience to the fundamental teachings of Christ. The second, putting these teachings into practice."

"Yes."

"Then how, for example," he asked, confident of his direction now, "are we acting particularly as Christ's disciples by using only German in our church services?"

The Pastor smiled for the first time in their conversation.

"You talked to Joseph too long. There's nothing Christian about the language itself. God did not use it to speak to Adam in the Garden! It happens to be the language our parents spoke and we speak, but any other would do as well. The fact is, it's a barrier between us and the worldly English surroundings we have to live in. There is merit in that, for it makes our separation easier; keeps it before us all the time. That's the reason Deacon Block was so insistent at our church meeting."

"Yes," the mention of the Deacon diverted Thom's thoughts from his original intention, "but he insists on other things too. We are never to do anything that has not been done before, *in the church;* yet for his farm he buys a tractor, and everyone agrees it's very fine—"

The other sobered. "The Deacon has done many great things for us here in Wapiti—never forget that, Thom. He started us all when we had nothing. Ask your father how Mr Block started him when he arrived here with a big family. Without his leadership, we would not be a third as far as we are now. To the young people he sometimes seems to insist on trivialities, but he does so for everyone's good. Obedience to authority goes against our human nature sometimes, but godly behaviour is always difficult. Discipline and restraint can only strengthen our spiritual convictions, even though the things we wish to do may not be terribly wrong in themselves." The Pastor spoke for his own benefit as well as the youth's, staring steadily across the noon-blanched meadow. He glanced up at the sun. "We've talked right into dinner. I must go. Let's put the knife back in."

Thom, breaking from his thoughts, looked back at the stack his father and Hal were bucking together half a mile away. The horses were feeding and Hal's small figure came running towards them. Thom went round the machine and bent with the Pastor, wondering how he could begin again. He said, slowly, conventionally,

"Thanks very much for helping me. Would have been awkward by myself."

Lepp laughed. "You'd have done it alone as quickly, what with our talking."

"Thanks." How could he ask?

The Pastor paused in his turn, thoughtful, then spoke rapidly, as from impulse: "Everyone has difficulties—I too. Remember that in the end, only your faith in Christ can help you. You may doubt our day-to-day expression of Christianity here in Wapiti, but you can never let these doubts affect your basic belief in Christ. If they do, Satan has you where he wants you."

The words, touching Thom at his deepest hurt, stirred him to plunge into his question. "Sir, that's just it. I don't doubt Christ, but our expression of our belief—that's why I really wanted to ask you about the Bible class—the one I'm holding with the—other children on Sunday afternoon—"

The older man looked up, face as if wiped blank. "Yes?"

Thom hesitated, intimidated by the look, yet caught by the faint encouragement of the "yes." "I—I don't really know how to teach very well. I only sat in on two classes with Joseph before he left, and he's such an outstanding teacher—the stories just live for the children. With me—I was wondering if perhaps—" he paused.

Lepp said distantly, looking squarely at him, "Didn't Joseph leave you his lesson booklets?"

"Yes."

"Don't they explain how each lesson is to be taught?"

"Yes—but the lessons really are meant for children that know more about the Bible than these do. They know exactly as much as they can remember from the few months Joseph taught them. He said that when he began they hardly knew who Jesus was. You have to explain everything so simply—I'm not a teacher like he is."

"Why don't you stop?"

"No!" Thom burst out, dreading he had somehow given the wrong impression. "I have to go on—I just need help."

The Pastor's sternness broke in a great smile, "I know, Thom, but I wanted to see how you were taking it. I've two very good books on teaching Bible classes: certain sections should help you a great deal. One of them is even written in English!" His voice became grave. "But personally, I cannot really help you. When it came to the attention of the church council last spring that Joseph had begun the class, never mentioning a word to the church, the council was strongly opposed to him. Joseph no doubt acted on the assumption that the fewer questions asked, the better. As far as his plan was concerned, it was definitely better. Several years ago—probably before you can remember clearly—your brother David asked such a question of the church council—and that one was too much."

Thom said, grimly, "I remember."

Lepp sighed. "Yes. Well, this time a few of the brethren were able to persuade the others at least not actively to oppose him—or you now. But as leader of the church I can give you little help, other than such private advice as I can offer. What you do, you must do on your own."

They could hear Hal's distant shouting, as he approached, "Thom! Dinner! Com'mon!" But they did not turn. The Pastor continued, after a moment,

"I think that you, and Joseph, are doing the finest Christian deed ever done in Wapiti. But I must stay with the opinion of the church. They will surely see some day—all of them."

Thom said, amazed, "But sir, why don't you just get up on Sunday and preach until they—"

"No!" Lepp's voice rasped strongly. "More is involved than you young men can dream of. It takes more than a sermon. And who would take it upon himself to smash almost every single belief that a man—that a group of people hold essential. But one man, young—alone—he can start it. And with time—" the Pastor turned abruptly on his heel. "—God bless you, Thom. You can do more than I."

After a time he said, his tone oddly rough across the noon hush of the meadow, "Come on Saturday evening. I'll have the books for you."

As Hal trotted up, gasping questions, Thom's eyes followed the retreating back. He had seen, heard, talked to the Pastor times without number, but he could not remember having met him before. Annamarie's father.

CHAPTER SEVEN

"My, it's been a lovely summer. And almost gone. I look forward to berrying, but when we do go it seems sad because the haying's done and summer is about over then."

"Yes," Annamarie answered Margret after a pause. "I was thinking that just this morning. But there's still bindering and stooking and perhaps even nice fall weather." Her fingers flicked among the low blueberry bushes, stripping them expertly into her large syrup-pail.

"Uh-huh." Margret stretched, trying to get another bush without rising. "Weather's been lovely. And after the one storm in church, there's been nothing to disturb us."

"Of course. With Joseph gone, what would happen? 'All's right' with our world." The other girl moved quickly to where the berries winked in blue profusion.

Margret continued, unheeding, "Thom sometimes gets a letter from Joseph. About once every long month, huh, Thom?"

Thom had been quietly picking in his corner of the patch, content to be within sight of Annamarie and occasionally hear her low voice. As Margret repeated his name, he looked up, Annamarie's inflection festering.

"Huh?"

"You get letters from Joseph, don't you?"

"Well, I've only had the one last week." He hunched nearer the girls, picking the sparse but plumper berries around a willow-tuft. "He's in Basic Training—whatever that means. Something where you have to train to shoot and crawl under barriers and that kind of thing. Toughening up, he calls it."

"Does the Restricted Medical Corps have to train like that too—with rifles and all?" Annamarie asked, glancing up just as he looked at her.

He said, picking, "No. That's one of the odd things about their training. The restricted medicals never handle fire-arms of any kind. He writes they run around with stretchers and medical packs while the others carry rifles and shells."

Margret rose to move farther. "Wow!" she yawned, "this is a good patch. Wonder where our mothers are. And the kids. Bet they're just playing among the stumps. At least Hal is."

They were in the wilderness north-west of Wapiti School, beyond Herman Paetkau's lonely farm and Poplar Creek between the lake and the river, the wilderness which decades before had been stripped by fire. Tall and crooked jack-pines murmured over great tangles of charred logs and spired stumps. Among the skeletons of razed forest, under the new pines, blueberries flourished wildly. With saskatoons, they were the chief winter fruit for all Wapiti.

Annamarie said, "I think Cornie would have gone into that service too if it had been open when he was called up. He's sick of CO camp. He writes that to hear the news is awful for him, yet he can't tear himself away from the radio when it comes on. Buzz-bombs falling on London, the French ruined, Germans killing in retreat, the Chinese starving, while they sit in Jasper planting trees that could wait as easily as not. But the worst is the way some of the men, our people often too, don't understand or care what is really going on outside in the world. They're happy that their own conscience is satisfied—they care for no more." The girl paused a moment. "He wrote in his last letter, 'Am I to be concerned only with the final redemption of my own soul? Have we progressed so far as to call *that* Christ's teaching? Or do I do something for my neighbour also? Sometimes I think that planting trees is not enough of an answer to that question.'"

Thom said slowly, watching two birds wheel, high in the sky, "What else can a Christian do, the wickedness of the world being what it is? Surely not join in the killing and add to the misery."

"Of course not. There are far too many persons already doing that. But we should be as aggressive as the others, just in the opposite direction. Sam is quite content to work in that boot factory and one evening a week help at a down-town mission, but sometimes our refusal to have anything to do with the War means only, 'Well, I'm doing the right thing and am bound for heaven—let the rest of the world go to hell as it wishes.' Occasionally Cornie's letters are more cheerful, but after weeks of only doing the same old thing and the War worse than ever, the mountains around Jasper are 'like a wall sheltering me from my duty in the world.' "

Margret said, "At least the Canadians treat the CO's decently. Rita Wolfe told me the other day that her uncle—he lived in the States then already—was called up into the United States Army during the First War and they sent him to a camp and beat him terribly because he and six others wouldn't take orders to cut down weeds in the camp."

Thom gulped, "What? They wouldn't cut down weeds because they were CO's?"

"So Rita said. Mr Wolfe said so too."

"How in the world were they expressing Christianity by refusing to cut down a weed?"

"Oh, the other Mennonites at the camp got along very well. Only these seven refused to have anything to do with the Army. Mr Wolfe said his brother was a fanatic."

Annamarie said sadly, "But men like that stick in people's memories and the ones that really are sincere get a bad name."

They picked in silence for a time. Margret thought of Sam. If the War were soon over, he would be released perhaps within a year. Then he would be home!

Thom wanted to think of Annamarie; with her there before him, he wanted somehow to fit their friendship into the simple customs of the Mennonite people her father had talked of. Ordinarily, if a Wapiti boy considered a girl, he prayed to God earnestly and then, if convinced, asked for her hand in marriage; yet Annamarie's openness completely nonplussed Thom. A boy and girl just did not drive out casually on a moonlit night. He had looked forward to the berrying because he would then be near her for a whole day, but now the talk of war usurped his thoughts, as always.

Four days before he had been at the store for the mail. He had turned from Lamont's smiling face behind the wicket, and there on the wall a red cardboard youth stared into space from his poster, head propped thoughtfully on hand. Words leaped into focus: "HAVE I THE GUTS?—ask yourself this question. One look in the mirror will give you the answer. Am I one of those who lets the other fellow face all the danger? Look yourself straight in the eye. The Canadian Army needs you NOW and needs you for overseas service."

"Nice posters they're sending out, eh?" Old Lamont had come round the partition and blinked at him over the cluttered counter. "Pretty desperate for overseas recruits, I'd say. What do you think of it?" The rheumy voice needled slightly. He had fought his war thirty years before.

"Guess they can send out cheap posters if they want."

"In the Great War they had no need to send posters like that to every smallest post office. Now—" The old Scot turned, his hand in a candy jar. "Mr Block has me put them up about a day to fill regulations." He shuffled out suddenly and jerked the red-blue poster from the wall. "Stupidity! Them as are gutless it won't bother. And for the others it's no' a matter of stomach."

Thom looked up, surprised, into the blinky eyes. He read the old friendliness and understanding there, mellowed with something like pity. For a moment Thom could not fathom that last then he turned quickly towards the door.

"Thanks, Mr Lamont." As he closed the door, he heard the cardboard crumpling.

Thom stirred, looking up at Annamarie as she picked swiftly. Her slender figure seemed hardly to touch the ground.

The girl was thinking about her brother's struggles and what answer she could return. She gloried in friendship. Marriage, which in the Wapiti situation of male initiative dominated most girls' thoughts after leaving school, was to Annamarie a natural consequence of life and so she did not bother herself thinking about it. She did not for a moment doubt she would some day marry; she was so unconscious of her own charming femininity, so occupied with what to her were more pressing matters, that she had no idea of Thom's upheaval. She had enjoyed the drive of two months ago beyond expression, but she had reacted to the beauty of the whole evening, not merely to Thom's presence. Her whole character conspired to conceal from her the effect she had had on the youth.

She arose now with her brimming pail. "I'm going to empty—are you?"

"Oh, you're always so fast—but I'm about full too." Margret laughed, "Thom's only half!"

"Well," he said, pretending discouragement, "I only come along to drive you anyway."

"If you'd let us try, you might lose that job too," Annamarie laughed as the two girls walked toward the milk pails in the shade of a pine-clump. The team and horses were out of sight in the trees.

So were the two older women, who picked with the greatest rapidity. Since coming to Canada they had acquired their families' winter fruit in this way. They tried to keep the smaller children in sight, if not within admonishing distance, but with Hal to stir the Lepp twosome into action, either task was impossible. Bent on their work, they contented themselves with occasional halloos.

The three children were beyond a low ridge and a thick stand of pine, happy in their isolation. Since they had grown up in a wild country, the bush held no fears for them. Though the youngest, Hal was clearly the leader. He had conceived a Great Plan that morning and had been trying ever since to get nine-year-old Johnny away by himself to reveal it, but Trudie, two years older and equipped with adequate intuition, stuck with them tenaciously. Finally Hal blurted his idea in her presence and she, habitual superiority forgotten, cried,

"Oh-h yah! Look at these pines here! The cabin could be right here and we've lots of trees to build it and for fire-wood in the winter—"

"Shucks," Hal sneered, "I guess any *girl* would build on the north side of trees so she could have all the wind and snow blowin' right on toppa her. It's right in the open—anyone could see it an' they'd find us right away an' get us home. Na, we've gotta build it in the thick bush, in that hollow we come through that's so thick all round—"

"Yah," Johnny echoed, eyes agleam, "an' me an' Hal would be trappin' all winter like the Indians an' come back at night with our furs in the snow an' you could be here in the cabin all day cookin 'an' doin' stuff an' we'd skin 'em in the evenin' an'—"

The three sat silent on the moss, faces rapt in the dream, pines whispering above them. They were alone on earth and theirs was one great happiness of anticipated life. They thought of the small open hollow they had traversed among the silent pines and the completed cabin already stood there thick-frosted with snow, smoke curling around the ice-rim of its chimney and up between laden trees. Johnny reached into the pail beside his sister and thoughtfully ate the last berries.

"How much do you get for a mink, huh?"

Hal considered profoundly. "'Bout five bucks."

They had, occasionally, seen that much money when their fathers took them along to the store. Hal said, in wonder that they had never thought of running away before (it was not that they disliked their homes: they were not thinking of their parents), "'Magine! We could get 250 taffy suckers for *one* mink. 'Nough for a whole winter!" They sat in silent awe.

"Aw, how could you two shrimps build a cabin?" the momentary charming of Trudie's habitual superiority faded. "An' what would we live on all the time—suckers?"

Hal had known it would not do to tell her. For a moment he had succumbed to the obvious asset of a cook and dish washer, but they'd never wash anyway and she'd just want to boss them. He said, caustic, "I never asked *you* to come. You can just keep quiet—tha's all—we don't want any stinky girls—"

"I'll tell your Mom on you an'—"

"No you won't," Hal yelled, "I'll smash you to pieces before—" and he flew at her with daring intent, not caring that she could always throw him down, when Johnny, who in wise meekness always sided with the winner, hissed sharply. The children froze, listening.

A horse trotting in their direction. In a moment the legs of a bay were visible through the tree-trunks, and then the rider emerged. It was Herb Unger. He jumped his horse over a log and reined up, grinning at Hal's war-like posture.

"Hi, kids. What're you fighting and hollering about?" He lounged on his jaded horse, face friendly.

"Hi, Mr Unger," said Trudie, shifting swiftly into her as-one-adult-to-another attitude. "It's just Hal—always makin' a fuss." She talked as a mother would speak about her week-old infant. "He just got the idea of running away from ho—"

"Shut up, shut up, you ol' sow!" Hal fairly screamed, only the presence of an adult restrained his attack. "You ol'—"

"Now hold on there, kid," Herb's voice soothed. He was alone enough to enjoy talking to children. "No use to get mad. Running away's all right—every kid wants to, but it's a big job if—"

"You can keep quiet too!" Hal shouted, past all caring. He glared up at the rough figure above him in the saddle, at the gun slung in the scabbard under the stirrup. "You think you're such a Bigshot ridin' around all the time with a gun." Herb's grin broadened and Hal, completely infuriated, could only scream, "You wait till Thom gets you!" The little boy's frantic thoughts caught on an incident. "Can't even keep your fence fixed! Thom was mad enough to clean you up that time. Just wait till he gets you! He'll do it right now if he sees you hanging round here."

Herb's face darkened as he looked at the two Lepp children. "Yah." He muttered half in his beard. "He'd be here—picking berries with the women." He spoke more loudly, Hal jubilant at the anger in his voice: "Where are they?"

Trudie directed importantly, "They're over the ridge. Mom's over there, the others there."

Without a word, Herb wheeled his horse stiffly and trotted into the trees, ducking the supple branches. The children listened to the faint thump of hoofs on moss, then Hal whispered, rage forgotten, "Maybe there'll be a fight! Com'mon!" All three raced after the rider, their empty pails left blinking in the empty clearing.

Thom and the two girls had picked their way into the open where only the stumps and half-burned logs lay under the long sky. Margret looked at the sun, high and directly in the west. "About one more pail—then time for chores."

Thom thought, And the day will be over. He looked at Annamarie, picking steadily, and she glanced up and smiled. He could not have enough of looking at her; he was thinking that a whole lifetime would not suffice to see her, when the snort of an approaching horse marred the quiet. As they looked up, wondering, Herb emerged from among the trees.

Without particularly trying to avoid Herb, Thom had not encountered him since the picnic two months before. Herb now drew rein near them, looking in silence at the girls, and Thom suddenly comprehended a shade of this man's need. Here was a man as lost and forlorn as the haif-breed children that squirmed tousle-haired and ragged on the school seats every Sunday afternoon. Concerning the beginning of their antipathy Thom could not remember anything, except that childish matter about the two fish and then his own even more childish behaviour at the ball-game. How a mole-hill had mushroomed! He said, smiling, longing for friendship, "Hello, Herb. Out for a ride?"

The other returned, without a look, "No, I'm diggin' ditches." Margret blushed slightly under his gaze. "Hi. How's the berries?"

"They're good here," with a wave of her hand. "See for yourself." She busied herself with picking as Herb slid in one motion from the saddle and hunched down near her. Margret had never told anyone except her mother that Herb Unger had once asked her to marry him. She could still remember the question as it had confronted her one evening the preceding summer while the sun flamed out in the west. Alone, she was idling along the grain-field where faintly-pink roses bloomed thick among the rocks, when he appeared beside her as if he had followed all the evenings that she had walked there, a ghostly attendant. As she understood, the question pushed stunningly into her shock. He accepted her silence as hesitation and repeated the question gently, adding he now had a farm that could be fixed up, that she would be close to her parents. She could only think of the smell of his greased hair stifling the fragrance of wild-roses pinned at her breast, then she abruptly burst into running across the growing grain towards the house, not caring for anything save flight, her broken, "Oh-h, never—never!" seeming to stretch thin and snap in the twilight air between them as she fled.

She had no inkling of how he had stood, feet in the green grain, listening to her stumbled steps, and then shuffled back to his hovel like a whipped animal. She only knew now the dreadful distaste she had felt then, as out of the corner of her eye she saw his black-rimmed fingers rooting for berries. Now she hunched away.

Annamarie asked, in her warm voice, "What do you hunt this time of year?"

His voice broke in an unaccustomed laugh, "Well, I got tired o' the same old thing, so I thought I might find me a small deer strollin' around eatin' berries maybe. Must ha' heard me comin' though."

"Hunt out of season?" Her voice was reproving.

"Have to eat every day, dontcha? An' Indians can shoot year round."

"You're no Indian, and it's not right to do it, Herb."

"We-ell, some people don't think I'm much better." He spoke in that peculiarly expressionless voice that he could employ on occasion; to each of them his words meant something quite different.

"Go on with you! Nobody thinks that. And if you'd behave yourself as you—"

"But that's just the trouble. I don't. The Wienses here are my neighbours—they know. That's why they're both pickin' berries like mad! Look at 'em."

Annamarie said coolly, "We're your neighbours on the other side and we haven't complained. What makes you think—"

"Yah, but the Wienses," Herb paused, looking only at Thom, "have to put up with my poor fencing—so that they blame near chuck their love-for-all-fellow-men overboard and get all riled up in their house, which is just far enough from my place so I can't hear them. Don't they, Thom?" The sarcasm jelled thickly. Herb stood up, gnawing savagely on a few berries. "Why didn't you come right over when you found my stock in your oats, Thom, and tell me to get that fence wired? Why send your Pa and the Deacon and my old man? Need the whole confounded church to tell one sinner he has to fix his fence?"

Annamarie, looking at the square grimy figure and then noting the fumble of Thom's huge fingers among the berry-bushes, thought, Wouldn't you be the surprised one if he ever took you up on your big words? It was clear to her that Herb talked because he rather depended on Thom controlling himself, yet that very restraint was partly what needled the bachelor to his baiting.

Thom said evenly, getting up to move with his pail, "When I run my own place, I'll do that. You know the way we have of settling among ourselves."

"Your kid brother there tells me that's not quite the way you felt that morning."

All had been so intent that only Herb had noticed the children approach. Thom, standing now, with Annamarie seated directly between him and Herb, turned with the girls to see the three grouped beyond the grazing horse. To Thom, Hal's face said, as if he had shouted it, "Plaster that Herb!" Thom knew the expression only too well; half his mind was urging with Hal, but he said, taking a step nearer the older man, "We all make mistakes in more ways than we know. I know what I wanted to do that morning, and I'm very sorry for it now."

Herb nodded. "Yah. Nice speech." He turned towards his horse, not looking towards the girls. "Probably be a preacher some day. I hear you're already tryin' it on the breeds—oh, hello, Mrs Lepp, Mrs Wiens."

The two women had come up unnoticed, carrying their brimming pails. As they greeted Herb in their quiet way, Mrs Wiens added, "It's time we were going too. Look at the sun."

Herb had mounted and, with a jerk, pulled his horse around. "Nice talkin' to you folks. Hope my visitin' doesn't sour your fruit."

Mrs Wiens laughed, "Now why should it do that?" She pitied him with all her mother's heart, this embittered man who was like an evil genius to her children, a man unloved and battering his better nature against the wall of what he knew he should do. Somewhere, along the line of his life, some Christian had possibly made a mistake. Or perhaps many. She looked down at her pail, misty-eyed.

"Never can tell," Herb answered in the same easy tone, but his glance at Thom was quite different. For a brief choking instant, Thom almost heard him say, "Not only your Pa's pants, but now behind women's skirts!" Aloud, Herb only added, as an afterthought, "Well, well, well." Then he kicked his sweat-roughened horse into a gallop and was lost among the trees.

Annamarie, the fading hoof-beats drumming in her ear, looked after Thom's tall figure retreating to the wagon with the berries, and she could only think, You've started, Thom. But you will have to let go more—much more.

CHAPTER EIGHT

"This is the Trans-Canada Network of the CBC. CBQ, Saskatchewan.

"We bring you now a re-broadcast of the BBC reports on the liberation of Paris. This is a compilation of various programs heard during the past three days. The program is transcribed."

Overseas static blared, then martial music, triumphant and stately, poured out of the brown radio. Thom stretched and twisted the volume lower, conscious of Hal sleeping above him with only the saggy paper of the living-room ceiling and the floor-boards above to absorb the sound, Head profiled against the western window by the sun sinking livid behind black spruce, he sat in the worn corner-rocker, listening. Up from the floor, from the depths of the corners, shrouding the organ-hulk, edging up the sewing machine with its crested flower-pots by the double window, wrapping the squat heater next the bedroom door, along the tin-pipe reaching into the ceiling, crept the summer darkness. Only at a blotch of sunlight did it hesitate, tentative as a leaf-flicker on the white-washed plaster, then moment by long moment it seeped in darkeningly. His eyes unseeing on a fading sky beyond the silhouetted flowers, Thom listened.

A high English voice was speaking: "At six o'clock this morning of the 25th of August—a day to be remembered—we were in an American jeep behind General Leclerc's armoured car, moving into Paris. Ahead of us, the tanks cleaned up a few pockets of the enemy. By nine o'clock we drove through the

Porte d'Orleans. We were in Paris at last! It is quite impossible to imagine how the French people . . ."

Meaningless names shrilled from the radio. The Germans had finally been pried from Paris. As Old Lamont had said in the store, gaunt arm reaching for the baking soda on the shelf, "Germany kaput!" As if he were spitting. And Block echoed, entering at that moment, "It looks that way," regret faint in his voice. Thom felt the regret too, for he knew his family had been among the few last to escape the Communists in 1930 because of German government pressure. But that had been President Hinderburg, not the Hitler regime. Yet regret persisted, faintly.

The Deacon would doubtless be speaking a great deal in church tonight. For a moment Thom wished he was twenty years old. When he thought of all he knew about what was being threshed through that evening, he could almost have laughed at his staying home because he was too young, supposedly, to know about the problems that arose where a man and a woman were concerned. As if at one magic moment, you could suddenly freely discuss people's intimate affairs. They had to set the line somewhere, he supposed. How Mom hated the meetings, where, layer by layer, private affairs were scratched open until only enough was left hidden to provide certain imaginations with lurid possibilities. But she had gone, with Pa and Margret, for the church had to decide what stand it would take. And he, within six months of the age, was sitting at home while knowing more of the matter than any church members. They would soon know enough.

". . . merci, merci, merci!" A massive swelling of sound like the prayer of an innumerable multitude, then the voice of the announcer: "Those were the people of Paris, shouting their welcome to us. I wish you could see them! All around the square below me, everywhere embracing soldiers and newspapermen, tears streaming down their faces. And everywhere the solid chant, 'Merci'. It is enough to make . . ."

Not understanding the word, it seemed oddly out of place to Thom when they had just been freed from four years of German control—but he could not concentrate. His own thoughts, liberated at last, dominated. Both he and Herman Paetkau had wanted it known what Herman had done, but neither of them expected it to be seven long months before another Mennonite visited Herman and found out. All the breeds knew, for Herman was their friend, but they never told the Mennonites anything. Knowing the Mennonites' rigidity regarding man-woman relations, the breeds had probably had many a laugh at Mennonite expense during those seven months. Thom could still see Herman's face that frozen day in February when he had ridden into the bachelor's yard to warm himself after the futile hunting of wolves that wandered around the rim of their corral every night. Thom could not remember having been in that yard more than twice in his life. In the northwest corner of the district, a mile beyond even the breed homesteads, the bachelor lived on his half-section for reasons Thom could not imagine. Herman, having heard the dog bark and the crack of frozen saddle-leather, tumbled from his snow-heaped cabin, pulling on his sheep-skin parka, face open with welcome. And Thom had perhaps spoken to him ten times in his life. Not only the cold made him clumsy in dismounting and leading Nance into the smoking barn and rubbing her down while Herman broke into a bundle of green-feed. It was amazement at the hospitality.

"That's good. Give her a nice rest where it's warm. Now come in and we'll thaw you out with a cup of coffee." Herman led across the small yard and Thom slid off his rubbers to step from the lean-to through the board door that Herman drew open and there, putting a stick of wood into the top of the stove as she turned to smile at him entering, had been Madeleine Moosomin.

". . . Eiffel Tower, and the great open area before it, the crowds were almost overwhelming the small cavalcade of cars. High above, the Stars and Stripes and the Tricolor waved side by side. The Germans were almost rooted out. Only here and there a sniper fired from a window, and immediately F.F.I. would fire back with their old rifles while others rushed in. No sniper could stop the crowds from spreading. A little girl handed us a Tricolor as we eased past, and one of the soldiers in the car leaned over and kissed her laughing face. The people were cheering, 'Merci'!"

Thom had gone in and sat down at Herman's gesture. He opened his parka, bewildered. It was not that he did not know the woman, for when he entered grade one she had been struggling in an upper class in Wapiti and had left school shortly after. For years, behind barns the white riff-raff of Beaver district had spewed rumours, smirking, of why she did not marry. Thom had seen her only occasionally, at a Christmas concert or a picnic, where her clean healthy appearance always surprised him. He had assumed, with the other Mennonites who noticed, that she was too young to show her degeneracy; that the years would clamp down in abrupt harshness as they did on all half-Indian faces. Yet there she stood at the stove as if she belonged.

Herman said, his voice warm, "I guess Madeleine being here rather balls you up. It's okay, we both understand. She's been here since the blizzard in January."

Thom ventured quickly, "It's just that I figured you'd be alone and, since I was so far from home and about chilled through—those crazy wolves—"

"Goodness sakes, you're welcome! Don't get me wrong. Haven't the nerve myself on a hard day like this to ride out after those robbers, though they bother me more than you people. I haven't had a Mennonite visit me since a good while before Christmas."

"What?" Amazed. "They don't come to see you—not on Sunday afternoon?"

"Oh, they usually have relatives or close friends to visit. I'm old, and a bachelor—or rather was (with a ringing laugh)—and it's a long way up here."

"It's not really so far, just three miles from the school—"

"Far enough if you don't want to come. But never mind—you came. Must be about the first time—no, once David came out years ago, just before he left for India, and you came along then, a little shaver. I was sorry in a way when David left—sorry for myself, I guess, mostly. Everyone must do the work given him."

They talked for some minutes of David and his wife. Because of the war, instead of returning to Canada on furlough, they had had to accept a brief holiday in northern India, and were now on their second five-year term. And as they talked, Thom could not contain his wonder that all the Mennonites, even his own parents, seemed to avoid the lonely bachelor. Herman was a grown man when he came to Canada, thirty-seven or -eight years old, as Wiens told him evasively later; he really belonged among them. And Herman, calmly smiling as the coffee-breath richened in the room, had told him.

". . . General de Gaulle's day, this 26th of August, 1944." The radio voice was different now. "While the shooting of snipers and the French return-fire is heard down the streets to the right, the General has laid two wreaths of gladioli on the tomb of the Unknown Soldier in the Arc de Triomphe. They are marching now toward Notre Dame." After an interval, the voice changed again. "The procession is coming down the Champs Elysees. At the head is General de Gaulle, marching briskly. They are now entering cars to proceed to the Cathedral. Cars piled high with people, tears and laughter evident everywhere. Listen to the cheering—" And the great voice of the Parisian people blossomed in the room. Thom could not help but listen. To be free after four years. The idea held little meaning for him.

His fingers running the familiar groove in the wooden rocker-arm which he had ground there with a long nail once many years before during a small-boyish fit of temper, he remembered Herman over his coffee in the scrubbed kitchen. "It's a long time to live fourteen years alone, even in the bush of Canada. But you get used to it—or think you do, and then something happens and you know that you're really not at all." Madeleine sat on a stool beside the red stove knitting, her serenity like his mother's late on a winter Saturday night when the heater cracked, and they all had finished bathing in the tin tub on the kitchen floor and the buns lay under the clean tea-towel in a great heap on the side-table, high, where Hal could not sneak the brownest as handily as he might wish. "You know that storm about a month ago? It hit here just like that!" and Herman slammed his hands together. "The Moosomins get milk from me all the time. Madeleine usually came to get it every two days or so. She came early on Wednesday because the storm looked bad in the north and they needed the milk badly for the baby—Jacq's, I think, isn't it?—but that storm hit with a screech while I was filling her pail, and I had trouble getting her horse to the barn for shelter, leave alone her riding home." Herman thought for a moment, then added, "She liked it here, didn't you?"

"Yes." She spoke gently, without looking up. It was the first word she spoke, but her silence was not really noticeable for she seemed taking part in their conversation.

Thom, sitting now in the living room with an occasional lost mosquito droning on the screens in the last flicker of day, wrestling with that day when he had sat in the small kitchen, brilliant from sun on snow, caught a vistage of the human depth the bachelor had suppressed into a sentence. Herman had lived alone since his aunt and uncle died in their first year at Wapiti. For him to have another person in the house, one who did not leave hurriedly but peeped into his neat cupboards and fingered the cotton window-curtains, a woman who had just been there as slowly he must have grown conscious of her whom, as he had laughingly put it, he had before merely considered as the "Moosomin-girl-who-gets-the-milk," the raging storm must suddenly have seemed a thrust into humanity. As he watched her, perhaps with the comb from his wash-stand soothing her black hair to gentleness about her face, the deft movements of her woman's shape began to stir the long-buried longings in him, longings whose very existence he had probably forgotten.

The remembered look on Herman's face had said that, and more. What the "more" was, Thom could not capture, but Herman's words hammered now as they could not before because he had promised to forget the whole incident: "Those three days of the blizzard, I read the Bible with her. She knew nothing of it, really. Yet she'd kept herself clean—those rumours were just the jealousy of the men with whom she would have nothing to do. I asked her. And Thom, every night, when I heard her stirring there in the bedroom as I lay here on the kitchen floor, I knew that that storm shrieking outside was God's blessing on both of us."

On that February afternoon, not having then thought about these matters, Thom had only felt instantaneous revulsion at the man's action. Looking at Madeleine, he could not recall having seen a more noble woman, yet his conscience insisted. Herman was a member of Wapiti Mennonite Church; church members did not live alone with and then marry any half-breed woman that rode into their yards. Though his reason could formulate small argument why a man, as good as avoided by his community for fourteen years and never visited except by accident, should not return the affection of a woman who, once she heard clearly, accepted Christianity and whose keenest delight after thirty years of squalor was to learn more of what Christian living entailed, his conscience reared, violated. Herman said, noting his face darken, "We drove to Hainy when the storm let up and the J.P. married us. You're the only Mennonite in Wapiti who knows."

That had exceeded all limits. To call himself a Christian and be married outside the church. His thinking had bogged, blind to its own illogic. Even now, his mind rebelled, blindly.

". . . Notre Dame. The procession is before the main entrance. On either side of General de Gaulle are Generals Leclerc and Koenig. The General is being presented to the people. They are receiving his salute—" From the radio a sudden rattle crashed, and the announcer's voice tensed to hysteria, "Machine-guns! They've opened fire from the Cathedral! Down on the General, the people—they are rushing—crushing to get in—" The radio buzzed a moment, then the voice of the announcer: "That was the most dramatic scene I have ever seen. As General de Gaulle walked down the main aisle, thrusting aside all who would detain him, there was a hail of fire from above *in the Cathedral*! No one could stop him—it was as if he walked into a curtain of bullets. Yet his life was charmed. His shoulders thrown back, he never missed a step. Even now as the organ plays the Te Deum, bullets spit from a few corners

—one smashed into the cornice by his head!" The organ music, rolling, was staccatoed by cracks. There was the buzzing for a moment, then, "The short service is over. The General is marching up the aisle. The guns have been silenced. The people stand huddled about. This is the most extraordinary display of courage I have ever seen. General de Gaulle has taken Paris."

The sound of wheels and trotting horses outside roused Thom. The music rolled on; it was ten o'clock. He could not recall the time passing so quickly, and for a moment he wondered if the broadcast were true. It seemed incredible; shooting and murder in a cathedral while a service was going on. But then that was war. Once you were killing, what did a church matter? He wondered idly why the great general had gone to the cathedral. Could one kneel and thank God for having killed more of the enemy than they had been able to kill of you?

The door squeaked and the steps of Mrs Wiens and Margret entered. Thom could discern only their shapes darkening the darkness of the kitchen door-way. His mother's voice asked, "Is Helmut sleeping?"

"Since before nine." Thom turned off the radio as Mrs Wiens' form crossed to the bedroom. Margret threw her coat on the couch in the corner and slouched beside it. Thom asked, "How did it go?"

"They argued—back and forth. That poor man—and her." Margret's voice was listless.

Mrs Wiens came back, faceless in the gloom. "Now Margret, these things have to be talked through in the church. There must be discipline."

"But why in the world do you—" Margret hesitated as Wiens slammed the door. "Oh, you don't know, Thom, what it's about with Herman."

"I know all about it." He sensed their astonishment as he dropped his words into their unawareness. His father's shape pushed into the room as Thom explained the day in February. Somehow, he had to add, "And Margret, I don't care if there was disagreement: a Christian can't just up and marry any person the storm blows into his house. There have to be rules."

"So what's he to do then? Tell her to stay out and freeze because if she comes into the house he may not be able to control himself? And why shouldn't he marry her?"

She had lanced him to the quick. Why should Herman not have married Madeleine? The reason lay painfully open now: she was a half-breed, and a Mennonite just did not marry such a person, even if she was a Christian. He stared at the bared thought. Despite this summer's work with the breed children every Sunday afternoon, he suddenly knew that he had not yet seen them as quite human. At times a glimmer of it had been there, but not reality. Abruptly his vague relief at the last Bible class of the summer the Sunday before rose to his memory in stark, dreadful simplicity. Public school was beginning within a week, and he had felt relieved to conclude the summer lessons because if one of the children had become a Christian, what would he have done with that child? Had he even taught them as if they were capable of belief?

"Thom," Mrs Wiens spoke into his heavy silence, "why did you never say anything about your visit? Herman has always been friendly with the breeds, but how could you see all this—even at the picnic and all, and never mention anything to us? You're almost twenty; you should have come tonight and explained what you knew."

Wiens said heavily, "Well boy, what possessed you to put on you knew nothing? There wasn't a word said about you."

For a moment Thom wished they would all not say another word; simply go to bed. He was suddenly prostratingly tired. Having pried so deeply into his own subconscious and having recognized such monsters there, he now wanted to say nothing. How could he now explain, even to himself, why he had agreed to silence when Herman had said, as he mounted Nance that winter day, "Thom, I wish you would not say anything to anyone. We'll be living here; anyone can visit us; I'll explain myself if anyone asks. Please, don't mention it now—until some older member has been to see me." Herman's narrow face looked up at him; he knew he did not wish to be involved, but then every church member was responsible for his church; otherwise he was too young to be in it. Now, considering the past eight months, he realized he had been agreeing to an experiment: does my church live up to Christ's injunction to visit the lonely? And more. Though he had never admitted it to himself, Madeleine had sealed his lips. When Herman mentioned that she was, on her mother's side, the great-granddaughter of Big Bear, of whom Thom had never heard, the woman had spoken softly and without show until the sunlight paled on the snow in the brief afternoon. She told of the great Indian who had ruled the Plain Crees as a true monarch; who had signed the treaty with the white man and given up a territory as great as many European countries; who, in his old age, could not prevent his blood-maddened warriors from massacring nine white men at Frog Lake because they believed that the Great White Mother had betrayed their contract. Hearing her tell of Big Bear, Louis Riel, Wandering Spirit, Thom glimpsed the vast past of Canada regarding which he was as ignorant as if it had never been: of people that had lived and acted as nobly as they knew and died without fear. For a few moments, she had become a person to him as she spoke, and unwittingly acting on that comprehension, he had said to Herman, "Yes, I will say nothing."

Now, understanding for the first time, he seized the simplest half-truth, "I didn't want to get mixed up in it."

His father said immediately, "Thom, that was not right—"

Margret interrupted, "You'd have done it exactly the same, Pa. There's no point blaming him now."

Mrs Wiens, knowing them all, soothed sadly, "Don't let's quarrel." She added, as an after-thought, "But it was a long time."

Thom felt ire rise within him, "Yah. Eight months and not a soul visits Herman. How can they call themselves—"

Margret, her face fleetingly revealed as she rose from the couch and sat down rigid on the organ chair, broke in, "What about yourself? You didn't go see him either after you found out—by accident."

Thom's mind leaped to a justification: he had thought about revisiting Herman—several times, but there was never an opportunity at the moment of thought and—he caught himself, ashamed. He could judge others well enough.

Chagrined, he asked, "Who did find out?"

"Block. Who else?" Margret's voice could be aspic. "Last Wednesday."

"Wednesday?" Thom did not understand.

"The Deacon didn't explain right away, but during the evening it became pretty clear that he went there to check up on a bill Herman owed at the store. In the lull before harvest."

"But Herman said he got all his stuff in Calder. I never see him at the store."

"Oh, probably some little thing that everyone had forgotten about—except Mr Block."

Their mother said, "Margret, be decent. There's no need to talk like that about him."

"Mom, he made me so mad today—the way he talked. He wanted Herman just plain hauled through the mud, if he could only find enough. Why couldn't they do what Mr Lepp suggested—talk to her, and if she is really a Christian, let the matter stand?"

Wiens said, hunched on the couch and noisily removing his boots, "Lepp's a good preacher, but I wonder where the church would go if he had his way. A church has to know where to draw the line. You can't just have anything happening and pat it down with a few nice labels."

"Mr Lepp didn't want to bend any principle. And why did the Deacon do it like that, after Herman explained and went out? As if he just wanted everyone to see how terrible it was—miss no detail of blackness—dragging Louis in too, about his drunkenness and being in jail. Can Madeleine help what her brother does? Even Elizabeth had enough. She looked downright sick. She told me she'd begged not to have to come, but he made her."

Wiens returned, with a short humourless laugh, "She should be there! She wanted him badly enough years—" he caught himself.

"What?" both Thom and Margret exclaimed at once.

Mrs Wiens said, distressed, "Pa, you have to drag that out now."

"Mom, what are you talking about? Did Elizabeth and Herman once—" Margret leaned forward in the darkness. Thom sat rigid in amazement.

Dark, earthy matters. Mrs Wiens could not have spoken of them, the eyes of her children intent on her face. Now, it seemed they were just known voices—voices in the darkness. She said, sorrowing, "I guess the whole affair will come out now, one way or another. Well, perhaps not—since only we and the Lepps really know of it. Not if you keep your silence, Pa. But you'd both be too young to know. It was a year after we came; Dietrich Paetkau and his wife had just moved here. They lived on the quarter Aaron Martens has now. And Herman came with them as son."

"They both weren't very strong," Wiens said, his voice reminiscent. "He died that winter of blood poisoning in his foot—no good handling the axe in the bush. They didn't even get to the doctor. She died a few months later—never was strong. Herman lived there alone all winter—let's see—'30—'31—about twenty-three then. Hmm—that was a hard winter—"

Wiens always bogged easily in remembrance, his head thrown back to stare at the ceiling. Mrs Wiens continued. "And David told us (they were very good friends) that Herman wanted to have Elizabeth, so he went to the Deacon and asked if he would say yes if his daughter agreed; that they would have to start very poorly on the farm but—"

"Huh!" Wiens snorted in his odd manner, proud of their desperate beginnings, his very inflection reminding the children that they could never know the labours of pioneering, "We were all as poor as church-mice—only Block had a good start. Well, he had been here four years already."

Mrs Wiens said, "And Block hemmed and hawed and gave Herman no real answer, David said—"

"Guess he was different then than now."

"Margret. Anyway, Herman talked to Elizabeth alone and she was willing, but her father said no. So Herman went to Pastor Lepp to ask what he should do. He said, well, perhaps they could talk to the Deacon together about it. But when they three got together, the whole affair broke open."

"That must have been something!" Wiens laughed shortly.

"And you laugh!" Mrs Wiens' voice sharpened. "It's dreadful that such a thing should even happen!"

"True enough," the older man said thoughtfully. He laughed easily, usually contented with the immediate superficial humour of a situation. Often, as now, his wife had to interpret for him. "It's certainly sad enough."

"Mom, what happened?" Margret said anxiously. Thom's fingers traced the groove in the chair, stiffly.

"Herman was so persistent, I suppose, that Block finally blew up. He told him straight to his face, in front of Pastor Lepp, that he was a—bastard. Said he would never let his daughter marry the child of a slutty Mennonite and a heathen Russian farm-hand."

"Na, Mother," Wiens interjected, "to use such language."

"That's exactly the way he said it—to hurt as much as he could."

"Herman—in Russia?" Thom was jarred from his silence, staggered.

"It's a sad story. Block knew the family in Orenburg in Number 17, north of where we lived." Wiens blew his nose noisily, emotions honestly affected.

"It was a Quiring family. He was Elder in one of the larger villages, and he was so terribly strict he would let his girls do nothing. And one day they found out—with the Russian he used on his big farm and who slept in his own barn. Of course, the scoundrel ran away. The girl died a little later—the older married sister, Dietrich Paetkau's wife, took the boy. They had no children of their own."

"He'd rather let his daughter ruin herself slaving for him on his farm and die an old maid than see her marry a decent man who can't help the fault of his parents. Oh-h—" Margret sounded livid with rage.

"Well, we just saw how decent he was," said Wiens.

"What should he do? Mennonites ignored him for fourteen years. The man is human."

"Don't quarrel," Mrs Wiens repeated. "There's nothing we can do now. Mr Block is probably convinced that he was right then, all this having happened. Herman was so struck, he sold the farm Paetkaus had started and moved out to that homestead in the bush."

"Did he know before?" Margret asked.

"David said no."

They sat silent. There was only the shiver of leaves in the poplar-tree beyond the yard-fence and on the window-screen the probing whine of a mosquito that could not understand that summer was gone. The dark bulks of his parents and sister like presences about him, Thom stumbled, unbelieving.

"Did—things—like that happen—in Russia?"

"Sometimes," his mother spoke as if only to him. "Everything wasn't perfect there, either."

"Well, it didn't happen very often," Pa was convinced. "Not like around here—Unger boys tramping off to war—Herman having to be expelled from the church for living with a breed woman—that sort of thing."

"Oh, Pa, he's married to her, and she's a Christian—"

"So he says. Why doesn't he ever bring her to church? Hasn't been in church himself nearly all summer. Why didn't she come then tonight and tell us herself?"

" 'Cause she can't speak a word of German. What should she do there—sit and be gawked at? You heard yourself that they're expecting a baby next month."

"So it's clear that we'll never know exactly what went on there before they were married."

"Can't you take the man's word? What would he gain by lying—"

Mrs Wiens broke in. "Stop it! It's far too late—we should be in bed."

Wiens said, as if suddenly weary, "Yes. Gret, get the lamp for reading."

As Margret moved into the kitchen, the three in the living-room sat silent again. Thom stared unthinkingly at the black bulge of the radio. A match burst in the kitchen. Margret re-entered and they sat in the wavering light of the coal-oil lamp, staring at their laps, as Wiens thumbed through the worn Bible. He read, in slow German, without comment:

"My little children, these things write I unto you, that ye sin not. And if anyone sin, we have an advocate with the Father, Jesus Christ the righteous: And he is the propitiation for our sins: and not for our's only, but also for the sins of the whole world. And hereby we do know that we know him, if we keep his commandments. He that saith, I know him, and keepeth not his commandments, is a liar, and the truth is not in him. But whoso keepeth his word, in him verily is the love of God perfected: hereby know we that we are in him. He that saith he abideth in him ought himself also so to walk, even as he walked. Brethren, I write no new commandment unto you, but an old commandment which ye had from the beginning."

After a pause, Wiens placed the Bible beside him on the couch. "It's after eleven. We'll stand and I'll pray alone tonight."

His head bowed to his father's prayer, Thom vowed, Immediately after I get back from the harvest crew, I'll start the Bible class again. The Sunday after.

When his brief prayer was completed, Wiens shuffled into the bedroom. "Don't stand around long. Mother, did you put the church papers in the cupboard?"

"Yes, you can lay them right tomorrow." Mrs Wiens picked up the lamp and moved into the kitchen for the alarm clock. Thom turned slowly to half lean on the radio. Through the open window, the sky looked clear like a great dusky band, but the scrolled clouds at the western horizon poised in a massive thunderhead.

Margret said, at his shoulder, "Storm?"

Thom shook his head, "Huh-uh. Too late—and not hot enough for a thunder-storm. No more 'God talking,' as Hal calls it." They looked out across the garden and the road allowance and over the tips of the spruce. "In a few days, comes the harvest."

Margret said, "Poor Elizabeth."

He had not thought of her part in the story before.

"Yeh," he said. They crossed the room and ascended the ladder-like stairs in the corner of the kitchen, one by one. In the boys' portion of the space under the rafters, Hal was breathing peacefully.

Autumn 1944

PRELUDE

An owl-shadow flitted ghostly across the farmyard. Over the tree-tips, glaring like a red-faced giant, leaned the September moon. Frost faintly threaded the trough water and fingered along the rims of the poplar leaves. The owl call, weird, came shivering the silence of the clearing. High, wisped by some stratospheric wind, clouds fled through the night.

In the autumn morning a wagon bumped northward behind two trotting grays. The road skirted a long yellow field immobile in the sun-sprayed hush. Balancing beside the man at the front of the wagon-box, the boy said,

"I heard an owl last night."

"You did?"

"Yah," after a long pause. "In the middle of the night. I woke up and it was bright as anything and you were sleeping and then an owl hooted across the yard." The boy's stubby fingers edged along the man's trouser-leg. "I was scared."

"In bed? Why?"

"I dunno. It sounded—like when we found Bowser with the tree fallen over him, and he died."

The man said abruptly, pointing north, "See the geese—beyond the grain—there."

The boy stared, fascinated, high into the morning sunlight.

The V of the wild geese wedged through the autumn sky, honking south over the prostrate field that waited ponderously ripe for harvest.

CHAPTER NINE

Wapiti School, two windows flanking its door, half-ruined steps below, peaked roof above, stared loggishly down the road, south over hills towards the church, south over the bush towards the world. The yard bristled with weeds of the neglected summer; there was no one to disturb the neglect. Only the flag, collapsed on its slender pole, revealed summer gone.

The quiet broke with a rumble of feet. The door banged open and boys poured over the steps, spilling through the broken railing out towards the ball diamond. A few girls followed primly down the steps, lips curled at the screaming boys shoving about home-plate. "Scrub one!" "Scrub two!" "Three, three, three-ee!" "I'm pitcher!" "You're not!" Those late in yelling their number because of seats near the front of the school were already fist-backing their claims when a dark boy dashed through the gaping door, leaped from the steps and charged towards them, waving a bat and white ball. Chaos merged into order at his barked commands. "I'm one. Who's two? You, Hal. We're up—you're pitchin', Jake—" and everyone filed to their positions, the more fortunate jabbing the others and racing off to dodge the flung fist. Some mouthed revolt, but no one argued with Jackie Labret.

"Children!"

All motion ceased. Jackie, waving the bat, turned slowly.

The new teacher stood on the porch, slender and stern. To the little girls standing just below her, she was the most beautiful lady they had ever seen. They had been awed beyond expression when they came to school that morning and saw that narrow face framed by sweeping yellow hair. "Just like a fairy princess," Trudie whispered to Linda Giesbrecht in rapture.

"Boys, you know that when school is out at three-thirty, you are to go directly home. Don't pretend you can stay to play after school. Your parents want you home. You can play again tomorrow at recess. Bring in the ball—Jake, isn't it?—yes—and you the bat, Jackie. Why do you think I put them away in the cupboard? I'll have no more sneaking like that, Jackie. Come along."

They shuffled back. For one day at least they would have had an excuse for playing after school. Heavily they filed up the steps past her to get their jackets and books. Jackie lowered the flag and, as he came up the steps, alone, the teacher said confidentially, "I'm counting on you, Jackie," and her hand rested momentarily on his grimy shoulder. Startled, the boy glanced up, eyes black and fathomless; then he ran quickly into the school.

Razia Tantamont watched them straggle from the yard, shouting, pushing, swinging their lunch pails. The breeds vanished north and west, the Mennonites east and south. Seeing Jackie and Hal Wiens trot together towards the east, she wondered for a moment if the former lived in the Mennonite area. She remembered Mr Block's explanations to her as they rode in the rough truck from the railway on Friday. All about half-breeds, and what Mennonites believed. Her luck to be dropped two hundred miles from nowhere when she wanted a city school! In the bush, as quiet as a midnight graveyard.

Slightly panicked, she turned on her pointed shoes and, leaning against the door-frame, flicked her eyes over the vacant school with its home-made desks, dinted gas-barrel heater, stove pipes sagging from wires, blistered blackboards, library of coverless books tilted against the wall. These poor bush-buried kids: there was plenty to teach them about the world. Reading and the radio would conquer her loneliness. She pirouetted at the thought, proud of her grace, and walked carefully down the steps towards the teacherage. The head trustee, so grimly handsome with splendid steel-like hair! He would be about fifty-five. And so concerned to explain things. Competent as she felt herself, Razia sensed, very strangely for her, that she had few resources to cope with the oddness of the community she was beginning to understand from his words and the behaviour of the Mennonite children, where one glare from the oldest in the family quelled any young rowdiness in the class-room. And, though many travelled by at the cross-roads, no one except Mr Block and his tired-looking wife had visited her—on Sunday afternoon. The woman had not voiced a monosyllable, even when they inspected the school. While leaving, the trustee seemed oddly embarrassed, which she could hardly have suspected him capable of, when he mentioned they could not invite her to the Sunday evening church service because it was held in German. He had added, careful, "Of course, we do not side with Hitler, though we speak German. As I explained—killing is never right." She puzzled momentarily, then she swept the pirouette again. The people could not possibly be as staid as Mr Block tried to impress her. Surely they would hold some dances—she would be the first to start them, if nothing else. And if Peter Junior, who was to come to string up her aerial, was as striking as his father! She swung the cabin-door wide.

The mirror had just smiled her reflection when she heard the hoofbeats. She patted her hair, brushed the chalk-rim from her skirt, and turned to rummage about in the wood-box. When the knock came, she paused, then opened the door, a piece of wood as if forgotten in her hand. She said, "Hello."

The man outside the screen-door nodded, as somewhere behind him a horse snorted. He said, through the sheer maze of the screen, "Hello, Miss Tantamont. Papa said I—ah—" The words caught on his heavy tongue.

"You're Peter Block Junior, aren't you?"

"Well, yes—Pete, really."

"Do come in, Pete—I'm so happy to see you. Goodness—I've still the wood in my hands! I was trying to make a fire in the stove, but really—you just don't know what a job it's been getting that stove going. I'm sure there must be a simpler way of making it burn—do come in."

She held the door wide for him, smiling, his face directly opposite her as he hesitated an instant. His mother's expression drooped his rounded face, but the bruising body was certainly his father's, even the beetling brows that hunched together as his eyes accepted the contours of her face. He was dressed decently in the checked shirt and heavy denim of a farmer. If only he were a bit taller!

She stepped to the stove, three paces from where he stood near the door, cap clumsy in his hands. "I don't want to keep you from your work, but," she paused, "could you show me a bit about this stove?"

"Sure." He was at the wood-box, motions purposefully quick. "You need kindling and split wood. I'll get some," and he was out the door. While she rummaged for the coffee-kettle in the cupboard, she was annoyed at leaving herself vulnerable to his thought of why she had not asked his father to explain the stove. She glanced swiftly out of the window; he was chopping wood with great strokes. She barely had time to busy herself at the cupboard again before he was back with a heaping armful of wood, kindling grasped in his hand. His shyness vanished while he worked, actions suiting words.

"First, you set the draft open. Then crumple paper—once you know how, you can use wood-shavings just as well if you haven't paper—then small kindling, bigger stuff, a few pieces of wood. Always make sure the first bunch is dry. Close this and light from the front. Don't look at it—listen."

The fire caught and roared. She laughed, "I always look to make sure!"

"And then it goes out," his laugh grumbled in his chest. The stuffiness in the kitchen had evaporated. "Once it's really burning, put on more. Close the damper to keep the heat in the stove. But you have to chop a lot of wood."

She looked out at the sprawling mound of blocks. "Doesn't someone—the janitor—?"

"The kids take turns doing janitor work. Didn't Papa tell you?"

"Yes, but cleaning the school—"

"Aaron Martens' family does it every month—wash and stuff. They're half a mile east of here." He looked at her slender figure, carefully, and it astonished her unpleasantly that she could not read his thoughts on his face. He said, surprisingly, "You should have boarded out."

"No," she returned, too quickly, and recovered. "It's not that there aren't nice people here—I'm sure I'd like to live in one of those cosy log houses (he'll think me a fool—why do I muddle into such drivel), but I want to live as I want to. Not bother other people—have friends visit me when they wish—you know—"

Looking at her, he said nothing, as if the thought she expressed had never occurred to him before. He became aware of his glance and his eyes shifted towards the door, a slight redness creeping up from his collar.

Her laugh cut across the tension. "I'll have the children chop wood for me instead of having them stand in the corner doing nothing!"

He grinned without looking at her. "Papa said you wanted your aerial put up?"

"Oh, yes. Looks like the radio will be my only contact with the world. You people seem to have moved as far away as you can." She laughed again, but his answer, as he examined the coil of wire on the table, was quite serious.

"It's still too close, usually. You want it here on the table-corner?"

While she began her supper, he worked with quickness that amazed her. Once he asked her for help. While he held the pole steady, she pulled out the bottom bolt of the two that held the flag-pole erect between its two supporting posts. He then lowered the pole to the ground, attached the wire to the tip above the flag pulley, and again hoisted it aloft. The other aerial pole was wired to the teacherage. She could hear his ponderous tread on the roof. One slight redness! she was piqued at her inability to touch him. He appeared so different from any men she had ever met, almost as if he did not know how—or did not quite dare—to look at her as a woman. Before he went he would betray some acknowledgement. So she did not invite him to a cup of coffee, as she had first intended. She said nothing at all; merely thanked him seriously and, as he was about to wheel his mount and she leaned in the open doorway, his glance slid down her figure. She said, half-joking, "How does a big man like you stay out of fighting the Germans?"

She knew then that the falling sunlight from beyond the school framed her as it should. He sat motionless on his horse, look riveted for a gathering moment. Then he muttered, rapidly, "Papa's got a big farm—I've got to get milkin'—so long—" and he broke his glance from her with a jerk of the reins and galloped from the yard.

As the hoof-beats faded over the south hill, Razia watched the dust-swirl settle before her, a smile tinging the corner of her lips. That was not quite what "Papa" had explained so carefully.

On his home quarter two miles from school, the Deacon was bindering the last of his green-feed. The horses moved steadily as the heavy oats shuddered under sweep and blade to the rolling canvas. Though the field was almost completed and they would start cutting the ripe crop in two days, he could find little of his usual joy at the harvest. He passed Elizabeth, slowly stooking, her back bowed under the green bundles, skirts sweeping the stubble. He thought, in a sort of parenthesis, Tomorrow there will be no interruptions: she and Pete will get more done.

A snip of a girl: skirts almost to her knee, face whitely smiling. The way the Superintendent had written, it had appeared they were sending a sedate older teacher with fine teaching ability. Her recommendations were excellent, but—his frown deepened as the binder clattered down the field. There had always been Mennonite teachers available before, but now the war disrupted that also: it forced some to camps, some to a denial of their fathers' pacifist position. A limited knowledge of the world was necessary for the children, but what would this worldly girl, fresh from training, emphasize in her teaching? In the unmolested prosperity they had enjoyed at Wapiti, he had almost forgotten the fury that in 1927 drove him to the wilds of Saskatchewan, or why he had begged the first Mennonites to join him there in the desperate hope of perhaps again building a community such as their fathers had known in the golden days of Russia. The need for the community had grown to be a driving imperative to him as his dread increased that if he were left alone to grub at a homestead for the rest of his days, he must sink under the thought of what he despaired to forget. No girl would disrupt the community he had built up; she could be dismissed after a month if necessary. He shifted his thoughts to the necessities of the coming weeks of threshing work.

But he had now tangled himself in the coils of his memory and he could not escape by forcing his look to the thick-erupting bundles. It had been for his son, after all. It was not for himself or his wife or Elizabeth or anyone: it was for his son who had been so long, so despairingly long, in coming.

The irony of Peter Block's existence was, though he would rather have suffered death than participate in war, the World Wars of his time had shaped his life. He recognized this, yet, but for one stumble, the fact had never overcome him. Ironically too, it was the cruelty of his professed "brethren in the faith" that jarred him into consciousness that as an individual he was not sufficient to himself.

It began in the forests of Siberia where he had been sent as a conscientious objector in World War One. Knowing about the initiation to which the Mennonites of Forstei groups, in a desperate attempt at amusement during month-long isolation, subjected newcomers, he drew his iron determination about him and wordlessly faced the veterans on arrival. That evening at supper a kindly older man whispered to him, "Just give in quickly—they will not do much then," but when in the middle of the night he was jerked awake and hoisted, blanket-muffled, from his bed, he disdained capitulation or resistance.

He felt himself drop sharply; he flung out his arms and almost choked in the wall of water that seemed to collapse on him. He splashed out of his wrappings in the slivered ice of the horse-trough and, returning to the absolute quiet of the bunkhouse, shivered to sleep under his coat. Morning brought only their wordless stares; after the forenoon's work he knew not a man on the crew could stay with him, stroke for stroke, except the long-jawed leader Heinz. At dinner they seemed to have accepted him, for several solicitously and quite needlessly advised him on sharpening his axe, but that afternoon, as he caught a moment's breather on the clearing's edge, his arms were abruptly seized from behind: the ring of them faced him. The wolf-jawed leader, now seated on a stump, ordered, "Get on your knees—here!" As he was hurled forward, Block barely got his foot up to kick aside the leg stuck swiftly before him; he stumbled sharply but ended upright before the monarch. "Smart one, eh," murmured Heinz, staring into silence the low laughter of the gang at their comrade's bruised shin. Block returned no word. Heinz studied the expressionless granite of his face. "Okay," he rapped, "the hard way."

He was forced arm-breakingly to the stump. Heinz stood now, eyes afire: "No," he growled, "no blindfold." They pried his head face-down to the stump; at the last gleam of sunlight on the fir-dark above the crowding heads, he glimpsed the axe-blade glint swinging aloft. "Count to five, Jake. Slow."

The whipsaw-dust sweet in his nose ground down on the fir-stump as the count tolled above him, he did not believe it. At "Five!" he heard the swish of descent and that second such fathomless terror seized him that he almost twitched his head. The jerk and thud crashed through him grovelling on the stump-face. He was kneeling there with no hand to hold him.

The wolf-ring stared in the lonely clearing as he pushed erect, only his legs betraying. He deigned no toss of his head to clear the hair-straggle from his face. He looked at Heinz, then at the stump where the half-buried axe drew the wide diameter of his black hair's half-moon. His hand lifted involuntarily to the hair-line of his throbbing scalp. The stubble was about a centimeter long.

"Good with the axe," his voice steady.

Then he saw his own number on the handle. With a one-handed heave, he jerked it out; they scattered like chaff as he swung about. With no more regard than if they were stumps, he strode to his place of work. Slowly the terror oozed from him as he chopped, doggedly.

That night as rats scrabbled under the bunks of the snoring men, his son-necessity hammered through him. Little Elizabeth was not enough; she would help form someone else's family. He, the lone survivor of thirteen children, was a mere vacancy without a son. If that unerring axe had slipped—the answer was the first in his life he could not face. And for the three unending years of Forstei duty, he knew himself clamped in the relentless fist of God; he could but read of the promise to Abraham and pray to live.

Yet, following Russia's abrupt withdrawal from the war, the relentlessness ground down more obviously than ever. He returned home as the Civil War stamped into their community on the western fringes of the Ural foothills. To either Red or White army they lost, one by one, horses, stock, wagons; their lives balanced on the sword-tip of a captain's temper. Into the anarchy of 1921 stalked famine. Once-prosperous Mennonite villages formed food-pools to feed the flights of beggars until they themselves had but ground-wheat and water to stir together for one midday meal and roast-barley "prips" to drink. Horses, cattle, dogs were long since gone; the granaries swept clean. As winter advanced, children lay limply abed while the mother huddled beside a scrap of brush-fire and the father drooped in his cavernous barn, not opening the door to the skeletons of Russian and Bashkir frozen on the village streets.

Suddenly for Block, in this climax of seven years' harrowing, there flamed the hope of a son.

When in spring of 1921 he knew his wife was with child, despair vanished. Work for his son was the only religion. He surrendered to the government requisition barely enough grain to avoid suspicion; that other villagers would be forced to make up his deficit he cared not at all. All summer he heaved water from the creek-trickle to save a corner of his burning grain. When in fall the village food committee questioned him concerning the two scrawny cows they knew he had butchered, he gave them a partly-spoiled front quarter. "We ate the rest before that happened in the heat. I'll share the few bushels of wheat I winnowed."

John Esau, head of the committee, his fourteen children like a millstone chained to his neck, gazed heavily to him. Block thought savagely, May my soul be damned if I lose my one son to feed his eight! After they filed out, he bolted the barn-door and turned to stare steadily at the horse-stall where they had stood. Fifteen feet below their foot-sole lay the narrow slabs of salt-crusted meat, enough for one thin broth a day for the winter. He stood in the aisle, trying, in the stifling silence, to hear the cows breathing at night and the horses shifting their weight as they dreamed. But God's grim irony could not crush him. He *would* have a son.

Before the new year fourteen Mennonites had died in the village. Almost all were grown men. Without lamentation, they were carried to the graveyard, box unopened. Almost a quarter of the neighbouring Russian and Bashkir villagers were dead by the last day of 1921 when the midwife emerged into the kitchen where Block was pacing. Swaying gently, the woman crooned as she held up the curled red body, "Cry, you darling little heart —you don't know all the reasons you have to cry."

Block did not hear her. He was looking at his only son.

Robbers descended on the desperation of 1922. Since the Mennonites were known to have pooled their resources and were openly non-resistant, more and more the slender caches vanished in the night. Driven beyond endurance, the younger men of the colony banded together to prevent the depredations; they beat unmercifully whoever they captured. A few faithful protested such aggression, but the church-elders did not even raise their heads. Life was one unending stomach-gnaw.

On the last day of January, when a letter was read in the village promising relief by spring from the Mennonites of America, Block discovered the hole gaping in his horse-stall. All within was bare, save a trickle of mouldy wheat in one corner.

Numbly he walked through into the kitchen where his wife sat by a tiny fire; Elizabeth was drawing designs on the stove with a dampened finger. Little Peter slept in his cradle. As Block looked down at him, a soundless belch formed on his lips.

"Did you hear anything in the barn while I was gone?"

Her look jelled into fright, "No, not until you came—what?"

"They got it all—every bit."

"What—who—?"

"The Bashkirs." He was too weak for rage. "There's no bit of food left in the barn." He sank to a chair in a long silence.

"There's a sack of wheat behind the stove."

"Yes. We'll eat wheat-soup with the rest."

She said, strangely, "I'm glad they got it. Pretending to have only flour and a few potatoes when we really had some meat: it wasn't right. When others have nothing."

"The American food won't be here till the end of March. We had just enough—"

"We can live. Perhaps now we can even believe God will help us again. We've nothing to lie—"

He heaved erect. "How do you expect to feed him on mouldy wheat?"

"Mrs Dick has—"

"He's two years, and almost dead! The Bargen baby died yesterday—three months old and never a drop of milk. He can't live!"

"God will help." Nothing, not even her child, mattered. Only God.

Block looked down at the rosy face. He had seen babies starving: seen the arms that lay like twigs; heard the thin cry that slowly stretched away. His fists balled as he turned to his wife, as Elizabeth stared fearfully from behind her skirts. "Someone's helping them. They wouldn't just know how to get in like that." He buttoned his shaggy coat, black beard jutting over the collar. "I'm going to Heinrichs."

"Peter, don't!" Her plea was a meaningless movement of air.

"Go to bed." He went out and closed the door. Down the cold-barren street, past the feeble lights of a few windows, he strode toward the house of the protective association leader.

On the night of February 12th they caught two Bashkirs prying at the barn-door of the village Elder.

In the lantern-light of a long-deserted barn, both faces bulged swollen in the final stages of hunger. Block rapped in Russian, "Who helped you in the village? A Mennonite?" The boy looked at his older companion, who said nothing. Block gestured. Gaunt faces gleaming like savages, the Mennonites ripped off the thieves' tattered coats, trussed them solidly against the barn-pillars while their flung shadows leaped grotesquely across the wall. Animal-eyed they circled the older man, only Block's authority restraining them. Block raged, "Who helped you?" The boy quavered from the gloom. "It won't help. Tell him."

The Bashkir said nothing.

They took turns beating with ropes, for they tired quickly.

After the man gasped out that John Esau had told them of prospects in turn for a share of the booty, they beat the boy. Names of Bashkirs came as the night ebbed. When morning dawned they left the senseless thieves roped rigid in the barn and marched to Esau's yard.

Leaving the others outside, Block and the two oldest banged on the door, then crashed it open against its bolt. Five boys, oldest perhaps seventeen, lying in the large "summer-room" into which they burst, peered out from among the rags of the beds, faces glazed in terror. Block bellowed, "Esau, come out!" The flurry in the next room ceased. After a long moment, as the three hunters stared at the door and the boys huddled away, their skeletal bodies sinking out of sight in rags and straw, Mrs Esau appeared, wrapped in a bare-worn sheep-skin, bent, shivering. She said, pathetically, "Please, John is very weak—"

Block's scar flamed livid in the morning gloom. "We're three. We can carry him—but he comes!"

Her face broke soundlessly, then ,"No."

Her eyes flew to the children, then she stepped back into the other room. As Block filled the doorway she said, her back to him, "He'll come. Wait."

When he came at last, wearing the same coat, they clamped his arms and pushed him out to the waiting men. There was no sound in the barren house as Block yanked the door shut.

By noon, after having beaten Esau into confession in Pretoria, the colony administrative centre, Block stood in the only sleigh left in the colony, driving the two Bashkirs to Suworowka and the Russian authorities. In dead cold the plains stretched white and empty to fade into the horizonless day. He felt his body consuming itself, cell by cell, as if each nerve quivered erect, longing, searching. Reeling slightly, he turned to look: the two Bashkirs crumpled behind him, and two Mennonites crouched half-sleeping at the rear of the sled. He said, "We'll stop at Klassen's in Number Three. The horses will drop if they don't eat."

One of his companions looked up. "So will we."

"Yah." Block thought of his son, without milk for a week, wasting visibly. The American relief seemed as remote as ever. His numbed mind rolled with fury unabated at Esau's alliance with heathen. Then, in the village, as the farmer led the horses around to shelter and the three Mennonites paused by the sleigh, the older Bashkir jerked erect in a frenzy, leaped down and beat Block in the face with his bound fists. The two men wrenched him away, but something burst in Block. He had lashed the thieves with ropes, as was the judicial custom, but now he sprang at the man, seized him away with a strength that knew no source save madness, and smashed the crook-nosed head back and forth, his frozen hide mitten like a club on his hand. The Bashkir collapsed to the hard snow with barely a moan when Block hurled him back. The three men stalked into the house.

When they returned, potato soup sloshing in their stomachs, the Bashkir still lay there by the sleigh. With his worn boot, Block poked at him. He was dead.

In the coolness of the Canadian autumn twilight, the Deacon's face glistened in sweat while the four fat horses hoofed their steady pace and the binder chewed at the field. He drove mechanically, knowing nothing but the remembered horror.

Only after he returned to the village, as day after day there was nothing to be done but sit and feel his body tearing itself, did his action edge into meaning for him. Not the inhuman brutality of the Mennonites towards their enemies when once they cut themselves from their convictions, nor the condemnation of the church stirred to activity by their Moscow representative, not even the ten Bashkirs dying under beatings, and Esau's starvation in prison, affected him. These happenings were too far removed from himself. What overwhelmed him was one scene. And on an evening when the American relief had come and both children slept, contented, in their room, with a convulsive movement he buried his head in the blankets beside his wife and cried like a child. It was the remembered way the Bashkir's whole body had squeaked over rigid on the snow when he prodded it with his foot, the thread of spittle frozen across its swollen face. With his own hand he had killed him.

He was driven by furies then. Driven to confess and repent, driven to labour for the Widow Esau and her family as for himself, driven to lift the village out of the morass of poverty, driven to bring them back to the paths of the fathers that they had missed over the years, driven to innumerable massive efforts, alone, that he might be an example for his son. But it was no use: Russia was ruined for him. They were in the first group of emigrants to find exit to Canada in 1925. Yet even finding a homestead in remote Wapiti was not enough. He wanted to raise his son as he himself, neglected by a careless father, had not been, and he knew this was impossible in what he saw as a mixed district. To have a colony of true Mennonites again! In the last stragglers to escape Moscow he found the people he wanted: poor, but with the convictions of faith on their conscience. The colony was grown now. No snip of a teacher was going to disrupt it.

Suddenly, as he looked up, he saw his open field again. The harvest sun was fading in glory. He was opposite Elizabeth, who still stooked unceasingly. He halted the team and called, "Elizabeth!"

She set up the two bundles and turned, rubbing her forehead with her arm. "You've stooked enough today. You and Pete can finish tomorrow."

Surprised, she said slowly, "All right, Pa." He chirruped to his span as she walked towards the house, pulling at the sweat-soaked gloves. Over the binder-clatter he could hear the dogs barking as Pete drove the cattle home for milking.

CHAPTER TEN

In the last week of October the threshing crew was working at the Block farm. When they concluded there, the harvesting for the year would be done.

Thom squirmed under the body of the massive machine to get at a grease cup. Running tractor and thresher with Block, he had been with the crew almost a month and, though he would have been happier on the open field, he wanted to know as much as he could about tractors. Capping the cup, he pushed out, wiping his greased hands on the chaff snowed about the machine.

The stillness of the noon-hour quivered in Indian summer haze. The vanished bedlam that usually engulfed the outfit gave the world an almost timeless hush. The men ate in the house. The horses chomped on oat-bundles around their racks. As a harness shivered, a blue-jay called through the autumn trees; Thom felt the peace of the world. The smell of threshing in his nostrils, from where he stood he could look across the half-threshed stack of bundles to the garden, now mounded and sprawled with empty vines, beyond the house and along the line of poplar and willow and birch in mottled yellow and white and dull-red stretching far as in smoke. The geese were long gone, but a covey of sparrows, swooping round the granary at the heap of cracked wheat by the elevator of the thresher, spied him, and vanished in a swirl. Another day, and the harvest would be home.

The door banged. He looked up to see the men straggling from the house. Placing the grease-bucket in the machine-box, he dropped the lid into place and walked to the house to eat.

On the path he encountered Block. "I took a link out of that loose chain, as you said."

"Yes." Block hesitated, as if preoccupied. "Good. I'll have to get a new chain there for next year."

Thom looked after him, puzzled, then strode on, washed roughly at the bench outside the door and stooped into the lean-to that served as kitchen. He slid behind the long table in the living-room to Mrs Block's murmured direction. Over his shoulder through the windows he could see the men hitching up; the coughing start of the tractor echoed through the house. Elizabeth came in noiselessly to clear the dishes. He said, half-joking, reaching for the potatoes-with-peelings, "Hardly fair you should work on the crew and in the house too. When will you eat?"

She smiled slightly, "Pa said I needn't work outside this afternoon. They'll get through by tomorrow night anyway. I'll just help Mama." Her quiet voice dropped tiredly; he looked at her as he drew the knife through his meat. She walked back to the kitchen, her arms laden, and he almost called after her, "Pitching bundles from a stack is no woman's work anyway," but he held his peace, now knowing what her father meant by work. Never before in his young life had he so exerted himself merely to keep up. Elizabeth entered from the kitchen with a clean plate and cutlery, placing them on the table across from him. "Hope I don't bother you if I eat here."

"You sure won't. All this month of threshing I've hardly ever had a chance to eat with anyone at noon. Have some meat." She blanched suddenly as he proffered the meat-platter, and he stammered, confused, "Is anything wrong?—I—"

"No," she gasped slightly, her hand seeming to press her abdomen, "—it's nothing. Just a pain I get—sometimes. Nothing." Her colour faltered back slowly, and she reached for the platter he was still offering over the wide table. She set it down quickly and picked a bit of meat with her fork.

Thom said, eying his food, "This is really good bread. Just like Mom makes it. Did you bake it?"

Her voice was quietly colourless again, "No, I'm outside too much to do baking. Ma baked the bread."

They were silent for a time, she picking at her food, Thom working at a second helping. He had never before been so close to her, or ever noticed, despite the dark formless outdoor clothes, the womanliness of her face. He said, without thinking, "You and Pete put up all those bundle-stacks?"

Suddenly she spoke, "Yes. It was fun. To drive out in the morning and load up and watch the birds fly south over the wide field and then come back to the house. Pa was gone with the thresher—"

He said, across the odd silence in the room, the cries of the men welling above the distant din of the threshing, "Pretty hard, wasn't it?"

"What's there to do if you don't work?" She did not even shrug.

He was silent, remembering once again Margret's words after the church-meeting in August. The month of grinding physical labour under Block, of learning about tractor and thresher, had absorbed Thom completely. The Deacon was so phenomenally efficient: an actual expert in anything. If a problem arose, he stood motionless in thought for a moment, then rapped out precise orders. Invariably, his solution worked. Thom, thinking of his own father, could only envy Elizabeth hers. But Margret's quiet-felt words, "Poor Elizabeth." Sitting now across the table from her, Thom's mind drove him back irresistibly to the many autumn-cool evenings when, as he settled himself beside the other men on the straw of the temporary bunkhouses, head filled with admiration at the Deacon's efficiency that day had revealed, he had nevertheless hesitated on the brink of the thought, You cannot run people like machines. Remember the past summer. Then welcome sleep would wipe all away, and the new morning broke to simpler necessities.

He shook his head slightly. She was there before him. A slight allusion she had made caught in his thoughts and he asked, hoping for diversion, "What kind of sounds do you like?"

"Sounds?" her voice hinting interest.

"You know—things you like to hear when you're alone?"

"It's hard to hear them now." Dishes crashed in the kitchen. "But you mean geese honking in a V—"

"Uh-huh! Or the frogs on a spring night. The stir of spruce when you lie in the damp moss of the muskeg. Cattle breathing in the barn as snow piles to the rafters." She interrupted quietly. "You know the most peaceful sound? I heard it once long ago when I visited my uncle beyond Saskatoon one summer. They lived about a mile from the railroad. Every night the train blew for the crossing."

"A train whistle?" He could not remember having listened to one. "Isn't that just men and machines—"

"No, it's not harsh at all. That long 'Wooooo' of the train on the prairie at night—as if all the world—and men—are as they should be."

Mrs Block entered from the kitchen to collect another stack of dishes. Pushing his wiped plate forward, Thom slid out from behind the table. "Have to get back to work." He glanced at Elizabeth as her mother shuffled out on worn felt-socks, but her face was grim in tiredness. Her eyes on vacancy, her fork traced wearily in the spot of gravy on her plate. He could not deny his thoughts now. He murmured a word to Mrs Block as he ducked out the door into the threshing.

"Wolfe! Can't you handle that team?" A mighty laugh roared above the puffing of the tractor and the hammering of the separator as young Reinhard struggled to back his wagon from the flashing carrier. Franz was feeding from the opposite side.

"Better than you any day, Reimer!" Reinhard hollered as by degrees the half-rearing horses jabbed the rack away from the drive-belt.

Franz bellowed, "You'll have to *show* me sometime. Not just yell." The rest was lost in clatter as Reinhard bounced away and Pete wheeled his top-heavy rack expertly into place. Never pausing in his pitching, Franz shouted, standing on the last layer of bundles, "You're really gonna have to work to keep up with me!" Pete grinned as he reached for his fork.

"Say that when you've a full load!" The straw sprayed and the grain poured into the granary.

Block knelt in the bin, checking the grade of wheat. After the late spring rains, all the Mennonites, except Unger and his care-nothing son, had bumper crops. Well, the land had to be worked properly. Kernels sliding from his hand, he considered the Wapiti harvest, but his thoughts slipped aside. What could be the matter with her?

The scene of the previous night aggressed across his memory. The outfit had arrived late from near Calder and they had manoeuvred the thresher into position between stacks and granary by lantern-light to get the usual early start in the morning. Not having been home for a week, he was draining his coffee-mug when Elizabeth entered the room. As he watched her walk towards the stairs, he felt strangely stirred. Pete and she had taken good care of the farm; had stacked all the bundles from the south quarter for threshing. The long years she had silently spent on the farm abruptly tumbled over him. He had never noticed her cracked, men's boots, shapeless dress and, the thought suddenly shamed him, her habitually bowed head. Pete and Elizabeth were all he had, really. She was at the stair-turn when he said, from his gratitude, "Elizabeth."

She paused, raised her head. In the yellow light, her face held, as in a faded copy, the lineaments of his wife. The memory drenched him: of the night when he had asked her father, the rich miller of the village, and she had walked into the yellow light, as Elizabeth now stood, and he had seen the gentle loveliness of her face. He could not remember when he had thought of that; or if he had ever discerned it in his daughter before. She looked wind-worn.

"What's troubling you?" His tone was warm. "Have you been working too hard with the harvest?"

She looked dully at him, as at a lump of mud. Then she dropped her glance away.

"It's not the work—" Her face crumpled suddenly under his look and sobs burst as through a dam. "It's—nothing," and she fumbled blindly, as in desperation, up the stairs.

He could hear the straw of her bed rustling above his head as he turned to his wife, silent as a shadow in the kitchen doorway, "Go see what's the matter with her."

Scooping another handful of grain unthinkingly, he thought, now as then, That fool Louis! He should not have allowed him to go: a breed with ten dollars in his pocket was dynamite with the fuse lit. But Louis, sullen across the barn-aisle, eyes never quite meeting a glance, the dead-pan look hardening on his face, as it had once before when he stated flatly he would walk to Hainy and get the Mounties if he was not given his wages, could be dented by no argument about saving. Ten dollars was better than having the fool blow up everything he had earned. But six months in jail! And Joseph and Thom trying to teach half-breeds Bible lessons. It kept their Sunday afternoons occupied, but what could you teach them? He had hammered at Louis for three years.

His wife had backed down the stairs into the room, and he looked up. "She won't say what's the matter; just says it's nothing. She did stop crying, but—"

"Well, if she says it's nothing. Likely some momentary womanish thing." He cut off her words as Pete entered from the barn; they discussed the stock. But his wife's half-haunted look returned to him. And there was something about the ungainliness of Elizabeth's work that morning. He did not know whether to ascribe it to his new-found perception or—

"Mr Block." Thom's face peered over the rim of the bin; he flushed slightly as he rose. "Everything's running fine. Perhaps I could go out with Pete and help there a bit?"

"They have a field-pitcher. But—you got the gas barrels from the shed?" Thom nodded. "Okay. But come back with him."

Thom's head dropped from sight as the Deacon reached up to pull himself out. He should not have had her pitch that morning, but the west-quarter haul took so long for the men—he had never known her so awkward before. Well, she was thirty-three. He heaved himself over the bin-edge and dropped into the doorway. The chaff was snowing slowly from the hazy oil-and-wheat-smelly air.

They had tossed up the first stooks before Thom, alive to the quiet of the field, said fervently, "Wish I could have done this all fall."

Pete was silent, pitching double-bundles from the opposite side unerringly, regular as a pendulum, unwasting of motion. Thom shouted, "Giddap!" and the two horses pulled along between the rows of stooks. Two mice scurried; Thom swung ildly, but they vanished under the next shocks. Jabbing his rk deep, he hoisted up three bundles at once, the third caught ingling by the twine on the last tine.

"You wouldn't have lasted a day, working like that." Pete ılmly swept the stray stalks together with his fork.

"Aw shucks," Thom was thoughtlessly jubilant. "What's the se of forever being so calm and steady about everything. ou've got to get rid of it somewhere. Don't you ever feel like elling like mad and maybe riding for about five miles with the ind in your face just as fast as your horse can go?"

"How would that get the work done?"

"Ah well—" They forked steadily. Thom thought, There iould be more to living than work, and more work. Friendship erhaps? He could as well forget about trying to regain that eep serenity he and Pete had known, past now as an age, before seph had come and gone. Pete, plodding in his father's ways, ever changed. But Pete's activities somehow lacked the edge f brilliance that, despite growing conviction, attracted Thom the Deacon. When he was near Pete, Thom found it increas-igly easier to discover flaws in the Deacon's methods. Savagely, hom speared a bundle one-handedly, as no harvest worker ver would. Work. What had work given Elizabeth, for xample? A pain in her stomach?

"Hal like school?"

Thom looked up, surprised. Pete pitched strongly, dust ran in tripes down his shirt-back. "Oh yah. I guess so. Haven't been ome for two weeks before last night. Mom said last night they're oing all sorts of things. Things he likes. Like making Indian illages in class. Don't know what good that does—"

Pete did not answer as he expected. "Yah. Guess the kids vould like that." The words hung in the air as if begging another uestion. Thom could not imagine why Pete should ask about Ial. "He like the teacher?"

"Oh yah. Mom says they all do a lot." They worked silently or a time.

"Annamarie left yet?"

Thom hurled two bundles on the half-filled rack and walked o the next stook. "Yes," he said casually, "about a month ago.

She's in training at the Battleford Hospital." Pete knew this as well as he, but Thom could not stop himself. If he could only tell someone about Annamarie; merely talk about her in an uninhibited manner as about anyone else. There were so immensely many things he wanted to know: he had racked his mind trying to remember all he could of her in the lower grades at school, but she had been just some faceless little girl below him. If people would just mention things about her, so he could feel he had known her before last June, but single Mennonite men did not talk at length about girls to one another. He did not want to ask Margret who, since having been announced with Annamarie's brother Sam, occasionally flicked a roguish wink at him. It was no winking matter for Thom.

"Does she like it?"

"Guess so. Hasn't come home yet anyway." Despite himself, he had sealed the topic. Minutes later they were jolting back towards the farmyard, talking casually about the harvest, both longing desperately to speak of something else.

As the afternoon ebbed away, Elizabeth came from the house with the cardboard box of lunch. The men, one by one, gulped food hastily and returned to work. Her face was pallid as she poured coffee in the lee of the granary. Thom, his teeth crunching through a thick bread-crust, saw her hand hover repeatedly over her abdomen. Except for the incident at dinner, he would not have noticed. Reaching for a last cookie, he said, "Soon the harvest will be in and the peaceful winter here."

As he picked the cookie from the tin in the box, her hand reached out almost as if she was reaching for his. Then it paused, and she whispered, as if there had been anyone to hear in the threshing,

"Thom—go away from here!"

"Wha-a—" His hand could not rise with the cookie. He was nonplussed, as if an elderly woman had kissed him. She did not notice his confusion but rushed on:

"Go away from here—Wapiti—for a few years. You're thinking right—to teach those children from the Bible—Pete told me you want to take correspondence school again, like last winter with Joseph—you'll be buried here under rules that aren't as important as this chaff. Go! while you can!" A terrible urgency suppressed her voice; she seemed to see to the bottom of his soul as if it were water.

"I—I don't know—" Stunned, he found no protest for an echo of his thought.

"Your brother David couldn't work here—Joseph had to go —Pastor Lepp—Herm—Aaron Martens—look what they are! A church is supposed to be a *brotherhood*—all equal—that gets its direction from Scripture—not rules!"

"Elizabeth, to go—" he knew not a word to add, his hand holding the cookie, her eyes transfixing him. He stared, crouched forward in his tallness before her.

"God in heaven! Can't you see what's happened to me?" The passion of her voice was as a surge to heave him from Wapiti. Her face was old.

He straightened up, stuffing the cookie into his mouth without thought, the eyes he could not face holding him as at a consecration. Abruptly Block turned the corner.

"Thom, get those few sacks out of the empty bin—the other's nearly full." Thom was gone before the Deacon had finished speaking.

Block swallowed coffee. "There's two teams in the field. Leave the box here and I'll tell the men. Better get the cows before supper, otherwise it will get late. And bring that limping steer in too.'

Elizabeth leaned forward and placed the empty mug in the box. Block turned to go. As Thom at that moment rounded the corner to ask about the chute-extension, his eye snagged on the motion of Elizabeth as she crumbled soundlessly to the ground. Seeing her in the fall, it was as if she had been falling always and the last instant of it had been revealed to him.

"Mr Block!" he gasped.

The Deacon swung about. "What—Elizabeth!" he was beside the motionless heap, and then, with a lurch, she rolled over, straightened rigid in spasm, shameless in pain. "Elizabeth, what is it?" Block pulled her skirts over the coarse stockings, kneeling beside her.

"It's—here." Her hands groped, face contorted to the sky. An animal groan twisted between her clenched teeth.

Block rapped at the paralysed youth, "Get Pete—before he drives to the field," and bent back over his daughter. He smoothed her hair straggling from beneath her kerchief. "Elizabeth," he soothed, leaning forward as the threshing thundered on, "is it your stomach?"

"Yes." Bitten short in pain. "It's—in jerks."

"I'll help you get up—get you to the house." He put his hand under her shoulder, but her head shuddered a silent "no". The chaff from the blown-straw drifted down on her face. She was lying pole-like; "Is it so bad?" helplessly.

Pete ran around the corner, Thom at his heels. Block, sensing his son, did not look up. "Take the truck—get Mrs Wiens. Tell her Elizabeth has stomach trouble." The usual sickwords sounded inane to him, looking at the face of his daughter. "Bad. Tell her if she's got anything to bring it to kill the pain."

"The team—"

"Right now! Thom can tie it up." They were gone in the lash of his voice. He bent down. "Can you get up if—" and then he realized she had fainted.

He looked at her an instant, her face fallen over against the box. Heavenly Father, what can this be? He gathered her clumsily into his arms and pushed erect. The threshing hammered on unabated as he started towards the house. The truck roared off. Somewhere, far from his thoughts, he sensed Thom run up behind him.

"The bin—" Thom could not pull his eyes from her face bumping against the grime of the checked shirt-sleeve. Merciful Father, he prayed.

"Yes," answered the Deacon automatically, "Sweep it—get the extension from the box-wagon. Use it when the first's full. You'll have to stop the machine a minute." He walked on with his burden draped in his arms. She seemed oddly lumpish and ungainly, almost as if—the thought was too absurd to be considered. She stirred; he quickened his step. As he passed the well and strode up the path, quite irrelevantly it became essential to remember when he had last carried his only daughter. His mind had no idea where to grope in his memory.

He kicked the gate open, and at that moment his wife emerged from the kitchen with a pail. She stared, frozen.

"Elizabeth's very sick. She's fainted—hold the door." He bent the limpness through into the house, and again the suspicion—but he sloughed it aside.

Mrs Block said, "Put her on our bed—it's bigger," and for the first time in his life he unthinkingly obeyed her. Under the cooling cloths she brought, Elizabeth began to stir on the bed. He passed his hand over his face, dashed at the sweaty glue of grit and chaff.

He said, "Get her undressed. Pete's gone for Mrs Wiens. I've got to get to the threshing." But when he stood there, alone, in the kitchen cluttered with supper preparation, he felt oddly useless: the work outside no longer seemed so important. He stared a moment at the half-filled water-pail on the wash-stand beside the door, then he dumped the water into the basin and strode to the well. The tractor puffed on while men yelled above the din as they pitched.

"Don't let the machine run empty. Pitch!"

"Hey, get your team movin'!"

"John, drive to the east field, this one's done."

Block did not hear them for his praying.

In the house again, he was setting down the empty dipper when his wife broke into the kitchen, eyes wild.

"Peter!" The proper name startled him as much as her look. "Peter! Elizabeth's in child-birth!"

Blood burst on his scar: "Woman, you're mad! It's imposs—"

"Peter, I've seen it all my life."

"It can't be true!" and a faint-wrenching oath tore from him. But even as he wheeled towards the bedroom, he knew it true. Her ungainly body.

He took only one step. His wife thrust past him, "She's in it now. Stay here! Pitching from the stack this morning!" She was gone.

He had not heard the truck, but Pete jerked the door open at that moment and stepped in, Mrs Wiens with her satchel behind him. Pete blurted, "How—"

"She's in there," and he shoved the woman across the corner

of the living-room toward the drapings of the bedroom, her face like a pale streak in the harvest afternoon.

"Is it bad?" Pete hunched forward in his anxiety.

"Drive to Calder. Phone Dr Goodridge in Hainy—tell him who you are and that Elizabeth's—sick—very sick. No matter what he's doing, he *has* to come. Now. Drive!"

"Can I see her just—"

"Drive!" His son was gone at the blast of his voice. As the truck burst into life, the Deacon blocked the doorway of the living-room, staring at the door-curtain, hearing, his mind blood red.

Mrs Block appeared finally, her face ashen. "It was a boy—or almost."

"A boy. And Elizabeth?"

"It was dead. Six months perhaps. All the chores and hauling bundles—"

"Elizabeth?" seething.

Mrs Wiens came out, wiping her hands on a bright towel, not looking at them:

"Elizabeth, we should wash—"

She broke off as he jostled her aside. He strode blindly through the drapes. He comprehended nothing save her, lying under a grey sheet pulled to her chin. Her long dark hair seemed glued across her forehead. Her eyes did not change under his glare.

"Elizabeth," voice flatly mad, "who is the father?"

A spectre of pain seemed to brush along her form, but her face remained graven. His terrible rage burned his eyes; he blinked and glared, seeing the face dissolve slowly in pain.

"You are no child of mine. When you can walk, get out of my house. I will never look at you again." He wheeled and strode out: his wife confronted him beyond the door.

"Peter, you're not talking to your only daughter like that. It's your fault as much as hers. If she goes, I'll—"

"You get out too—both you and your whore of a daughter!" Mrs Wiens was a blur as he stamped from the house.

Down the path, into the melee of threshing, his mind a chaos and only one thought, Get back to work—you can do something about this yet, he fled to the normalcy of labour. As he rounded the granary, Thom stepped before him. "Is Elizabeth all right?"

"Yes." He spat the lie from him. "Second bin going?"

"Yes, just after—" Block left the youth with the bared question still on his face and, ducking under the heads of the near team, made his usual round of the machine, around the back, away from the men and the racks, checking chains with his eye, opening vents to stare at the grain-straw shaking past. But it was no use. The racket and the dust and the grit was like the swirl of his mind where only one item whirled like flotsam to the top. Who was the father? After all he had kept her from, who could have dared? No one had ever been around the farm except Lou—not that scum of a half-breed gutter!

The vent he was holding crashed shut. He would get it out of her, if he had to beat her within an inch of her life. Louis left the second week in June—his mind caught in a moment of startling calmness. How many assaults had he withstood in the community? He had wondered about the new teacher, but that was turning out well; he himself had harboured the snake. His own daughter and a half-breed! The Devil would not break him, nor the church and district he had built for his son. Pete need never know; it would be worked out, somehow. Let the Devil take her—and his wife too. No towel-wrapped bundle on a chair was going to wreck this separated community.

His mind frothed. He strode into the granary, swung wildly over the bin-door and, seizing the grain-scoop that leaned against the wall, began shovelling. The small heap and the slow run of the grain from the spout made shovelling quite unnecessary, yet he laboured fiendishly, slamming each scoopful against the far walls and corners of the bin. The sweat burst from his livid face. If the man had stood before him, he would have bare-handedly torn him limb from limb.

He did not know how long he worked. Once Thom looked in and he bellowed, "Get to work! You got nothing to do but look around?" and the youth's frightened face vanished before he could catch himself. The grain was cleared to the floor under his feet when he heard the sound like a sob. He wheeled, the few kernels ground under his boots.

"Peter! Peter!" His wife's face wept uncontrollably abov the half-boarded door as he floundered up the wheat toward her. "The hemorrhage—we didn't know, and then we couldn' stop it. She's dead."

Stunned, he said, "Dead?" There was too much to this after noon. Comprehending, "Dead! Pete's getting the doctor. Sh can't be!"

He was through the opening in a shower of wheat and run ning up the path to the house in the thunder of the threshin machine and the chugging tractor. The truck whirled throug the gatė with the doctor's grey Ford behind it, but he had n time to wonder at the sudden arrival as the screen-door slamme behind him. Mrs Wiens, tear-blurred, left without a sound a he charged into the bedroom.

He need not have rushed.

Then the doctor was there, and in one smooth gesture ha whipped back the corner of the sheet and had his hand on th wrist. Block waited. Far away he could hear the threshing an the indistinguishable cries of the men. Dr Goodridge turned hi wrinkled face up to the Deacon.

"I'm sorry, Peter." He pushed the bag he carried among th towels on the sewing-machine. "It was really only luck tha your son caught me coming from a call in Calder. I don't know if I could have done much. I have to check—for the papers If you'll go—"

Block turned to go, and found Pete standing directly behin him in the doorway of the tight room, staring towards the bed He put his hand on his son's shoulder and they went out to gether. They sat down by the long table. Pete put his head dow on his arms, wide shoulders heaving. The Deacon stared a nothing.

The doctor was not long; he said merely, "Could I talk t you, Peter?" and Pete got up, tear-marked, and went into th kitchen. As the outside door banged, Goodridge said, "Yo know what she died of?"

"Yes."

"I don't think it would have gone badly, except for the hemor rhage. The women did their work. It would have taken a docto

—maybe a hospital—to get her through the other." He paused, and Block said nothing. "Who knows of this?"

"My wife and Mrs Wiens."

"Pete?"

"No."

"Did you know it was coming."

"No."

"It must have been the worry—and the work that brought it on. Did she work in the harvesting?"

"Yes, but my wife—"

"I know—all your wives do, but it's the worry above that that does it. This will really hit your people here, Peter." The doctor's arm gestured; he knew Block as none of the Mennonites could.

"What do you have to say?"

"The official report has to state everything. But nobody here sees that. Otherwise, I don't have to say a thing. She's gone now; there's no need to drag her through the mud. That—man—shouldn't talk much."

"What do we say?"

"Whatever they believe." The doctor turned on his heel and went into the kitchen where the two women were trying to finish the evening meal for the threshers. "I'm sorry, Mrs Block." She nodded dumbly, weeping as she peeled the potatoes. She could not have replied, even if he had spoken German.

Thom was waiting at the doctor's car, but Pete was nowhere in sight. The youth said, "Is she better?"

The doctor paused, as if pondering. "What's your name?"

"Thom Wiens."

"Is your mother in there?"

"Yes. Is Elizabeth—"

"She's dead, Thom."

Thom stood without breathing as the doctor pushed his bag across the seat and eased himself wearily down behind the wheel. He said, "Was it—work?"

The doctor squinted up at him in the fading sunlight, then looked slowly across the yard at the toiling men. "People don't die from working." Goodridge turned the key slowly and placed his finger on the starter. "It was just an internal disorder that got out of control. The thread of life is sometimes very thin. Good-bye, Thom."

As Thom nodded, numb, the doctor backed his car around swiftly and drove from the yard. He moved back toward the outfit. He could only think: The person I ate dinner with is now dead. He pulled out his watch: ten past five. An hour ago he had stood beside her drinking coffee.

Block could not endure the house. After a few words to the women, he went out and walked down the hollow path to the well. The stupor settled on him; his talk with the doctor had been an involuntary mental reflex. Then, before he could comprehend, he was at the well and there was Unger, filling the threshers' water-pail. The cheerful voice rang high above the threshing.

"Well Peter, your harvest this year is the best you've ever had!" The older man lifted his heavy face, "Oh—Thom said something about Elizabeth. Was that the doctor's car? Is she—?"

"She's dead."

The Deacon left the other man there, mouth agape. He moved away from the threshing, across the yard into the empty barn. He could hear the chickens singing as they scratched in their enclosure. He gripped the rail of the manger and, tilting forward, slowly bumped his forehead against the smooth-worn logs of the wall.

CHAPTER ELEVEN

The grey clouds of autumn tumbled low that Sunday afternoon as the Mennonite people of Wapiti drove into the church-yard for the funeral. They arrived in silence; the women and children clambered over the high buggy-wheels at the church-door and walked up the steps while the men drove to the barn and put the horses away. Except for the cry of an infant or the voice of a youngster, sharply hushed, there was only quietness and sorrow in the yard. In the church, the people sat down, shook hands gently with their neighbours, and waited, gazing at the floor. At a suggested song-number from one of the congregation, their warm German voices lifted a hymn of comfort.

No one was to be seen as the funeral procession turned into the yard. Only the empty buggies lined before the long barn and the song from the church reaching out in greeting.

I'm a pilgrim, and I'm a stranger,
I can tarry, I can tarry but a while.

Thom halted the truck at the church steps and got out. The two buggies were close behind. Pete sat on the edge of the truck-box, steadying the coffin with one hand. They waited as the teams drew up and the others descended. Pastor and Mrs Lepp, Wiens, Mrs Wiens, the wives of Ernst and young Franz together with Margret went silently into the church. The rest stood bleak, the black box swallowing their thoughts.

"It's time we went in, brethren," Block said.

The men eased the narrow coffin from the grey blanket on the truck-box; they were ready to enter: Jake and John Rempel at the feet, Franz and Ernst in the middle, Thom and Pete at the head. Usually there was a long procession of relatives after the coffin, but here only the Deacon and his wife followed. The congregation was singing as Thom and Pete stepped through the opened doors and into the church:

. . . For I am only waiting here
To hear the summons, "Child, come home."

Razia Tantamont, inside the church for the first time, turned with the others as the short procession entered at the doors under the balcony and filed down the aisle towards the pulpit where the Pastor waited, head bowed. She could understand no syllable of what was being sung, but the tune spoke their sorrow. She scanned Pete's face. For once it was not her near presence that sentenced him speechless, she thought with grim humour, then pity welled in her. Elizabeth had been his one sister. Razia's glance shifted: Almighty stars, she thought, what a striking face! She could see only the man's profile as he walked beyond Pete, but she did not notice the home-made coffin that Mrs Block had herself draped. She noticed nothing then but the broad back, as she arose with the others at the gesture of the minister. The sounds of the prayer tumbling past her ear in the stillness, she thought, What a body he must have under those out-dated clothes!

The coffin had been placed upon the bench before the pulpit, and as the congregation sat, she watched him step up into the last row of the choir. His head loomed above them all; he made the others seem puny, she noticed with delight. If he only wore some decent clothes! And a profile like a Greek. He doesn't look like a Mennonite at all. The choir sang some mournful tune she had never heard: at least she had someone to watch during the service she could not comprehend. But really —this was a funeral. She bent her mind to consider Elizabeth. On Razia's one visit to the Block's for supper, Elizabeth had seemed even more colourless, if that were possible, than the Mennonite women of Wapiti. She had been truly kind and gentle, but she had carried an incomprehensible aura of old-maidish resignation about her. Yet, considering Block's age, Elizabeth at most could not have been much over thirty. Listening to the chatter of the older girls at school, Razia had sensed that if a Mennonite woman was not married by twenty-five, she could look forward to nothing but spinsterhood. The corner of her eye caught the woman beside her, Hat seven years old. And hair like coiled slough-hay. No wonder.

Pastor Lepp was speaking: "We had planned that this Sunday should be our annual Harvest Thanksgiving Festival. God, in His Wisdom, has seen fit to move in a very different way. We cannot know why, but we must accept. We are far removed from the rest of the world here, and when sorrow strikes one of us, it comes to us all. How often our brother Deacon and his family have helped us in our trouble and in our grief! It stands written: 'As for man, his days are as grass: as a flower of the field, so he flourisheth. For the wind passeth over it, and it is gone; and the place thereof shall know it no more.' We cannot know when our days are numbered, we only . . ."

Pete, sitting beside his mother in the pew opposite the coffin, stared at it, thinking. It was almost as if she had known. He remembered the long days they had worked together that summer and autumn: milking cows in the smoke-choked corral, caring for the stock, hauling bundles as the geese flew south overhead and leaves drifted from the poplars. Tired, they occasionally lay in the stubble while the horses nosed the stooks with their hampering nose-baskets. She said once, out of nowhere, "Are you going to farm here all your life, Pete?"

He was amazed, "Why sure. Where else?"

"Wouldn't you like to see something of some other place? Wapiti is so small and away from everything in the bush. Don't you sometimes wish you could get away from here like Lou—Louis and do some—"

"Talk about that breed! Just a good for nothin'! Why should a Christian want to run everywhere in the world like a heathen? We're here to prepare for the next world. We should be happy that we have such a separate place to stay as this, where we're protected. You see what happens to Louis—gets thrown in jail for six months."

"Things can happen to you here too." She spoke strangely, looking beyond the patch-work trees edging the field at the wind-wisped clouds.

"What?"

She returned nothing; then, "Well, people die here too. You can't go on just working forever."

He had not understood her as she pulled herself up against the wagon, and now, he thought, he never would. He believed as the other Mennonites: people died, sometimes for a discernible reason, sometimes because God took them away and not even a doctor could explain how. She seemed to have known, somehow. He had never known what life was like without her: she was there, to care for him, as far back as his memory could stretch. When his father disciplined him sharply, she would slip him a cookie and hold his hand until he slept. Grown up, he had not thought about her presence in any particular way, for she was still always there, occasionally speaking a helping word. Last night he had gone into the cleaned tool-shed where they had laid her, there being no room in the house, and he had looked at her stone face in the black box under the lantern-light. Home was unimaginable without her. He felt tears starting deep inside him; he could force them back no longer. He bowed his head to his hands.

". . . gone on to be with God, was an example in her Christian walk to us all. Not one of us will have the remembrance of a bad or vicious action she did. Since our church began, she taught her Sunday School class here with true devotion. Could we but live as she did, that when we are called Home, the memory of what we have done will be an uplift and a happiness to those we leave . . ."

Mrs Block's thoughts were chaos. No one knew or suspected. Mrs Wiens had promised, but it would remain the open scar upon their conscience, festering to their last day. As she had never really comprehended the massive mental power of her husband, she now had no idea what he thought. He was as steel in everything he did. But the subterfuge: to unscrew the coffin-lid at night and place the towel-wrapped bundle in the empty lap. Had she but persuaded him on that night years before when Herman had asked for Elizabeth. If she had died in childbirth married to Herman, it would only have been the lot of a world of wives before her, but now—she could not think of it. It was inexpressible even in her thoughts. Had she but been able to move him that night when Elizabeth begged him for Herman and he was as ice that finally, abruptly, blazed facts like fire. She had thought, There will be another man. But never; only at the final brink of her daughter's womanhood, this. She had to live with the thought, tomorrow and tomorrow—

The Deacon took her arm as she sobbed, drily. She shuddered at his touch.

". . . but she is not silent, even in death. Though her spirit has gone to be with her Lord, her body here before us teaches us a solemn lesson. It says to us, 'You must all die. You have no dwelling place here, but through the Grace of God you can triumph over Sin and Death at last. You need not . . ."

Block heard no word that was being said. He was staring at the bench-back before him, his eyes ashen-dry. In the three days, the stupifying shock had worn away. Those three days he roved in madness, for Elizabeth had said no word before she died and he could not but see her as eternally damned for her sin. If she had only confessed and asked forgiveness when it first happened—or when she knew—before the work and the silence ruined all. He set his mind: the matter was beyond all change. Yet, despite the racking longing that he might have had the opportunity to forgive her, whenever his mind led him to what must have occurred that spring on his very farm-yard (he could have no idea how long the affair lasted)—how she must have stolen away to that room in the barn-loft when all were sleeping and there, on the sheets his wife washed every Monday, they must have taken their carnal lust of one another—he knew that if he had discovered them in that animal embrace he would himself have sent them to the deepest wallow of Hell. Or perhaps they had met during the day under cover of the silent bush. As he sat in the pew by her coffin, the scar blazed at his temple. He leaned on his hand to cover it.

The breeds must go. Too many years he had allowed them to remain on the edge of the settlement, where their dark wolfish faces could betray weak women. It must have been Louis. There was no other man possible. He would buy them out personally, every one of them, and send them all to wherever their animal natures could destroy themselves without involving others. His fist clenched at his temple.

Old Franz Reimer was slowly reading the brief life-history. "Our sister, Elizabeth Anna Block, was born on the 15th of March, 1911 in Orenburg, Russia, the first child of Peter and Elizabeth Block. She was a quiet child, and at the age of eight she confessed her belief in Christ as her personal Saviour. She was baptized and accepted into the church at the age of fifteen. She was an obedient daughter, and her work in the church and in the home will ever be remembered as one of the finest examples of Christian living this community has known. She died unexpectedly on October 25th, 1944, aged thirty-three years, seven months and ten days. May her body rest in peace in the earth, and her spirit in the bosom of Him who died to save her. She is mourned by her parents, Peter and Elizabeth Block, her brother Peter, and everyone who knew her in Wapiti district."

The choir sang:

Safe in the arms of Jesus,
Safe on His gentle breast;
There by His love o'er-shaded,
Sweetly my soul shall rest.

The book blurred before Thom's eyes. He could barely sing.

Pastor Lepp said, when the song was concluded, "The family has requested that, for personal reasons, the coffin not be opened. We will honour that request, and proceed to the grave-yard. Let us stand to pray." The stir of wonderment from the congregation was suppressed by the closing prayer.

They were pacing out then, between the standing row of grim men on one side and weeping women on the other. Thom looked straight before him, the coffin-handle smooth in his hand. The weight was nothing for six men. He was the last person she had talked to on earth, and that knowledge gave her words an eternal significance. She had said he must get away from Wapiti to learn other ways; he would be ruined otherwise. And that last impassioned outburst, as if torn from her being, "Can't you see what's happened to me!" Almost as if she knew she was speaking her last word. Elizabeth, only vaguely pitied before, had that last day branded him forever with her personal being. In that moment when her eyes held his, the colourless woman had vanished and the human stood, naked, starved. He could not forget that. As he carried her body in the coffin down the church steps, that look reached after him and he knew himself eternally committed to something. Stepping to the ground in the sullen afternoon, he did not know what.

Heads bowed, Block and his wife followed. She was weeping convulsively into her balled handkerchief. The Deacon, leading her, looked only down, but under the shadow of the balcony, as if drawn forcibly, he raised his head an instant towards the last pew. Herman Paetkau and his wife Madeleine stood there. Herman, head bowed, held in his arms their slumbering baby.

The people ebbed out, curious at the unopened coffin, but hushed. Old Franz Reimer lifted the dirge, and they sang, the women's voices high and thin, as they followed across the yard to the corner enclosure where the mound of earth humped above the grey grass:

Es geht nach Haus, zum Vater Haus,
Wer weiss, vielleicht schon morgen;
Vorbei, mein Herz, ist dann der Schmerz,
Und weg die Suend und Sorgen.

Es geht nach Haus,
Wer weiss, vielleicht schon morgen;

Es geht nach Haus,
Wer weiss, vielleicht schon morgen.

The song was never sung except when they followed a coffin. Though the words were to be a comfort, to Thom the sound fading in the dead-grey afternoon was harrowing.

The wind stirred as they stepped through the gate, lifting the hair on the bare heads of the men, swirling a twist of dead leaves about their feet. The pallbearers placed the coffin carefully on the two planks across the grave. Looking past his feet, Thom saw the rough box in the bottom, the lid half-pushed between it and the wall of earth. He waited motionless as the people grouped about. Pete left his place to stand beside his mother at the grave-foot. Block stood solid on her other side, his cropped hair stirring, his eyes like a desert, staring at the black box.

Pastor Lepp read slowly over the coffin, his voice moving among the silent mourners: "Remember now thy Creator in the days of thy youth, while the evil days come not, nor the years draw nigh, when thou shalt say, I have no pleasure in them; while the sun, or the light, or the moon, or the stars, be not darkened, nor the clouds return after the rain: in the day when the keepers of the house shall tremble, and the strong men shall bow themselves, and the grinders cease because they are few, and those that look out of the windows be darkened, and the doors be shut in the streets, when the sound of grinding is low, and he shall rise up at the voice of the bird, and all the daughters of musick shall be brought low; also when they shall be afraid of that which is high, and fears shall be in the way, and the almond tree shall flourish, and the grasshopper shall be a burden, and desire shall fail: because man goeth to his long home, and the mourners go about the streets: or ever the silver cord be loosed, or the golden bowl be broken, or the pitcher be broken at the fountain, or the wheel broken at the cistern.

"Then shall the dust return to the earth as it was: and the spirit shall return unto God who gave it."

There was only the sigh of the wind in the naked poplars.

The pastor turned the leaves of his Bible. "So when this corruptible shall have put on incorruption, and this mortal shall have put on immortality, then shall be brought to pass the saying that is written, Death is swallowed up in victory. O death, where is thy sting? O grave, where is thy victory?

"Let us pray." Thom stared down past his feet. He heard only the last words, "May she rest in peace—in the bosom of her Father."

He leaned forward and reached his long arm under the coffin to take the rope Ernst passed to him. He and Ernst, with Franz and John, lifted the coffin on the two ropes; the planks were withdrawn, and they lowered the coffin into the earth. It settled in the box and, before another could move, Thom was down in the grave, his feet precise on the edge of the white box framing the black, pulling the ropes through carefully. Then, balancing on the edge, he levered the lid up and over the black coffin. As he looked up and caught the screw-driver, bending forward, he saw the elongated bodies and heads of the people dividing the slate sky and the grave's rim, staring down at him. At a corner, beyond the granite form of Block, he glimpsed a woman's face he had never seen before. It terrified him, somehow, to hunch in Elizabeth's grave, feet on her coffin-box, and look up to see all Wapiti—and that sharp new face. Shuddering as before a premonition, he stooped to turn the screws, two at each end and one on either side. The men threw in loose straw as he did so; he straightened up, and spread the straw evenly over the white-wood box. He paused a moment, looking unseeingly at the mound of straw under his feet, then, even as he grasped the hands stretched toward him, the falling earth thudded dully in his ears.

The pale straw vanished under the rain of earth and the thud died away to the rapid shovelling. Swiftly, men exchanged spades. Thom stood there at the foot of the grave, the sound of Mrs Block crying brokenly on her son's chest mingling with that of the other women. He did not look at Pete. He saw his mother weeping while Margret held her close. Herb Unger was standing beyond them, away from the mound of earth and the shovelling men, looking steadily; Thom followed his glance. Herb was looking at the strange woman. Thom thought, in some remote portion of his mind, That must be the new teacher. Why did her narrow face look like a death's-head from down there, beyond Block's shoulder? He shook his head, gazing back at the grave, and saw it was nearly filled. Surrendered to dusty death.

He turned to go, and saw Pete leading his mother slowly down the path towards the church. Block stood alone motionless, by the mounding grave. The tumbled glowering clouds told that harvest weather was past; winter was about to break. Thom followed the silent people.

CHAPTER TWELVE

The chores were done; late-autumn night had encumbered the world. Washing his hands at the wash-stand by the door, Thom let the soapy water drip from his finger-tips. Behind him the house-kitchen lay quiet in the kerosene light. His mother came in from washing the cream-separator, and they were all in the house: Margret rattling wood into the stove, Hal reading a gaudy-yellow book, Wiens leaning on his hands over the table. No one said a word.

Hal jumped up from the bench, "Aw shucks!" his high voice broke across their thoughts, "There's no fun around here any more. Nobody says anythin'—everythin' just quiet an' quiet!—don't play no games—"

Margret said, where the faint light moulded the gloom by the stove, "You were at the funeral today too, Hal. We can't sing happy songs and laugh and play right after a friend has died, as if it didn't happen."

Hal pushed the reader over the worn oil-cloth. "Yah. It sure was sad, eh? Mrs Block was cryin' the whole time—an' even Pete. But Mr Block didn't a bit, even when the grave was filled up an' only a few men an' Mr Lepp were left an' Mr Block still was standin' there. Me an' Johnny sneaked up close an' looked, but he was just starin' at it like nothin'—"

"Sonny," Mrs Wiens admonished gently, "You shouldn't stare at people—especially in their sorrow."

"Honest, he wasn't cryin'. Doesn't he care that she died?"

"Of course he cares." Thom thought his mother answered quickly. "But some grown men cannot show it like others. In his heart he was probably crying more than anyone there."

Margret said viciously, "Yah!" Mrs Wiens looked quickly at her, but said nothing. She turned to Hal.

"It's late, Sonny; time for bed. Pa will read first."

Thom draped the towel over the spool nailed against the wall and moved over to drop to the bench as his father reached up for the heavy Bible on the shelf above the table. Margret sat on a chair in the gloom. Hal leaned against his mother. Wiens read slowly, voice rough and uninflected.

"And I saw a new heaven and a new earth: for the first heaven and the first earth were passed away; and there was no more sea. And I John saw the holy city, new Jerusalem, coming down from God out of heaven, prepared as a bride adorned for her husband. And I heard a great voice out of heaven saying, Behold, the tabernacle of God is with men, and he will dwell with them, and they shall be his people, and God himself shall be with them, and be their God.

"And God shall wipe all tears from their eyes; and there shall be no more death, neither sorrow, nor crying, neither shall there be any more pain: for the former things are passed away."

After a moment, they all stood for his prayer.

"Our Father, we can only thank You for this blessed hope of being forever with You. In your mercy, grant us grace, now and in the moment of our death. Let us sleep tonight under Your hand. In Jesus' name. Amen."

Thom had never heard his father pray so—he looked up at him, seated again at the table, staring into the hand-worn book —so—*personally* was the only concept that formed in his mind. Like the prayer of some new vision, almost.

Mrs Wiens said, "Now to bed with you, Hal, come." She took the boy's arm and started him up the narrow stairs before her. She had not gone to put Hal to bed in over a year.

As they vanished in the dark of the stair-hole, Thom rose and went into the darkened living room. Fumbling, he pushed his fingers under the heavy radio-battery and slid out a fat envelope. When he returned to the kitchen light with it, Margret said, sitting now on the wood-box, "You going to read that letter again?"

"Sure." Thom settled on the bench behind the table.

"I better write Joseph to send you another—before you wear this through."

Thom said, without a smile, "This will keep me occupied for a while yet."

Margret looked at him, past the silent figure of their father propped motionlessly against the table. Upstairs, Hal's prayer murmur was indistinguishable. The whole day repelled teasing. She slipped from the box and walked across the living room. He read, as the rocker squeaked forlornly.

"Dear Thomas:

"You asked me why I wrote 'Thomas' to you when I never spoke so formally. Well, to tell you the truth I really did not know how to write your name, since in Wapiti it's spoken 'Tom' in English and 'Thom' in Low German and 'Thomas' in High German. You can assume, therefore, that I am writing in none of these languages but rather am using the correct Biblical form of the name as given in the King James Version; the name of the man whose eyes were open but could not see. I wonder sometimes if our parents, when they label us thus biblically, really understand what they are about. Surely mine didn't. I'm convinced that anyone having glimpsed my face, even when a newborn infant, could have concluded on the spot that here was one male who would never be forced to leave his garments and flee away naked to preserve his unspotted character. There are other aspects of the Old Testament Joseph that might fit, but certainly that portion is, to me at least, a grim irony whenever I glance in the mirror.

"Enough of names.

"We are in the last week of basic training. We did a cross-country race today—seven miles with full pack. We Restricteds carried our stretchers instead of rifles. Most of the men are accustomed to us. They cannot really understand us, but they try to be democratic about it. After all, if you actually have a democracy, you're liable to end up with more odd-balls than conventional people. It seems to me you should, anyway.

"I do get off on tangents! The incident I wanted to write about happened just now. After the race, we were lying in the barracks when a whiskery man came in and began talking to the man on the first bunk. He talked and waved a book and sheaf of papers when suddenly the half-naked recruit said, loudly, so that everyone looked up, 'Go on—beat it!'

"Nothing daunted, he turned to the next. I told you about O'Hannigan; the man said three words and O'Hannigan gagged him with a stream of filth. Then the man came to me, his face almost happy; I nearly fell off the bed at what he said.

"He leaned over me, clothes looking as if he'd slept in them every night he had them, and whispered, 'Brother, are you saved?'

"I think I managed a 'huh?'

" 'Brother, the Bible says that everyone must be saved from the wrath of God to escape the fires of Hell. You're goin' into death, soldier and you've gotta be sure you're not goin' to end up in that fiery lake that burneth forever. The Devil's just waitin' to stoke you—'

"I knew him then. I got him by the collar and out the door, but not before he bellered a few snatches of 'eternity in Hell' and 'sin-ridden drunken soldiers.' Thinking of it, I'm sick. Bum from one army camp to another, shout 'Be saved! Be saved!' and imagine your job done. How utterly simple; and you are guaranteed to find enough persecution to make you a martyr! But where do the teachings and life of Christ come in?

"But I suppose a Mennonite should not complain. We don't appear in army camps to tell, or show, these men anything.

"I'm writing this in the heat. Don't jump to the conclusion that only the Mennonite branch of the Christian church has made mistakes. No church shows up here—only the chaplain, and all he does is speak about 'our glorious opportunity to die for our country.' What a travesty of religious position! Other churches seem to be bound as rigidly by tradition as our Mennonite church: they in insisting that, if there is a war, their members should use force to end it, we in holding to 'peace' at all costs. Our tradition is made more obvious by being in opposition to that of the majority. I am convinced that their position is contrary to Christ's teaching, but am not sure that ours is very much better.

"We make great use of the word 'peace.' We quote Matthew glibly: 'Blessed are the peacemakers, for they shall be called the children of God.' Yet how can we 'make peace'?

"I dug around a bit in some books I bought. In the English Bible, 'peace' is often used in a general statement 'to hold one's peace'—that is, a state of restfulness which includes silence. Our people, reading Luther's German translation, may not know of this specific meaning of 'Frieden,' but certainly you'll find it frequently applied in our church meetings when a difficult point arises. As long as everything goes smoothly and they themselves cannot be blamed, 'peace' is being maintained.

(Thom did not have to be reminded of such a meeting.)

"Secondly, the word 'peace' means a state of safety and blessedness. This was one of the blessings promised Israel by God if they followed Him. 'Peace' to most Mennonites has, besides that mentioned above, only this Old Testament significance, if it has any distinct meaning at all. As long as God gives us good crops and we don't have to fight in any war we are at peace. We can squabble with our neighbour as much as we please. Or we can neglect him entirely.

"Yet the 'peace' of the New Testament is quite different. The angels sang 'Peace on earth' and shortly after all the babes of Bethlehem were slaughtered because of the birth of Christ. Explain 'peace' there, if you will! It sounds as if God was playing a horrible joke on mankind.

"According to Christ's teaching, peace is not a circumstance but a state of being. The Christ-follower has the peace of reconciliation with God and therefore the peace of conscious fellowship with God through God in Christ. Peace is not a thing static and unchanging: rather a mighty inner river (read Isaiah 48:18) that carries all outward circumstances before it as if they were driftwood. This was the peace Christ brought; he never compromised with a sham slothful peace, as we want to. He said, 'Do not think that I have come to bring peace on earth; I have not come to bring peace, but a sword.' He brought no outward quiet and comfort such as we are ever praying for. Rather, he brought inward peace that is in no way affected by outward war but quietly overcomes it on life's real battle-field: the soul of man. By personally living His peace, we are peacemakers.

"But I must stop preaching! I'm tremendously happy that you see the necessity of carrying on the Bible class after harvest. It may be a bit tough in the hard winter, but don't be discouraged. If it gets very bad, perhaps you could hold it in one of their cabins—they live close together—if the parents let you. It would be a wonderful way to get them to listen too. If the beginning goes well, why don't you try that? I found two books that I think may help you in your preparation and I'm sending them along separately.

"I can't afford extra postage! Answer when you can: I enjoy your letters tremendously in this barren camp. Tell me especially about the class. I cannot give specific advice, but I think perhaps that Herb's persisting in being angry towards you, as with the other matter, centres around your relationship to the Christ-given peace I mentioned above. Thom, who can help Herb but you? God help you. Joseph."

While he read, Thom had distantly sensed his mother coming back from upstairs, but had really comprehended nothing beyond the letter before him. The letter invaded his thinking more each time he read it, yet now he was numbed. Some days had too much.

Far away his mother spoke to him, "Go to bed, Thom—tomorrow comes so quickly." She placed her hand on Wiens' shoulder; the older man still pored over the family Bible. Thom looked at them as he slowly folded the letter into its envelope. He pushed it into his breast pocket, turned and climbed up the narrow stairs. His mother's "Goodnight" drifted through the lonesome music of the radio.

Hal's body a ball of warmth beside him as he lay abed, he stared into the blackness of the rafters. How could everything, after many years of existence, in one short summer be so suddenly wrong in church, about Block? There was no finer man to work for; others' interests always came first; yet Elizabeth—

He was sick of it all; sick and deadly tired. He heard Margret creak the stairs, and soon her tick rustled. Safe in bed on a still night, miles away through the bush from the loud world of many men. He curled over against Hal and the little boy instinctively snuggled tight in his sleep. For the quiet of sleep after a harrowing day, Thom wearily thanked God.

Immediately he was lost in the bush that separated Wapiti from the world. The trees loomed about him like walls. He could not move around them for numbing weariness. Wild animals roared at him; he could not inch aside. He knew somewhere that it was a dream: he should wake himself, but his mind had no strength to force consciousness. A great brute with gaping maw leaped at him. He fell, despairing. The beast was snuffed away like a candle-flicker in the wind. The bush held him, bottling his spirit within itself so that he knew no escape from the terror and sin and the tiredness that he had never imagined existed, yet now found within himself. He fought endlessly, but knew he did nothing. The bush drew closer. Single trees merged and the bush-mass wrapped him away from all, cloaking his own evil and sorrow about him in tight-wound clutches until he sank in suffocation like a birth-heaving animal that cannot throw off its young in a final tearing of tissues.

Then all was gone. He was above the bush, as if standing on a high tower whose limbs did not reach down into the ancient trees below. Through misty air he saw dim outlines and far vanishing shapes. Abruptly, a pin-prick of light flickered at him, so tiny that he could not have seen it except in the blackest of nights. He looked away: another light pricked at him, then another and another, until the boundless black of the bush was split like the night with cracks of light while he stood on the legless tower, watching. And the lights grew fearsomely, drawing nearer, the lines of their growing as if distended in terror. Wind whiffed his cheek. Sparks winged up to fall on dry needles. Fire blossomed below him like a flame-rose. Then he saw sparks falling as hail and where each fell flames burst. The wind jelled with smoke. He saw the trees like patriarchs, limbs now yearning in petition where they had stood triumphant half a thousand years; and they moaned in terror, rooted immovable before the scourge. Then they blistered in light as fire raced to the tip, and dripped orange and blood-red into the black swamp-water as branches dropped hissing down. The fires ran together in gruesome patterns until all before him was a furnace moaning and crashing and hissing and breaking where the very light blotted his vision to blackness.

When he opened his eyes in his tower, not a tree stood between Wapiti and the world. Only the black spines of the patriarchs humped splintered, broken in dead-fall. A spiral of steam twisted here and there from a glazed swamp pool.

He heard a pop! Before his eyes an enormous spark arched through the air to fall at his feet on the tower. He could not stir while he stared in fascination as the glowing spark spread wider and wider its black circle to leap into flame with a tearing sound. Then the fire surrounded him on the tower he had thought limbless, and he could only grip the peeled-poplar rail blistering in the heat as the holocaust caught him. As his heart baulked in terror, he was wiped away.

He was awake in bed. He lay rigid while the death-fear dripped torturously from him, but long minutes passed before he could open his eyes at the darkness. He pulled Hal tight, but the sight would not leave. The sight of the wide miles of burned bush that opened Wapiti to the world. And the sight of the widening circle about the glowing coal before it burst into flame at his feet.

It was in the thin sunlight of the next day that an idea hit him. If they ever did have such a fire, they could clear the rubble, jerk out the stumps and really farm! He swung his hammer in a great arc at the corral-rail he was replacing and roared with laughter. When he thought of it a second time, he stopped laughing.

Winter 1944

PRELUDE

Into the numb days of November, dulling to greyness under the leaden bowl of the heavens, the blizzard tore. One day hung wan, the next howled in whiteness. The blast streamed and eddied round house, barn and bush; men ventured their lives to feed stock in barns and straw-sheds; they staggered indoors to thaw their faces. The storm squirmed through door-cracks, between window and sill in granular curls, prying at the people piling deep with wood their roaring heaters. It blurred pale the frozen face of night.

Abruptly, after three days, it ceased its showy violence. The wind dropped; hoar-frost blistered the tree skeletons. As the mercury huddled to the depths of its bulb, sun-dogs glared doubly through the crystals of the sky. Indoors, beside the blazing stove itself, wall nails stood capped every one with white fur hats of rime. At night wolves moaned under the faintly-bloody sprawl of northern lights. On November 29th the mercury stood fifty-three degrees below zero.

Now barns seeped cold, thick straw-sheds gave no protection. Bunched together, the stock crouched inside their heavy hides, stiffening, or stumped across the squawking snow to watering, stirred only by the desperate beating of men. The trough-heaters, under prodding pokers, plumed smoke into the air; without them each pail of water had spread solid in the trough. Every breath drew a knife-wound down the throat. No one thought of the howling blizzard now. The men, dumping hay in mangers and heaping straw under the bellies of their stock, knew that the silent malignancy was far more deadly.

CHAPTER THIRTEEN

The school, sparkling in blackish smudged shadows, hulked in the clearing as Thom slid out of the trees at the crossroads. Etched by moonlight, all was hazed in cold, save where the teacherage dropped its yellow light through the tight-curtained windows like damask on the blued snow. Smoke curled fearfully from the warm chimney into the clear of the hard sky as he kicked loose his skis and crunched on the step. He knocked.

He heard her steps above the radio music, the inside door opening, and the door pushed open before him. Her face appeared in the crack, as if she were ready to jerk it shut at any sound.

"Yes?" clipped, like a frozen branch snapping.

He cleared his throat, "Miss Tantamont, it's Thom Wiens. I was wondering if—"

"Oh, of course. I couldn't see your face with that big parka in the dark." The door swung wide, "Come in! It's terrible outside. Do come right in," and she stepped back as he entered, huge in the Indian parka. She smiled as he pushed back the hoared hood. "You look like an Arctic expedition. Please let me close the door—it's bad enough keeping that heater going when it's closed."

"Oh, I'm sorry." In the warmth and strangeness of her tiny kitchen he had not noticed that he still held the inside door open. He backed it shut, his hand on the knob. "I hope my coming's all right tonight. I don't want to keep you from your work, but as I said last Sunday, some of these correspondence courses—"

Her laugh pealed like bells. "If I can help you! What grade did you say you were taking?" She remembered well enough. Since he had begun the Sunday classes with the children in November, she had been planning some occasion or reason for him to come to see her alone. She had even listened to two of his lessons but his tremendous seriousness and the distant invariable politeness he presented towards her speared duplicity before it could develop. She had been forced to the very strange position of wondering how she could attract this man when he had abruptly approached her himself. He said now,

"Grade nine."

"I should know something about that! You didn't forget to bring your books?"

"No—they're in my knapsack outside. I skied out. If you've a broom, I'll clean my feet outside."

"It's by the door—there behind you. But don't bother so much."

He was gone, his head bending under the door-jamb, and she could have laughed for joy. He had the gentility of great strength. Her glance flew about the room: she tossed *The Sun Also Rises* behind a pile of texts on the shelf above the table. In the tiny bedroom she kicked off her slippers, stepped into the pumps which were the marvel of the girls in school, dabbed away a trace of lipstick, whisked the brush down the curve of her hair and paused, the kitchen light on the mirror wrapping her figure warmly in the darkness of the bedroom. As he fumbled for the door she called, "Come on in, Thom," and then from the bedroom she saw the cigarette box on the table beside her lamp. Tapping over, she dropped box and ashtray behind the texts with Hemingway. She turned as he entered.

"Let me take your parka." She moved towards him. He twisted out of the sheep-skin lined coat and the thick sweater underneath. "I've often wondered," she said, marvelling fingers on the bead-work, "where did you get this? And the fur around the hood!"

"It's fox fur—Old Two Poles, an Indian on the Reserve, north of the river, his wife makes these sometimes. I got it late last winter. Warmest—and fanciest—coat I ever had."

She folded the parka and sweater on the bed and returned. "I've never seen such a beautiful bead-pattern. Do you think she'd make one for me?"

"Sure—she'd want to do that. I see Two Poles sometimes when I go hunting. I'll tell him to come and see you. You can draw your own design if you want, and she'll work it in beads on the coat."

He sat down at the table, and she wondered again at his poise. So different from Pete! The blue-plaid shirt hung beautifully on his wide shoulders. It was better than the shiny suit on Sunday. He said, lifting his head, the hair glued down by the rim of the ski-cap he had worn under the hood, "English and Social Studies aren't bad, but mathematics is tough—for me, anyway."

She picked up the text-book he had laid beside his pencil scribbler on the table. "I always found math rough too, but I should know how to do this." She sat down, drawing her chair closer to his.

Razia's golden head bending to Thom's black one, they worked. She was amazed at his perceptiveness. After some time she rose to place the coffee-pot on the heater while he worked on, quite oblivious of her movement. A huge man bending over the schoolwork of a child. But for all his inadequate schooling, he could certainly impress the children with his Bible-story telling: the older girls talked among themselves about King David last week. And even his strange, impossible-of-explanation emphasis that Jesus was God, somehow gained a sort of credence from his tremendous conviction. To try to teach children something at which men staggered! She glanced at him again, in his hunch of concentration, and his appearance intruded on her thoughts. She jammed a piece of wood into the heater. He smells clean, like frost on a windowpane. And his fingernails are scrubbed, not like that pig Herb.

Her thoughts about Herb blackened as she measured coffee into the pot. To think that he could suddenly, on the night the blizzard blew out of the north like fiends fleeing, come stumbling in and assume he could stay the night without ever having done more than sit there once a week and drink her coffee!

As if all that was required was four evenings squatters' rights!

But she had at first pitied him that night as he sat near the heater after rubbing his white-blotched face with ice-water, rolling his cigarette with hands shakily dribbling tobacco-crumbs to the floor. "Gad, it was terrible. I thought it would snow a bit, yuh know, but all of a sudden the wind just come with a roar—I was about a quarter mile down the road, and Grease, he just stopped movin' and I kicked him, but he wouldn't budge an' the wind tore under my clothes, up high on the horse, so I slid off and led him. Couldn't see a damn thing for snow. All I knew was, stay on the hard road an' you'll come to the school corner. Gadfry, what a wind! About seventy miles an hour an' straight in my face." He finally got his cigarette, his grimed hands cupped as if he were still in the storm that howled outside.

As the evening dragged on she had begun to hate him intensely, for there was nothing to talk about but the storm and how tough it would be on the stock! The wind whined about the corners of the teacherage. Once he staggered out for wood, and almost floundered coming through the drift by the corner in the ferocious darkness. It was all very well for a girl to play Lady Brett Ashley when she was in Paris with a dozen men flowing about, panting, or in Saskatoon on a Saturday night with the airmen on leave from their base, but to be caught in a blizzard with a brute left the bile on her tongue. She should have rapped him into place the first night he ventured out, but she was sure she had met his brother Hank in Saskatoon, and after asking Block, once, about having a dance—Heaven knows nothing ever happened in Wapiti. But the better-than-nothing diversion had recoiled. He had never had a cleanly amusing thought in his head! Listening to his usual spill of hatred against the Wapiti Mennonite community, she said,

"What's the matter with them?"

"Who?"

"The Mennonites you always yell about every time you're here. You're one too, just like your father and mother."

His face convulsed. "I'm no Mennonite! Think I'd sit around and pray and read the Bible like a dumb Mennonite? That's why they can't stand me, all those pure churchgoers, because when I was old enough so my Mennonite old man didn't dare clobber me into readin' the Bible and goin' to church. I went fishin' on Sunday."

It was the nearest he had ever come to self-revelation. Interested, she said, in her clear uninflected voice,

"What did that prove?"

"Prove? It showed 'em that I could do as I damn well pleased. Nobody's going to tell me what to do. I'm my own boss."

She did not hide the tinge of disgust in her voice. "So you can do as you please—and live by yourself—without a friend to your name. Don't you think that someone like Thom Wiens has—"

He swore across her sentence. "Thom Wiens! That ratty coward claiming 'holy love' as an excuse for hidin' at home during a war—you been listenin' to him preach to those kids? He'll stuff you full of dish-rag Christianity. I'll tell you what—"

Angered, she cut his speech sarcastically, "You'll tell me nothing. Why—" she hesitated momentarily, glancing at his lour, catching the very understandable jealousy on his homely features, and flicked her question away from Thom, "Why don't you get out then, if you hate everyone so much. I wouldn't stay."

He looked up, startled. Baldly stated, it sounded childishly simple, and it seemed for a moment that he could not scrape together a mutterable reason why he had never considered it. She calmly checked through Grade two drawings. He shrugged, "Well, I get to Battleford once in a while, but if a guy has a farm started you just don't up and take off—"

She faced him squarely. "Why not?"

"I've a lotta money tied up in things—"

His scowl soured, almost as if he needed to remain in a place, among people he hated, to give some meaning to his existence. Merciless, she flayed him quite. "That place? You could earn it back in two months working in a factory! The army won't bother you, even if you leave the farm!"

Shuffling his feet, he cursed the Services, the Mennonites: viciously, as she had not heard him. She pushed into his oaths, swiftly, "Don't you swear in here! Get out—beat it to your precious farm." She swept his coffee-cup from the table beside him in one wipe of her arm. He rose, but otherwise remained motionless, and she knew with a heart-trip that her first impression of him had been only too correct. She should not have enraged him. His face turned toward her, eyes agleam.

"I was kinda plannin' to stay the night."

She ignored it, conceding, "The storm sounds bad—I'll give you two blankets and you can go into the school. There's a fire and plenty of wood." But, staring down the line of her body as if she were a mare he was about to buy, he growled,

"Don't act like you didn't know what I mean. You think I came that stretch into the wind's teeth just to drink coffee and be laughed at? We've taken it easy, kiddo, but this is a cozy night."

She fell back before his slow, confident step. She felt the corner of the wood-box in her back, and for an instant terror gripped her: she had always been in control and abruptly she realized what could happen to her in this wilderness. Then rage swept her—to be terrified by a brute! Her hand found the heavy poker behind her; she swung it in a blinding arc that caught him across the temple as he grinned at her, hand reaching, and with a bitten curse he reeled aside. She was past him in the second and slammed the bedroom door as he pulled himself erect by the table.

The dark bedroom with its pale-frozen window was a cell she could not escape. A rude door of half-inch boards: he would walk through it as if it were not there. She wedged herself against the door-diagonal, panting in her humiliation and rage. He did not even deign to batter at the door.

"Listen, you slut, I know you, floutin' your trim rear around for everyone to ogle at and then prancin' off like a high-steppin' dame. You can fool these other simpletons, but not me. I know you. Do I break the door down? You can scream till you're dead, or—" his laugh was coarser than any word he could have spoken. "Not a soul on earth to hear you—the storm outside. Listen."

He paused, exultant in what he must know was her silent terror inches from him beyond the flimsy door. She forced her thoughts. Suddenly, her mind gripped and immediately she leaned away to jerk the door wide in his face. His grin spread at her surrender as his hand lifted at her, but she rapped, "Don't touch me!" For a second her superiority held him, and she continued swiftly, "If you lay one finger on me, I'll go to Mr Block the instant the storm is blown!"

The very name stalled him a moment, then, "Haha—what could he do, after?"

"Bring the Mounties. You'd get jailed at least ten years."

"Your word against mine!"

"What kind of a word have you!" His glance wavered and triumph stirred faintly within her.

"He's a Mennonite—they never go to the cops."

"And he'd never get another teacher here! Think he'd do that for you? Don't be absolutely stupid!" For some reason she could not quite fathom, the Deacon's name squelched him. She said nothing to break the spell, hanging like a thin membrane between them, but stepped swiftly past to the chair and flung him his parka. Blackly silent now, he jerked into it. She said, in careful calm, "You can sleep on the school-floor or drift home before the wind. You said you could never get lost on Grease." He opened the inside door, and the wind-moan wallowed into the teacherage. Her voice tensed, "Don't dare to come here again."

He glared at her a moment, then, flinging a tearing insult, he slammed the door and was gone. "You filthy ignorant blockhead," she screamed hysterically against the door and the whining storm. Abruptly she rushed to hook the outside door, heaved the inner tight and feverishly braced a chair under the knob. Holding to the wall, she tilted into the chair where he had sat, her head collapsing into her hands. Sobs of humiliation racked her. Such an absolute pig! It was only after some time that she realized her pointed pumps were in the muck that had melted from his boots.

"Well, that's that. I should be able to do the rest at home." Thom's voice broke the thoughts she would have gladly done without. She turned to get the cups, her rigid features relaxing into a smile at his huge form comfortable in the chair. If he had, by accident, come that night, he would have tossed Herb out by the scruff—and then she remembered that Thom was probably "non-resistant"—which was a great deal better than being like that beast. She said, placing the two cups on the table beside his books,

"I've made coffee. Do have a cup before you go."

He protested politely, but did not insist. As she poured she said casually, remembering Pete Block three months before, "How does a great healthy man like you stay out of fighting the Germans?"

He said, studying the curl of steam, "My call hasn't come yet—should be here any day." Not another of those, she despaired, but he continued, "Anyway, that's neither here nor there. If I really felt I should go, I'd join up without the call. But I don't think that a Christian can go out and kill his fellow man, even if the government says he should. And I'm a Christian."

She was nonplussed for a moment, the simplicity of it dropping a wall before her thoughts. At Normal School they had sometimes discussed the "problem" of the conscientious objector, but this directness was odd. She said, groping for the arguments she could remember, "But musn't everyone do his share? Is it fair to believe that, when soldiers are dying for you?"

"I've thought about that." His frankness cut. "It's not fair that I sit here comfortably and drink coffee with you while men are under gunfire across the ocean." He thought for a moment, and she, watching, saw his face freshen as if a new idea had found him. "Look at it this way: we're very conscious of the misery of the Canadian soldier right now fighting the 'Battle of Freedom' for us, as the radio insists. What about the time when there was no shooting war and all those soldiers were here with us in Canada having a, comparatively speaking, comfortable time, like us now. There were still millions of this world's people dying miserably, for no other reason than that they happened to be born in the wrong country. Did we, who on the whole had enough—and some too much—to eat, feel any concern for them? My folks can tell a few things about Russia they lived through. Are we merely concerned now that some other Canadians are having a rough time? They at least have plenty to eat, which is more than most of the people of the world know about now, or will when this war's over." He scratched his black head. "Do you get what I mean? I'm a bit mixed up—I've never thought of this exactly before either. I don't think there was much talk about our way of life not being fair until our boys got into it and found out what misery is like. From what Pa says, death by hunger is quite a bit worse than by bullet, though it doesn't sound as spectacular to us, sitting about a full table. I should think more people die of the first, even now."

"Isn't there a difference between men dying so that you don't have to, and men dying because of the accident of their birth?"

"Probably." He concentrated momentarily. "But what I want to get at is this idea of fairness. Life on earth is not fair—ever. Advantage for one is always balanced by disadvantage to another. Canada can only hold so many people. If I—and you—live and eat here, in a sense that fact makes it impossible for someone else to live and eat here. The way people behave, there is not enough either of food or space for all to live comfortably. Joseph—last year's teacher here—he gave me a book written about World War One. It was to be 'the war to end war.' But look at the one raging on now. Man is always fighting such a war to end war, and the next generation has to fight it over again. The Bible says there is this lack of unity, space, food in the world because man has sinned. He is now sinful. I suppose this sin—this unfairness—becomes most obvious in time of war and that's why so many begin to act very nobly and want to kill off the tyrant of the moment to prove that they, at least, don't take part in this rashly open unfairness."

"So you, as a good Christian, can sit back and calmly accept your own comfort while—"

"No!" his earnestness precipitated him into violent interruption. "No. Certainly not that. But that's just where I—like a bog —get nowhere. I've read and thought—perhaps a Christian is on earth for a different purpose—" he gestured almost pathetically.

She smiled warmly into his sad face. She had been not at all prepared for the torrent that spilled against her, and now attempted a smooth shift: "Well, you seem to have thought about it a good deal, at any rate. You don't sound much like the usual Mennonite—at least not Pete Block, but—"

He interrupted again, his face jerking up at her, "What did Pete say to you?"

She laughed for his sake, inwardly disgruntled that she had not drawn him from his preoccupation. She stretched slantingly in her chair, her legs brushing his under the table as she put her bare arms behind her head and stared up at the ceiling. Good old Jim at Normal School had once told her, in a moment of insane infatuation, that she stretched as sensuously as an alley cat.

"Oh, I can't remember it too well, really. He muttered something last fall as he was putting up the aerial about his father having a big farm and he having to stay home to help—something like that. But about two weeks ago he came over to invite me to their place for a supper of—what do you call it? bor—"

"Borscht, our Mennonite soup."

"That's it—we had a tremendous meal. They really miss Elizabeth there—Mr Block said so as he drove me home in the truck. Anyway, Pete said something about non-resistance when he came to invite me. He said he was a Mennonite and the Mennonites taught their children not to resist their enemies and so he could not join the army to fight anyone. You sounded rather different—"

She knew immediately that she had lost him, somewhere. He was staring against the curtains of the windows, sinking into untrackable thought. She said, lightly, "In all my talking, you've finished your coffee. I'll get the pot." Willowy as a whip, she rose and walked to the heater, the cellar hollow under her heels, but he said as she came with the coffee, not having noticed her motion,

"I guess he can say that's his reason—if he wants. But it has to go beyond the mere teaching of the fathers—" Then he comprehended her standing beside him. "Oh, no," smiling forcedly, "I really couldn't have any more. Thanks." He rose towering beside her, and heaped his books together.

"Just one more cup," she smiled.

"No, really. Could I have my coat please? It's late and I should get home." She knew then her hints had not found him. Recalling Herb's vehemence, she made one last attempt to interest him as she held his parka while he pushed into it. "I've lived here for three months and I don't really know. Who is a Mennonite?"

He smiled wanly as he scooped up the books. "I doubt you'll get an answer in Wapiti—or anywhere. Some say only church members are Mennonites, others that we're actually a race of people. Most who are born with Mennonite names but refuse to join the church don't want to be known as Mennonites—guess they feel somehow it commits them." Then he was gone into the frigid night, his low thanks hovering in the empty teacherage. Why, in the name of Heaven, had she come to Wapiti! One Mennonite fool was so smitten with her he could only use his eyes but not speak a coherent sentence, another knew nothing but animalism, and the third, with a body like a Greek hero, knew well enough where he could go for help with his mathematics but no more saw her as a woman than if she had been an icicle dripping from the roof. What a sink-hole! She wondered what little dove in Wapiti Thom's manly coo had first roused to chaste emotion. She could conceive no other reason for his imperviousness. Probably some anaemic overworked "maiden" she had never seen! As she twisted the radio dial, her other hand groped behind the text-books for *The Sun Also Rises*. She scrounged for a pencil and, to a blaring fox-trot from the radio, leafed rapidly. She'd have to send him the book with significant places underlined! She laughed. The dunce would probably not even know what was going on. As a good teacher, she had better add footnotes. Detailed.

Thom, strapping on his skis, slid away from the teacherage. The school hill stretched away behind school and barn to lose itself in bush under the stars, somewhere. He recalled children's voices all over the hill, so high then! and how he could barely breathe when flying down prone on a little sled, and how they came stamping in at the bell, and how forty mittens dripped steaming about the barrel stove as he sat and read. He had known everything, in those days. Now he did not even know if a friend's way of expressing himself was correct. Should one say, I act this way because my father tells me so? Should one talk about Mennonite tradition before one spoke of the only possible basis for that tradition: the personal commitment to Christ? Especially to a woman who knew little about Christ's teachings and was ever telling the pupils in school that "everyone had to do his part to win the war"? His mind snagged there, at how Hal had come home to ask, as he forked hay to the stock, "What are we doing to help win the war?" Thom found small comfort in remembering he had at least not said they were raising stock to feed the soldiers. Perhaps he would have been more truthful with Hal if he had.

In his stride, he was about to push into the road when he noticed a fast-approaching team and he slid to a stop. The growing moon shone full in his face, he could not discern the driver's face, but as the horses came opposite he recognized the shiny bay even as the clear voice greeted, "Good-evening, Thom."

"Good-evening, Mr Block," he returned in Low German, then glided into his tracks for home. Where could the Deacon be going late on a December night? No one but breeds lived north of the school. Unconnectedly, a thought fell into his head: I should go see Herb Unger. The words of Joseph's letter had often stirred in him, but there were always possible excuses. Get that triviality cleared away, whatever it was, and perhaps even find some basis for friendship. Do it and done with, before easy alternatives lured. His heart pounded: if there's a light, I'll go in. His skis slipped swiftly over the drifts.

His horses trotting past the teacherage northward in the sleigh-tracks, the Deacon mulled over Thom Wiens' moonlit emergence at the school-gate. What was he doing there at this hour? The teacher? Yet there had seemed no embarrassment in his greeting. But he filed the thought away. For certain men the slim teacher with her narrow face and skimpy dresses would be very attractive. Despite her worldliness, her teaching was excellent: after that one request for a dance, she seemed finally to understand what was needed in his community. If that foolish boy now upset—he would talk to Thom. There were enough Mennonite girls in Wapiti.

With the formed decision, his thoughts turned. Face rigid to the night's stiffening cold, he drove because of the rumour he had heard that morning in the store. Again, as ever again, he endured that last hour of Elizabeth's life. He should have forced an acknowledgement, yet—he shifted abruptly. In the five weeks since her burial he had studied the people of his community as never before. He knew them, every one. Sexual immorality was for all Mennonites the nadir of sin; it was equivalent to murder. There was not a single Mennonite man or youth who could have fallen so low as to accept the embraces of—as they all considered her in their Mennonite way—his elderly daughter. His thoughts fled to their only refuge. Perhaps she had not—perhaps it had been the terrible shame that had sealed her death.

Perhaps. Bare face deliberately defiant into the streaming cold, dreadingly poised on the slim pin of hope, he turned his team down a snow-hemmed trail. In a short minute he crossed from the shadow into the clearing where the Moosomin shacks squatted in the hard moonlight.

Three dogs tore over the drifts in raucous greeting. Pulling the horses into the shelter of the house where the Moosomin sled stood, he stepped down, kicked the dogs aside, and tied up the horses. Straining heads interrupted the light at the tiny window, changing every instant as he moved methodically. No one emerged to welcome him; he had expected no one. He pushed through the snow that veiled whitely the litter of the yard, the lean hounds at his heels. Scurrying inside ceased abruptly at his fist-knock.

Old Moosomin himself creaked open the lop-sided door, his grease-shined face blinking up out of the feeble light at Block in the pale-blue cold. The Deacon said loudly, into the stares which could not comprehend him outside, "Evening, Moosomin. I've come to see Louis. He's home, isn't he?"

"Oh—Mr Block," snuffily, a tattered sleeve drew itself across the crumpled half-Cree face. "Yah, he's home. Jus' got here yesterday." There was a flurry of women and half-naked children in the room; several in rags peered from beds and trapping gear. The Deacon did not glance at their furtive movements.

"Tell Louis to get a lantern and come to the barn. I want to talk to him."

"The house warm—" the man gestured.

"I want to talk to Louis, alone."

"They were huntin'—I think maybe he's sleepin' jus' now."

"Get him up. I'll wait outside."

"Okay. Sure Mr Block. What you say."

Block's feet moved back out of the circle of yellow light and the door scraped slowly shut. The stale smell of small children through the open door had been enough. He pulled the heavy horse-blankets into position under the harness, hearing the agitation inside the cabin. There must be about twenty people living in one room: with miles of bush all round. Laziness: it saved them wood-cutting. He leaned against the bay, face uplifted to the open sky that cut like ice, waiting for the man he prayed had raped his daughter.

The door complained, and then the swinging light of a lantern preceded a dark figure around the corner. His mittened hand trailing off the nose of the bay horse yearning after him, Block stepped across the snow. He could not discern the face of the man, the lantern hanging low at the end of his arm, the peaked cap shading the visage. He stopped, "Louis?"

His voice, "Yeh."

"We'll go to the barn."

Without a sound the other turned into the path towards the barn, Block following. Suddenly the black shape stopped before him, doubled over in a tearing cough, spat violently, and then limped on. Block could not restrain a shudder.

As the Deacon pulled the low door shut behind him, Louis was hanging the smoked lantern from a cross-beam. The meagre warmth of two cows and four rake-like horses barely blunted the cold in the littered barn. Block saw only the face of the man before him, leanly dark, hair projecting from the cap-edge. Thinking of him so often, the Deacon had almost forgotten how Indian-like was his face. It was impossible that she—hope springing, without preliminary he said, as Louis stared beyond him at nothing, "When did you get out?"

"Friday."

"How did you get back so quick?"

"Bus."

"They give you a ticket to Hainy?"

"Yeh."

Block stood like a rock on the filth of the barn-floor, glaring. "No criminal works for me. You worked two months this spring and I paid you ten dollars when you went to town. You've fifty coming."

Louis said no word, and Block made no motion to give him the money he had earned. There was no sound in the shadowed barn except the cattle breathing thinly in the cold.

"What are you doing now?"

He knew immediately the question was wrong, for Louis shrugged and turned away, the glance no longer holding him. The Deacon knocked aside a dung-heap at his feet; it rolled clumsily into the frozen gutter. Without warning,

"You know Elizabeth died in October."

Louis swung at him, fear flicking across his face, then the stolid hood dropped back over his eyes. His voice was flat. "Yeh. They said."

The flash was enough. Block calculated coolly; in the three years of work he had learned to know this breed. He could overflow with words when something exciting happened; his terror of what he did not know or understand was clear from that hinted betrayal. Jail had not changed *that* a great deal, perhaps even added a little. Block said,

"How did you get on in jail?"

The abrupt change in questions caught Louis nicely off-guard. "Oh, it wasn't so bad."

"Have you been working hard—digging ditches and things?"

"Yeh—that was really nuts."

"Guards all right to you?"

The other seemed now to have forgotten the previous trend of the questions. His face hardened in hatred as his eyes unmasked at remembrance in the yellow light. He hissed, "Suckers! Standin' around with their guns that they sure as hell didn't know how to shoot and forever yellin' at us to work an' work—" Block, watching his face eagle-like, saw the skin taut over the high bones shade livid and he lashed out:

"What did you do to Elizabeth last spring?"

The whipped sound jerked the horses in their stalls; Louis stuttered, staring open-mouthed. Instantly his look twisted away: "Huh?—nothin'—wha'—" Block's glare shrivelled the thin film of resolve acquired in loud bragging sessions in the penitentiary. His force caught him:

"Don't you dare lie to me. You did it, didn't you, you miserable—"

"I didn't do anything! Not a damn—"

"Stop swearing! You forget yourself." The breaking cough erupted in Louis's chest, allowing him to bend away from Block rigid between him and the door. When the younger man straightened, spittle flecking his face, Block rapped, "You won't talk? Suppose I tell the Mounties. You know what happens to a half-breed that bothers a white woman? They don't just send him to the rock-pile—they take him to the whipping room first to see what they can do there. You ever been whipped in jail?"

Fear suffused the other's face, "No! Not the whip—I—" and then a thought seemed to click into consciousness. "I don't even know what you're yellin' about. If you know so much, why don't you go—"

Block broke in, having thought of this long before, his voice tense, low, "She's dead now, you know. I'll leave all as it is. The dead are everywhere—you told me yourself, remember we were scrubbing last spring? They're the spirits that dance the northern lights in the long winter; they're the spirits that drive the werwolf to stalk you on the trail; they're everywhere. When you sleep, she'll come in your dreams; when you're hunting, you'll sense her behind you. Everywhere. Maybe she's right in here with us—now."

"No! No! It won't be. She's dead—she—" and terror gripped Louis quite as he stared white-eyed around the barn, over the shaggy backs of the animals as if an apparition were wreathing there. Pigs grunted in their sleep beyond a wall. Then Louis's cough broke again, and when the spasm was over, the fear was bent aside.

"No, Block," the bare name hardly deliberate. On the fringe

of his consciousness Block knew Louis would never again hunt alone. But it was not now enough to hold him, and the Deacon was driven by his necessity. The gaunt face fronting him like a knife, he took one step forward in the narrow aisle, his shadow cast by the lantern hugely ominous over the other. His voice was barely audible.

"All right." Breaths hoar between them, Block's glance held Louis in bind. "If I had ever once had an inkling what you were doing, I would have taken you and with my two bare hands killed you." His glare unearthly now, the scar pale at his temple, he deliberately pulled off each heavy wool-and-leather mitten and dropped it on the floor. "There's always time. You'll never touch another woman." He took the next step, but the other faded back.

"No!" It was a cry; the long hand flashed to the hunting-belt. Block's pressure held him as his foot flashed out at the motion and the half-drawn knife clunked on the frozen aisle.

"Now, with your own knife, Louis." Voice and steps were nemesis, foot abrupt on the fallen knife. Louis's heels caught on the hay mounded against the back wall and he tilted backward, horror blanching his face.

"Mr Block! No!"

"You did it!" the scream torn as from a compelling madness, their faces a foot apart, the horses plunging in their stalls. It spilled then, stark terror banning lies:

"Mr Block! It wasn't my fault. By the sainted Mother of God! She came to me once at night—last spring. She cried at my bed—she had to have a man—she could not live—she had to have a man—"

"*She* came?"

"Yes, she—"

"Once?" The face pushed nearer, the long arm groping for the knife.

"Only once—I swear! She wouldn't ever even look at me—but that night she cried she had—"

"Shut up! Shut up!" Hoarsely, despair echoed in the barn, despair of ever ramming those self-forced words back down that dark throat.

Block jerked back, not a line to indicate him stripped. His hand fumbled in the mackinaw pocket and flipped a paper package on the litter. "There's your money. You've relatives on that reserve in Alberta. Go there—or anywhere—but if I see you around Wapiti one more day, I'll—" and he kicked the knife, glinting, into a broken calf-pen. "Tell your Pa to come to the store tomorrow. They're all leaving here by spring—your whole breed-brood."

His glance flashed down at Louis, still hunched against the wall where fear had pegged him, and then he turned, picked up his mittens and strode to the door. A thin laugh broke behind him.

"When I talk about this—"

The Deacon spun around, his glare in the yellow light spiking the other against the logs again. "No. You won't. Just get to Alberta." He motioned once with his hand, turned and pushed open the door. The frozen air wiped away the fetid barn. A cough followed faintly after him.

He strode to his team, untied it, slid the blankets off and stepped over the edge of the box into the bob-sled. He wheeled the horses sharply and, with the dogs loud about him, drove across the clearing. Erect in the withering cold of the radiant night, he did not care, in his numbness, that he had, by every standard he ever believed, damned his own soul eternally. Wapiti was clean for his son.

The horses trotted briskly into the shadow of the bush; he slumped to the bench. He prayed, Now, alone, at last, let me cry.

But he could not.

CHAPTER FOURTEEN

"Whoa!" Thom eased Nance to a stop where the deep sleigh-tracks to Franz Reimer's wound from the main road into poplars stuck paling-gaunt in the snow. Jake and John Rempel scrambled up from where they had squatted against the cutter-dash and, standing in the snow, shook themselves free from hay-whisps. Thom looked at them. "I'd drive you to the door but the road—"

John laughed, "I know. Four men in one small cutter on the main road is bad enough, what with all the snow. We don't want to kill your good horse. How would you get home?"

Thom grinned. "Oh, she can take it—it's you guys who don't do anything all winter and are lazy enough to need a bit of walking that—"

Jake, kicking profoundly at a snow-ridge, glanced up at Thom and Pete, blanket-wrapped on the cutter-bench, and interrupted with great seriousness, "Not only is *he*," with a shrug towards John, "lazy, he's also fat!" With a quick stiff-armed ram, he sprawled John in the soft drift and trotted down the sleigh-track towards Reimer's, his laughter echoing on the frigid air.

"You wait, you so and so!" Bellowing impossible threats, John floundered to his feet and roared after his tormentor, shedding snow with each lumbering step. But the narrow track defied racing; his perilously maintained balance escaped him near the gate and he plunged face-first into the three-foot snow. As he rolled, blinded, Jake yelled from far up the trail,

"Don't worry, fatso! I'm getting the team anyway. I'll drag you out!" and he doubled over in hysteria.

Thom, laughing with Pete until the raw air rasped their throats, held Nance in check till at last John again staggered up. As the cutter drew away Jake was shouting to the now deliberate John, "Not so slow, pokey. The folks will be waiting to go home—it's time for chores."

Thom's laughter eased, "Those twins!"

"Jake isn't exactly as thin as a spring steer either," Pete chuckled.

"Yah. Looks like he's been fed more grain than John."

John's voice drifted after them, "Just wait till I get you, Jake! We'll see who has to be hauled out of where!"

The sun was about to resign the brief winter day to clouded darkness. Nance trotted briskly homeward. Thom, washed clean for a moment by carefree laughter, glanced at Pete whose eyes were tracing a rabbit-run into the willows of the creek-bed they were passing. He looked non-commital, at any rate, just as he had looked throughout the lesson in the Mackenzie cabin that afternoon, watching the grimy children without stirring, moving only when another song was announced and then his warm baritone, as always, rolling clear and strong. Thom wondered again, momentarily, if he should have hesitated so long in asking his quartet to come and sing: the children had so evidently enjoyed the songs. But there were so many things—and people—to consider when you—

"You should have had today's meeting here in school," Pete's statement broke Thom's thought. The school they were passing pushed into Thom's consciousness. He studied the curl of smoke over the teacherage chimney as he replied,

"I guess so. It was a fairly decent day after all. But I arranged with the Mackenzie's last Sunday because it was so bad then and coming to their place saves most of the children a mile hiking. It's hard to tell how cold it will be a week ahead. Mrs Mackenzie was very nice about it all, I thought."

"Yah." Pete's inflection seemed thoughtless, and Thom saw him glance momentarily, almost furtively, at the teacherage as they passed in the swaying cutter. Thom's wonder had barely time to stir when Pete's voice interrupted again, "Must be hard for her—living there all alone in that teacherage and no one ever visiting her, snowed in and all."

Thom, recalling the teacher's cheery face and warm welcome just two evenings before, said, "She seems to be happy enough. Anyway, Margret's been to see her twice and they have a great time. She never complains."

Pete asked, rather reluctantly, "Does she come to your classes sometimes?"

"She's been twice. Hal says she's such a good teacher, I wonder how she can put up with my story-telling. It should do her good—she doesn't know much about the Bible. Anyway she's friendly enough—" he laughed in a cloud of breath, self-consciously. "Asked me for coffee even." He added quickly, "Of course, having to do the chores gives me a good excuse not to on Sundays."

Thom, eyes on the rhythm of Nance's thigh's, felt Pete glance at him swiftly then look away into the road-side shrubbery. He felt compelled, by the other's silence, to continue, "But I suppose, after years of living in the city, she does find it lonesome here. I guess you're right."

Pete said nothing further. Waiting, Thom puzzled, Why does our talk, when we're alone, lose itself where there is nothing to say? I wanted to ask him what he thought of the class. But now Pete's distant look repulsed such a question. As Nance turned into the short-cut towards home across the Marten's quarter, Thom, rubbing his face against the cold with his coat-sleeve, tried to re-balance his thoughts.

Oddly, in the one-room cabin crowded with children and grown-ups and a crying baby, he had felt freer in teaching the lesson than ever before. He stood backed against the chipped iron bed-stand in the cabin thick with the smell of drying furs and unwashed children and spoke of the man who had been born to prepare the way for Christ. But the story of John the Baptist seemed to interest the children very little. As he was drawing near the close, nearly discouraged, some strange biblical detail caught at small Judy Mackenzie and she, tongue loosened apparently by the home surroundings, for she had never before spoken even when questioned directly, asked with wide eyes, "Mr Wiens, you ever eat grasshoppers?"

"Why—no—I—" nonplussed.

Proudly, "I did one, last summer. Phooey! They're terrible salty!"

It was then that the twins, who at her question had ducked their heads hastily, snorted and roared. The older children had been smiling in their restrained way and Mrs Mackenzie, by the kitchen stove nursing her youngest to quiet him, was just reaching over to slap her daughter to silence when the mirth broke and convulsed them all. Thom, knowing the twins, had previously warned them to control themselves, but as the infectious laughter beat at him in the gloomy cabin and even Pete joined, Thom was pushed into it too, albeit with a sinking feeling regarding the story he must continue. But strangely, when the laughter eased and he explained that Palestinian locusts were quite different from Canadian grasshoppers and that the diet of "locusts and honey" meant that John, living in the wilderness, ate only such food as the region naturally provided, Jackie Labret asked quietly,

"Did he live like us when we go huntin' in summer—berries and fish and stuff?"

The unexpected parallel amazed Thom. "Why yes, Jackie. John the Baptist lived like that, simply, eating what God provided. He was too busy doing his job to be concerned with nicely cooked meals."

As he spoke, Thom sensed a new element of contact with the children which he had not brushed before. He could explain John's great urgency as he waited and taught in the Jordanian wilderness, preparing the way for the Redeemer, and the children found a kernel of truth in his story. Thom could but marvel at the attention on the faces before him, and the strange path by which it had arrived there.

Then the story was over and he, Pete and the twins sang a final song. He reminded them all to come next Sunday to practise for the Christmas program and the afternoon was gone. As he moved towards Mrs Mackenize, careful of the children twisting into their worn coats and parkas, she glanced up shyly and said, "You sing nice. Could maybe some grown-ups come and listen in the school sometime—with the kids?"

Thom's heart leaped "Why of course. And your husband and older sons come too—especially two weeks from today. The children will have a Christmas program then. Next Sunday will be mostly practice, but on Christmas Sunday you come—with the whole family. All right?"

She looked away from his friendly glance, holding the baby's tiny body tight against her. "Yes. Maybe he'll come too—maybe."

"I want to thank you very much for letting us have the class here today. But when I asked, I didn't mean that your husband and the boys should stay out. They could have listened too and—"

"Oh, they're workin' lots with the traps. They're never home in the day. If traps good, skin all evening," and she gestured into the gloom above the stove where rows of raw furs hung on their stretchers from the peeled rafter-poles.

He said, "You get him to bring your whole family. He can leave the traps to themselves on Christmas Day at least, eh?" He added, about to turn, "You don't know why none of the Moosomin children came today, do you?"

"Not been here. I don't know," her frank eyes faced him fleetingly.

He murmured, "The oldest girl has a big part in the program—hope they come next Sunday. Well, good-bye, and thanks again." She smiled briefly as he turned to the children surging out. He followed in their stream, patting a few heads, dropping an occasional word. They attended with amazing regularity and seemed to enjoy most of the stories, but their silence in his presence always depressed him somewhat. They so rarely spoke. He had tried every way he could imagine to understand them since they began with the classes again in November, but somehow his resources for coming near them were so inadequate. As he looked about at them, Jackie Labret, in the act of prodding his two smaller brothers towards home, turned and smiled up at him. "Mr Wiens, maybe Hal could come to our class too?"

Hal! Why had he not considered him before? Perhaps it would work. Neither Hal nor Mom would require much persuasion. "Would you like that, Jackie?"

"Sure. We have fun in school."

As Jackie trotted away Thom thought, Probably I've been too serious with them. They're not used to our ways of teaching Bible stories. The grasshoppers had begun to crack their tacit reserve. Mrs Mackenzie's words and Jackie's smile warmed him to his very depths, beyond the concern at the Moosomins' absence. He'd tell Hal to remind Marie in school. And Hal could come to the class Christmas program, then continue coming after New Year's. Response would come. He breathed deeply in the frozen air that cut away the smells of the crowded cabin. Joseph and his tremendous ideas! Then he walked out into the yard where Pete, silent and sober, was leading Nance from the barn. The children had all scattered.

Carlo's bark, as he leaped into the cutter, jerked Thom from his thoughts. They were home: Nance was stopping at their yard-gate. He shushed Carlo, who was avidly trying to tickle his face, as Pete clambered out and pushed through the snow to open the gate. Thom, mind falling upon some less cheering aspects of the afternoon, thought, I must find out what he's thinking. He looked so grimly watchful. The air in that cabin must have been dreadful for him. Perhaps I should have asked the quartet only to school, but I wanted the Mackenzies to hear us. They like to sing so much. Well, it's too late now to consider. But I have to find out before he goes home and tells his father who knows what. It's so strange to Pete. As he chirruped Nance to move ahead, Thom forced his mind to turn from the widening gulf of apprehension.

Pete leaned his weight against the gate-pole, slipped the wire over it and climbed back under the cutter's blankets. He said, "It's later than we figured. Guess I'll go home right away —do the chores."

Thom, eyes unseeing on Carlo's open-mouthed smile, answered while groping for an opening, "It is later than usual.

The folks should be home soon from Lepps'. Did yours go visiting today?"

"No. They're home every Sunday—since Elizabeth died."

Nance stopped before the house at the spot where Hal always halted her when he drove home from school. As Carlo hurled himself out and raced a madly happy circle around horse and cutter, Thom said quietly into the deepening dusk, "Perhaps they should visit a bit—forget a little—"

Pete said slowly, folding back the blankets and stepping to the snow, "Oh, they'll probably go visiting again." He added abruptly, as if forced to confide, "Papa wanted to last Sunday, but Mom just all of a sudden cried so hard—"

Thom, reaching to unhook a trace, spoke quickly over Pete's painful hesitation, "I really want to thank you, Pete, for coming today. The kids don't say much but I know they liked it from the way they listened. Adds that extra bit. And Mrs Mackenzie said it was nice."

Pete's wan smile was reflected in his voice as Thom led Nance from between the shafts. "You know how I always want to sing. Good if they liked it."

Fine granules of snow began to drift as they plodded across the yard to the barn, Nance's nose gently insistent against Thom's back. He put out one leg and neatly flipped Carlo into a roll in the snow. The black dog leaped up and at him in ecstasy. Trying with one hand to calm the frantic friendliness, Thom said to Pete, as if nonchalantly, "What did your father say when you told him you were going to sing with us at Mackenzies' this afternoon?"

Pete returned nothing for a moment as they turned the corner of the horse-barn and Thom pushed up the catch to swing open the frost-creaking door. The animal warmth lapped gently against them standing in the cold. Thom stood aside, flipped the halter-shank over Nance's hame and she stepped carefully across the door-jamb and swung into the darkness of her stall. Pete said slowly, as the two men followed her into the low black doorway, "Guess that's partly why I didn't say much now coming back. I just told him I was going to see you. Don't think he would have liked it—otherwise."

"Oh." Thom was glad Pete could not discern his face in the gloom as he pulled the door tight against the cold. He said in a sort of parenthesis, digesting, "I'll get your Prince out—soon as I get Nance fixed."

"Okay."

He reached out his hand for Nance and, mindful of his Sunday coat, pushed into her narrow stall. He tied the slip-knot and turning, spoke over her withers into the encouraging darkness, fingers swift on the icy harness-buckles. "What did you think of the class?"

The quiet familiar voice said, oddly careful, "Well, if you held it in the school all the time—"

Thom interrupted, "I told you it was because of the cold. They have to go so far every day to school that—" he caught his over-protest and wrong direction. That was not really the basic reason. "I'm sorry. Shouldn't butt in."

"That's okay." After a moment, "I don't really know, I guess. Why do you teach them? What's the point? Papa says there's enough for everyone to be busy in our own church. You could teach our children. Why—" The shrug was evident.

"There are plenty of teachers in our Sunday School for our children. They've taught for years. All I've done in our church is sing in the choir and make the opening twice at Young People's. Once in a while we sing a quartet. Is that usefulness? I've been a church member for three years. These kids never heard the complete Bible once." Thom unbuckled Nance's collar and pulled it down with his left hand.

Pete said from the far side of the aisle, "You'll have more to do soon, don't worry."

"What?" Thom pushed his right arm under the harness and dragged it from Nance's sweated body as he stepped from the stall. "What is there for all of us to do? We've got plenty of workers. But these poor kids haven't a single Christian interested in them. And I'm a Christian now—I can't sit around waiting to grow old." He moved past Pete's silent presence and straddled collar and harness unerringly over their pegs in the known darkness.

"There's no need to be in such a rush—"

Thom swung around to Pete, whose form was now just barely perceptible in the last stray light from the tiny frosted window. "Why don't you say the real reason?"

"All right." Pete's voice was abruptly hard. "What do you want to do with them—teaching them Bible stories?"

"I want those children, and their parents—Mrs Mackenzie was interested today—to become Christians."

"I thought that was why you wanted to have the class there so much. Okay. And then what?"

Thom skirted now, "What do you mean, what? They learn to live like Christians—probably join the church—"

"What church?" relentlessly.

"Well, there's only one church in Wapiti—I guess—"

"But you can't. They can't join our church." The words hung in the darkness a moment. "They don't live like us. You were in that cabin all afternoon—and she had even tried to clean up a bit. They're like—and they speak Cree and English. You know they could never become members of our Mennonite Church. Look what happened to Herman. They're just not like us."

"You know what you're saying, Pete? We sing mightily, 'It is Well With My Soul' and let our neighbours die as heathen because they eat moose-meat instead of borscht for Sunday dinner!"

"Aw Thom, don't get mad so quick. You know it's true what I'm saying."

Thom turned wearily to the stall for Pete's horse. "Whoa boy, easy there." Hand soothing he stepped beside Prince and reached down to the loosened saddle-cinch. He said, "I'm not mad." The situation was quite beyond a superficial emotion. For he knew exactly what Pete meant; he had been puzzling these many nights about making the Bible lessons more understandable for the children while respectfully avoiding the sure knowledge. There is nothing I can do with them, after. Once, last summer, he had faced it; but not again. And once, just a week ago, he had sensed that if he continued just a little longer, the second Razin girl, Laura, would stay behind to talk to him. He had ended the class abruptly; he was fully conscious now that he had been side-stepping the goal he was labouring towards. And his unconsidered enthusiasm about Hal coming to the class— Pete spoke into his thoughts.

"Thom, our people could not accept a half-breed into our church. Can you honestly imagine such a thing?"

Thom, his fingers clenching on the hard-leather cinch, did not counter that question. He could not. With a quick heave he tightened the cinch, slid the stirrup down and stretched for the halter shank. His mind groped, blindly, for some handhold to start him up this wall of known impossibility. "Have you ever thought of why God has spared us from military service? According to Canada's law, you and I should be in France right now." He backed Prince into the aisle and Pete's hand met his on the rope. "Why are we still here?"

Pete returned, fumbling for the bridle hung from the saddlehorn, "Because we believe what our fathers taught—"

Thom interrupted, concerned now beyond the words' momentary jostle of his memory, "So you say. But is that a good enough reason—our fathers? Other fathers have taught differently. Why should we listen to ours?"

"Because our fathers got it from the Bible."

"All right. The Bible also teaches 'Love your neighbour as yourself.' That means, if you're concerned about your own salvation, be concerned about his too. How can we avoid that?"

Pete had Prince bridled but paused as he turned to the door. "It also says we are to remain separated from the world. 'What has light to do with darkness?' Thom," he continued as the other was about to urge a question, "you can argue till tomorrow and logically you'll be perfectly right. But you can't change people with perfect logic. You know that as well as I. You know that the Mackenzies and the Labrets just could not join our church. It's impossible. And Papa said last week once, as he was talking about your class, that you'll only make things worse than ever. Instead of them caring nothing, as they do now, your going there all the time, maybe even helping them to believe they're Christians, would only show up the difference between them and us so much more clearly. Only bitter feelings could come of it. And we've lived peacefully beside them for many years. You saw that cabin today. Don't tell me you liked it. Maybe years from now they'll have changed—but not now. Why don't you end it now at Christmas? Papa says you don't know into what impossible problems you're heading."

Thom could not even marvel at Pete's long speech. He said, battered, "Why did you come today then, if you feel like this?"

Pete's hand clasped his shoulder, "Man, because I'm your friend. And I wanted to see what Papa said for myself. And he's right, Thom. Think about it—what we saw today."

Thom said nothing. He was tiredly thinking, quite beside the point, First time I've ever known Pete to check his father's opinion with facts. Odd.

Pete pushed open the door and led Prince from the barn. Thom followed them into the whiter darkness of the raw winter, closing the door behind him. Snow sifted against his face. Carlo trotted up from behind a hay-stack in the corral and rubbed against his leg. Pete said, having mounted, "Our quartet should sing for them on Christmas Sunday afternoon. The twins will like it. They never think much. And Papa will say it's okay—a sort of farewell program."

Thom looked up at him, black against the gloomy sky. "Thanks for everything, Pete. And for telling me what you think."

"Right. I'm late for chores already. See you tomorrow in the hay-meadow." He flicked his reins and cantered from the yard. His shape vanished into the black spruce that had long since swallowed the sun.

After a long moment Thom trudged heavily round the barn up the path to the house. At the narrow lane dug through the drift swirled beyond the slab fence, Carlo dropped a pace behind him. The shaggy cat, curled on the heater wood-blocks piled on the step, meowed at him forlornly, then spat as fiercely as the dog sprang lightly toward her. Thom murmured, "Carlo, behave yourself. That's okay Mietzy, I'll go milk right away. Just wait a minute." He buffed her head with his heavy mitt, lifted the latch and stepped into the dark silent house. Standing on the hooked-rag rug at the door, he stuffed his mittens into his coat pockets, unbuckled and stepped out of his overshoes. He moved towards the faint outline of the cupboard, found the match-box behind the curtain, and with a flare the match he struck burst into light. Holding it aloft, he reached the kerosene lamp down from the cupboard-top, lit it, and set it on the kitchen table. He lifted the lid of the fire-grate in the stove and let the spent match fall. He stared a moment into the stove. Abruptly he shook his head, turned, rummaged in the wood-box and turning back, pushed two pieces among the barely glowing embers of the grate.

He closed the lid. Before the table again, he took off his coat and fur hat and placed them carefully beside the weathered catalogue lying opened at the electric trains, where Hal must have been dreaming. He took the lamp and climbed up the narrow protesting stairs. Undressing, reaching for his chore clothes, he thought, A typical, smooth, Block plan. The Deacon's training is bearing fruit.

He sat on the bed and pulled on heavy socks. At last it stares me in the face. Pastor Lepp could not do anything for Herman; there's not even time to write Joseph. I have to make a choice. Suddenly the dreadful responsibility of being a man and being morally required to make a choice, either this way or that, thrust upon him. Whatever a man does, he is held responsible. He alone. Overwhelmed, he shuddered. Who would ever choose to be a man, if given such a choice. Why, being a man and having a choice, had he not chosen, like Pete, to walk the sure guarded path of the fathers? He knew why, but strangely he had to think hard for a moment to recall the weightiness of his former arguments.

Within two weeks he must decide again.

He took the lamp and went downstairs. He pulled on his worn jacket, lit the lantern with a wood-splinter, fitted the milk-pails together, turned down the lamp and, holding the pails in one arm, went outside. It was snowing more heavily now, the flakes falling in silver diagonals through the yellow pool of lantern light. He could hear the approaching ring of Star and Duster's harness just beyond the north knoll. As he pulled open the door to the cow-barn and the shaggy cat slipped in between his legs, he thought, At least I know one thing certainly. It would not make any difference even if the Mennonites of Wapiti spoke only English. Language one can learn, but love—but he did not want to think that.

The cows, struggling ponderously to their feet, stretched and turned their heads dumbly towards him as he stood, head bowed, in the aisle.

CHAPTER FIFTEEN

Eight Mile Lake shone stark white. Here and there scattered bulges of hay-stacks shored up the snow; all else was swept drifts from border to far border of frozen poplars. Sunlight glinted in warmthless irony.

Thom slipped the oat-bag cords over the horses' heads, drew the heavy blankets off, and hurled them all high on the towering hay-load. He scrambled up, arranged the blankets about him on the packed hay, and chirruped to the team. The big geldings strained for a moment; he swung them sideways and, with a snap, the runners broke free of the frost and they creaked from the stack. Just beyond the enclosure he remembered with a grunt, halted, dropped from his comfortable perch, and plowed around the load to fasten the gate. Not that it prevented much: snow buried a corner of the fence and the wild-horse herds could flounder over to the stack if they were desperate enough. But one did not leave a gate gaping.

Then he was up and they were treading the narrow trail they had broken after the blizzard, the sleigh-tracks now packed solid and high above the wind-wasted meadow. A flock of snow-buntings swept by in waves and, squinting in the dazzle, he followed their flight. He could not understand how, living on frozen seed from bush and stack, the tiny creatures survived, thick-feathered though they were. Winter was deadly cruel. Really, the whole cycle of the seasons was an endless battle to retain existence. The buntings stored nothing against the winter: they merely found out if they had the hardihood to survive. Man also —perhaps man even had a spiritual winter. If a man stored nothing—or perhaps the wrong kind of food—but he could not carry through the analogy as his hands numbed in his mitts. Besides, there was always the secure hope of coming spring. He looped the reins about the pole thrust up before him and clapped his arms about his body. The blood quickened, but the cold clamped viciously on his face. Pulling the parka lower, he rubbed his nose against his shoulder.

The team drew the ponderous sleigh across the rocky ridge that ran out into the lake-flat; the southern half of the meadow glistened before him. A man forked hay rapidly from the open Block stack. Pete had hauled one load that morning; Thom could not for a moment understand why they should drive themselves so mercilessly on a stiffening day, but the colder it was, the harder the Blocks worked. They had results for their efforts.

A black dot in the wide world, he drove down the track toward home. When almost opposite the stack, he made out that it was the Deacon himself loading the rack. Thom gauged the sun: the afternoon was early. Perhaps—at the thought he halted the horses, flung blankets over them, and walked across the hard-driven patterns of snow. The team perked its ears as he approached. He called,

"Hello, Mr Block!"

The other glanced up from his labour. "Oh, hello, Thom." He paused, leaning on his fork, then reached for the hay-knife, continuing in Low German. "Got your load finished?"

"Yes," with a run Thom scrambled up on the low bench of the stack. "We only haul one load a day—that's enough for the horses—and for me. Here, let me cut."

"Thanks. I've got the other team. Tomorrow's Friday and Pete can't haul very well and do all the chores too." The older man, working in a wool jacket, his parka draped on the rack-pole, dug up great hunks of packed hay effortlessly and laid them tightly on the basket-rack. Thom cut down a layer and waited, propped on the knife-handle, a glow of camaradarie involuntarily quickening in him. Even pitching hay, Block was so decisive, every motion precisely purposeful! In a few moments the loose hay was forked away; Thom shifted to cut again when the Deacon said,

"Wait a minute. I was going to have some coffee. Want a bit?"

"Yes! It's cold standing, even in the sunlight."

Block leaned over, dug a rock-warmed stone crock out from under the hay-covered blankets at the side of the rack. They squatted in the lee of the stack, where the sun smiled feebly warm on the open hay of the cut, and passed the coffee between them.

Thom ventured, the coffee glowing in his stomach, "Mr Block, I want to ask you what you think of my Bible class. Pete told me—last Sunday afternoon—some things. I wonder if you would—" He suddenly could not proceed for even as he spoke he wondered why he asked. He knew where Block stood; what was there to explain? And, somehow, his words were faintly gaining the "you-have-the-answer-tell-me-and-I'll-do-it" tinge that always caught him in his small-child feeling before the Deacon. Thom dropped his glance.

Block lowered the crock and passed it, staring slit-eyed across the white expanse to the ridge bristling black pine and poplar into the dead-blue sky. As the older man turned to speak, Thom knew startlingly, as by intuition, that every man in Wapiti community had, at some time or another, felt compelled to come to Block about his problems. There was more than competence or common-sense in this man. Thom shook his head to clear his thoughts. Block was saying, in High German,

"Let's look at the principles involved in what you are doing. Once they're settled, the details will fall into place. Now: every person on earth, generally speaking, lives in the way he has learned from his fathers. We live as ours taught us, the breeds as theirs. Each generation changes only slightly. If a people find something that they know is important, that way of acting or thinking will persist for generations, if care is taken by the parents to teach their children."

Thom, alert now, interrupted, "But we don't live like our parents. They lived in villages and had their barns built in one with their houses and—"

"Those are the outward things. They don't matter. Why should we live in villages here in the bush where fields are small and we would have to drive miles every day to work? Why should I not buy a tractor if it helps my farming, or a radio to tell me the meat prices and the weather forecast? Those are outward matters that change as men invent better ways of handling nature. I wear an Eskimo parka because it keeps me warm in this cold. These outward matters should change, but the great matters of moral and spiritual discipline have been laid down once and for all in the Bible and our fathers have told us how we should act according to them. They cannot change."

Thom hunched forward; Block continued rapidly across the question on his face. "That's why we have to remain apart from the world. And that includes the breeds, who are culturally and morally backward. They—the world—has been trained by its fathers to despise the things we hold precious: cleanliness, frugality, hard work, moral decency, peacefulness. Look at the filth and laziness that Moosomins—or Mackenzies—live in. You can barely stand in the doorway, such a frightful stench pours out at you. We have to know about the evil of the world—that's why no one objects to having a radio, if the parents are clear what type of program they turn on for their children (and not many are fit to listen to)—but we have to know about evil just enough to be repelled by it and be happy to live our secluded lives. We are not of this world, the Bible says. We have to live separated to prepare ourselves for the world that is coming. Our knowledge and attitude therefore creates a certain distance between us and—the breeds, for example. It is right that it do so."

"Joseph writes too that all people live by traditions, but does this—"

Block, drawing the cork to pass the coffee, looked up at Thom sharply, "Do you write to Joseph Dueck?"

"Yes, I do." Thom felt a flick of pride that the Deacon's look could not rouse his conscience.

Block considered him soberly for a moment, then said, as if more carefully, "You have to watch what he says. He's a very clever man—too clever. He wants to work everything out with his brain. Certain things cannot be done with brain power; objects of belief cannot be affected by logic. But he's right if he said most people live by the tradition they have received. But here is the difference. Most do not care if they break the tradition because to them it is not an absolute standard of right and wrong. In Rome, they sheepishly follow the Romans. But our fathers found the correct way of acting. Through the years, this action has developed into our culture. If we do not follow them in their way, then we stand in grave danger of losing our eternal salvation. That is why we are so rigid about certain matters in the church. The Russians around our villages in Russia had traditional ways of acting too, but when they came to Canada and once knew about acting differently, they let the old way slide because the new way suited better here. But we hold that our actions are eternally important; our fathers found the right moral and spiritual action. Therefore we withdraw from the influence of the outside world and train up our children in seclusion where they can learn the correct way unhindered. We want nothing from the world—either the English or the breeds. They will merely ruin the training of our children. Other Mennonite churches in Canada, not sheltered as we are in Wapiti, have many more problems. Especially in city churches the devil lures many young people from our teachings. More than enough men at the Conference have wept as they told me."

A faint whiff of the lost summer wafted to Thom as, rising, they stirred the dry hay. He began cutting another layer, momentarily unable to penetrate the forceful thinking. Then it caught. He probed, "Children must always be told what to believe?"

Block paused his forking, then continued, speaking as he did so, "Yes. How will they know what to believe if they are not told? I'll tell you something. My father was a huge man who did not care what he did, as long as the church elders did not protest. He never told me a single thing of what I should or should not do. As long as I didn't annoy him, I could do as I pleased. That was the trouble with my youth—I was taught no control or moral principles. And that's why when I was bigger—apparently a good upright member of the church—I still did not really know what Christianity and the beliefs of our fathers were, even though I thought sincerely I did. Then, a terrible thing happened." The Deacon said nothing for several minutes, then rushed on, "There, when in that upheaval my life was changed at last, I resolved that no child of mine should ever be forced through that agony of having acted in spiritual ignorance. They were going to have a better chance—be taught clearly, protected from the filthy lawlessness of the world, the straight narrow way to Heaven."

The Deacon, beyond himself, unworking, leaned intensely towards the youth, his bushy eyebrows bent in a black crescent. Only when he was through the burst of his emotions did his falsity strike home. He had protected Elizabeth?—from a bad marriage, but not a shameful death. He wheeled quickly from Thom, unable to bear the young man's glance leveled at him from under the brush of parka fur. As he threw the forkful of hay on the load, he was praying, Father, give me grace to keep quiet—that I do not lie outwardly more than is necessary—for the sake of people such as this. Sinkingly he knew he need say nothing, ever, and yet his whole life would be one long-drawn perjury. But his action had been right! Elizabeth had weakened, miserably; what good could now come of exposing her sin? He could not know how God would judge his living lie; and sometimes at night, fleetingly, the fear hooked him.

Far away, Thom spoke, "But it's impossible for me not to speak this truth to my neighbour, if I hold to it myself."

Block interrupted, recovering quickly, "But we do speak of it. Your own brother in India—"

"Yes. And how much could he do here at home with the half-breeds you're objecting to? They know no more about—"

Teaching throbbed strongly through Block. "I know why you've tried these Bible lessons with them. It's a noble effort, but be realistic about it, as David was years ago. Will our church gain more members for God's kingdom by doing everything in English and trying to get all those mixed people to join in our services, or will we gain more by secluding ourselves from their influence, preaching in a language only our Mennonites understand and carefully training our young people in the ways of peace? The answer is obvious. Some Mennonite churches have tried English services: they gained no English and merely lost many Mennonites who could not understand. Those churches that did gain a few members did so by sacrificing ethical standards. Soon a church member could do this, do that—no one really knew if anything was right or wrong. Don't you see, Thom? We must be concerned about *our* people, and then we can present an unblemished front to the world."

"But—"

"Listen. In a compromise it is truth that suffers. Always. In some communities members of our church have tried to bridge the gap between ourselves and other people—gaps that should never be bridged. You," the Deacon looked calmly at Tom, and the other, drawn, was compelled to glance up, "are, with that Bible class, trying to do the same thing. More is involved than you, in your young missionary zeal, have any notion. Our fathers always said that they had to maintain a certain distance between themselves and ungodly people. So must we. Your brother took a long time to learn this here in Wapiti—you couldn't possibly know what happened here six or seven years ago—but he knows he can do mission work in India now only because there is a strong, unblemished church community at home supporting him. You will undermine this community completely by trying to bring breeds—and Indians naturally follow—into it. They are basically different from us—qualitatively. No matter what you do for them, on the whole they remain children. Once you've lived long enough you'll know experience as a rough but effective teacher. Give a breed ten dollars and he becomes as irresponsible as a lunatic!" Block caught himself. In his drive to out-front Thom on his own ground, the example had slipped from him unthought. The Deacon would have given almost anything to recall it as Thom, leaning on the hay-knife, returned quickly,

"I don't think Herb Unger is any better than Louis. One look in his house, or barn, shows that. How can you make such a difference—"

Block, letting his fork fall to the hay, could not allow him to continue. "Herb's had a hard youth and hasn't been handled too well. Basically, he's rebelling against his Christian home. But he still goes there and I'm convinced he will some day become a Christian and then we'll welcome him into the church. But to have breeds members of our church? Can you imagine it? They're not the stuff." In the clarity of the evidence, the Deacon gestured with his fork and bent back to his work.

Within Thom, after five days of deep pondering, stirred the thought of whether such obvious simplicity of explanation could really suffice. Why was he never allowed to question that basic pattern? He said, carefully reining in the first twitches of his temper, "I hear Louis's come back now. What are you going to do with him and his people—let them just live and die as in the past?"

Block glanced swiftly at the youth with his prying questions, then deliberately heaved a wad of hay into the rack. "No, we won't." Thom stepped aside as the other reached for another forkful. "And you heard wrongly. Louis was here, but he's left again. We are not having drunken jail junk around here. I told him to get away and stay away."

"But his parents are—"

"They're moving in spring too. I bought their farm."

Thom said, dazed a moment, "The children weren't in class Sunday."

"Yes. Old Moosomin was a bit huffy. No matter. This jail business only proves that we should have gotten rid of them years ago. They just cause trouble—even for strong Mennonites like yourself who get the wrong ideas of what should be done for them. You didn't have any converts, did you?"

Thom said slowly, "No, but there will—"

Block returned, as if he had heard only the first syllable, "And there won't be. You'll have the Christmas program and that will finish it. They'll all be bought out by spring."

Thom stared speechless at the Deacon; his own thoughts startled him. Last spring he had accepted just such a buying as natural and inevitable, but now the scheme looked quite different. He said quietly, "You have been planning this for some time."

"Why, yes." The Deacon was slightly, but pleasantly, surprised at the youth's calmness. "Do you think I'd have allowed someone from our community to become as involved with the breeds as you have if I thought they'd be staying here for years to come?"

"Oh!" After a long moment, "But Brother Lepp—"

Block said quickly, turning from the rack, "This is no place to discuss our pastor." He levered loose a forkful of hay. "He's a good preacher, but I think you'll find him a bit short-sighted regarding the effects of many of his well-intentioned actions." He added, almost dryly, "We've had some examples this summer."

Hearing, Thom could not swallow; the year had mined at his beliefs. His eyes on the Deacon's labouring back, he tried to clamp rigid his tightening anger. All these months Block had deigned no mention of his plan. This man handled everyone, Mennonite and half-breed, as if they were pieces of farm machinery: each pawn had a particular spot in his scheme, and each was told what to believe and what to denounce. Each had small significance beyond covering his spot. You there, and you there! Could someone merely be ordered: Believe! Holding himself rigidly controlled, needing to know more, he said, "You say we must be taught to believe the right. What about the new school-teacher? She isn't a Christian. Is she going to go on teaching the small children—"

Block wheeled around to him, breaking in, face intent now, "Yes—the new teacher. I was going to talk to you. I met you coming from the schoolyard last week—late. Let me tell you, Thom, that is no place for you. If someone else had seen you coming from there, the story would already be about. The first way to protect a good reputation is to give no cause for doubt. I'm surprised your father allowed you—"

The straw broke the dam: Thom's blood charged to his face. "You should talk about my father and he being careful about what *I* do! What about what you allow *your* children to do?"

Block stiffened, whitely, "Wha—"

Thom was too furious to consider at whom he shouted. "Check up on me when I go to get my correspondence explained!" The crest of his rage bore him, inevitably; the whole summer's turmoil and now wasted labour convulsed his words. "You send Louis Moosomin packing because he isn't fit to live in your Wapiti. You push people around without bothering to tell them your plans. You tell me what my father does wrong.

Why don't you make sure you're doing well with your own family? You wouldn't even let your own daughter marry—she had to ruin herself on your farm! Elizabeth told me herself that day! And what have you taught your son? Just acting on the father's say-so won't get him through this world—"

The look on the Deacon's face finally hit through to Thom. Block stared lifeless, his mouth forming, inanely, the words, "Elizabeth—Louis—what do you know—"

Thom did not know what he had shouted; only that she had been dead six weeks. His own cruelty crushed him: "Mr Block, I— I—don't know what—how I could have said that—I just get *mad* sometimes— I—please—"

But Block's eyes seared him, voice pale, "What did Elizabeth tell you—that day at threshing? Thom, tell me!"

"Why—why—" remembering now, he wished the iron-frozen earth would envelop him; he could but speak the truth, and the Deacon's strangely paralysed necessity repelled the statement. But he had to answer.

"She said—I should get out of Wapiti—that I would be dragged down by useless rules and be buried here—and—I could not understand what she was saying at first—"

"She said something else."

"I— I—"

"Thom!'

"Yes!" Abruptly he did not care. Let him know what she had thought of him and his ruthless regimentation the day she died. "She said, 'God in Heaven! Can't you see what's happened to me?' "

The Deacon staggered slightly, almost as if he had expected a frontal blow and suddenly been savagely cut from behind. Silence froze the white world of the hay meadow, the men on the stack as carved from ice. No puff of breath stirred.

Block, ancient now, turned and tortuously poked another forkful of hay. But he did not lift it. His mittened hands gripped twice, about the gleaming fork-handle; he said hoarsely, "God forgive her—and you—" And me, he added, in the clamouring silence of his heart.

Thom, ashamed beyond comprehension, could only stumble

a few words, then turn, leap to a drift and flee to his team that still waited patiently on the trail to pull home. The sun was sinking in the brief December day. The horses moved at his whistle, even as he twitched off their blankets and clambered up on the load. Over the shoulder of the hay-load he could see the stack and the half-filled rack beside it. Block lifted a fork of hay, slowly, and put it in place. The cold burning in his nose, Thom's mind staggered about as he hunched down to the ride. The question stared through his widened comprehension and his heavy shame: what really had happened to Elizabeth?

CHAPTER SIXTEEN

"—an' we put up the stage all along under the windows an' there's a stair in one an' we climb *right through* to go to the teach'rage an' get dressed for the pl—uh—" Hal barely caught himself, ending weakly, "for the thing."

"Better watch," smiled Margret, dusting around the radio. "If you keep talking about it, you'll give the best of the Christmas program away."

"Nah. Don't you think I can keep a secret? Not like those silly girls. Why Johnny said Trudie had blabbed to her Mom almost the first day we practised the—anyway—an' she isn't even *in* it!" Hal ran his finger down the side of the organ but there was no dust for patterns. He crawled up on a chair by the window and began melting a spot with his tongue. "Wow, is it ever thick here! Look, Gret." He flicked the ice with his tongue again, then pulled back. "Look at the picture my tongue made—two bumps like on the camels in the—" he stopped dead, glancing pleadingly at Margret.

She pushed the rocker into place and said solemnly, not looking at him, "Have you seen pictures of camels with two humps? The book I read in school once showed them with only one."

"Oh, there's two kinds." In his relief, Hal was quite willing to benefit others with his knowledge. "I think maybe they found this two-hump kind after you got out of school (Margret gasped a laugh, caught herself, but Hal, designing the camel with a wetted finger, noticed nothing). We've studied about camels quite a bit; these new ones—like this—come from real far East and can carry big loads a long ways. We were studyin' about them in school," he repeated casually, again confident. He applied his tongue to the frost.

Margret, to get him away from the subject, asked, "Have you memorized that poem yet?"

"It was too long, so Miss Tan'amont give half to—somebody else to learn. I know my half."

"Does she know her half?"

"Well, it's a pretty hard poem but Elsie just about—aw Gret, you're a cheat!"

"Why, what's the matter?" she looked around at him, eyes wide, laughing.

"You tricked me—I didn't want to tell you she's sayin' the poem with me."

"Oh you little sniggle-fritz!" Margret reached over and hugged him fiercely. Hal pushed away and she said, "Got a hole thawed in that window yet? See if Pa's hooking up."

"Yah!" Hal attacked the thinner ice and soon discerned the outlines of the frosted yard. "There comes Pa with the team—he's drivin' to the cutter! Boy, I'm goin'!" and he dashed through the living room drapes, across the narrow kitchen and up the stair-steps to the landing. Looping his parka off the nail, he shouted to his mother, bent over the stove in the floating aroma of baking buns, "The Parcel will be there today, won't it, Mom?"

"It should be, Sonny," she raised her heat-flushed face. "It's been three weeks now—otherwise it might be late for Christmas. Only one more mail-day left."

"It'll be there—it couldn't be late for Christmas. Come on, Gret, you comin'?"

"Don't rush. Pa'll come in before we go." Emerging leisurely from the living room, she passed Hal fumbling with his buttons on the landing and climbed the stairs. Thom opened the outside doors just as Hal came hurtling towards them.

"Whoa there!" Thom gripped the little boy under the armpits and tossed him to the ceiling. "Want to run me down?"

"Thom—don't—I gotta get out—with Pa to the store! The Parcel'll be there an'—Thom!" Hal burst in laughter as he was tossed again.

"And maybe there'll be something in it for you? Okay, beat it."

Still gripping him, Thom backed out the door and tossed the boy, muffled in his thick clothing, into the snow-drift against the slab-fence. Carlo charged immediately. "After noon we go for the Christmas tree. Don't let the candy-case hypnotize you." Hal managed to struggle out of the drift despite Carlo's flashing tongue. Together they raced furiously into the yard.

Thom closed the door behind him as his mother, her arms flour-white to the elbows, said, "You shouldn't leave the door open."

"Sorry." Thom sniffed. "Buns baked yet?" She shook her head, hair tied back with a tea-towel, kneading steadily. "I'll just wait then—smells like they should be soon." Slipping the snow-shined rubbers from his felt-boots, he relaxed on the bench-end, unbuttoning his parka. "We sure fooled Hal, ordering that sleigh in October when he wasn't watching the mail like a hawk. We'd never get it past him now."

Wiens pushed into the house. "Is Margret ready to go? Margret!" he called, reaching for the water-pail on the wash-stand.

"Right away, Pa," her answer came down the stairs.

Lowering the dipper back into the pail, Wiens muttered, "Hope Eaton's send that whole order. At least substitutes." The War disrupted even the inviolability of the mail-order catalogue.

Thom lounged, waiting, and Mrs Wiens looked at him with a laugh. "They won't be done for a few minutes yet—you can carry the slop-pail out."

"Never safe from work, sitting in your kitchen," Thom grinned. As he emerged from the house, Hal shouted, trying to pause in his wrestling,

"We won't be long, Thom. We'll come home with the Parcel right away—we can get the Tree—" Carlo spilled him.

"Okay. But we'll eat dinner first." Thom went around the house and dumped out the pail. While he cleaned it with snow, he heard the door bang and then the harness-ring as hooves squawked from the yard. He had found a beautiful tree that summer on the far edge of the muskeg near the swamp; he would have to lead Hal round-about and come to it as if unawares. Like last Christmas. All the brief afternoon they had stomped through the snow-cloaked muskeg on their skis, searching, discovering squirrel nests and weasel slurs and rabbit forms, ducking beneath laden spruce-boughs where snow slid with a soundless *whoooooosh!* if they raised their heads. At last they had found it. Hal said, as he always did, face cherubic from cold's pinch, "It's been waiting all these years to be a Christmas Tree." Then Thom brushed him aside, sprawling, and before he could scramble erect because of all his clothes and the feather snow and the skis on his feet, the Tree was down. Grins cracking their faces, they headed home, Hal breaking trail and Thom following where he led, dragging the booty. When they reached the sleighroad at the gate where Carlo wagged in greeting, Thom perched the Tree erect in a drift and they studied it, green fluffed with snow. After a moment, Hal said, "That's the nicest we've ever had." And then he was sprawling in the snow again and had to ski madly to catch up before Thom and Carlo reached the house with the Tree.

Having stomped off the snow, Thom re-entered the kitchen where his mother was just removing the first pan of golden buns from the oven. He padded to the table and surveyed the smoking pattern of their bottoms, breathing deeply. With a long finger he tapped off the brownest corner-bun and tossed it back and forth from hand to hand. Mrs Wiens chided,

"You'll burn yourself. I've told you since you were wee tiny not to do that."

"I know. But it's *best* to eat them like this—see," he explained elaborately, "You crack open the soft centre, so, let it steam a bit, then you eat the middle as hot as—ouch!—your finger and mouth can stand. Then the crust is cool enough." Gingerly he suited words with action, slouched on the bench-corner near the glowing stove; she pushed in another pan and turned to form more from the dough. They were quiet in contentment.

Thom thought abruptly, I could ask her about that threshing-day. Even as he hesitated to blunder into her calm, his mother asked gently, "Have you ever gone to Herb and talked to him about your quarrel? It's so close to Christmas—the end of the year."

Jarred from his thoughts, Thom slowly peeled out the hot centre of another bun. "I tried, Mom."

"Would he listen?"

"At first," recalling the light that he had seen, the door he had rapped. "I stopped by that night last week when I got my correspondence explained. He seemed friendly enough for once, but when I mentioned about coming from the school he changed just like that." Thom flicked his hand. "Wouldn't hear a word I said—just called me two-faced and swore at me to get out. I don't know what it was I said—he even asked me in at first. Mom, he lives in filth—unbelievable."

"Poor Herb—his poor mother."

Thom recalled Block's words about the Unger family two days before; he voiced his disagreement now. "Ah Mom, I sometimes wonder if Mrs Unger cares much about Herb, one way or another. Hank's the precious boy."

"Thom, she's deeply grieved her son has gone that way in the Air Force. She—"

"Her words say she's sorry, but not the look on her face when she makes sure everyone knows how many Germans her 'lost sheep' has shot down. If she'd do a bit more for the son she has here—"

"Thom! We better be concerned about how we act." After a pause, "It's good you tried, anyway."

Thom could return nothing. Again quick to attack, and yet so fatally vulnerable himself. He remembered the quickening stir of his temper as Herb had seized the brown bottle and bellowed, 'Beat it before you get brained!' As Annamarie had told him once, glancing at him from under her brown-soft eyebrows, he was still trying suppression.

Times innumerable he had sat in that stove-corner when a child, watching her shape white buns on the table. "Mom," he said, wistful, "Why does God allow such a thing to sit beside us and bother?"

"What?"

"Like Herb. On the quarter next ours. If he were even half a mile farther away, it would not be so bad. But our nearest neighbour."

She was silent for a long time, knowing he knew the answer perhaps better than she, her hands flying from pan to floured table, forming the buns, row on row, doubled with a dimple in the top. She said then, as she often had, "To become mature in Him, God requires you to overcome obstacles. You can overcome this, but not while you go to Herb with your mind made up. You have to love him with all his mistakes in all the power of Christian love that you have. Your love for him should overpower your anger at what he does. If you really loved him, you would have no time to be angry; rather see him as the poor man he is, alone, miserable in his dirt."

Thom crumpled the shell of the bun in his fingers, staring at the worn-orange floor. The question pushed from him, "How can one person love another?"

There was only the crackling of wood in the stove.

"And why must we in Wapiti love only Mennonites?"

His mother looked up then, "Don't always be on the attack, Thom. No one has said that. The reason our men aren't in the Army—"

"But Mom, what about those people north of the school? Shouldn't our love for them as lost human beings overpower our revulsion at their squalor—rather help us to teach them something better?"

She said simply, "You know neither your father nor myself objected for a moment to your teaching those children." She worked silently, then continued, "You don't fit so well any more with the other young men, do you? I've seen you, after church, standing in their circle, without talking, where you used to lead the laughter. And then they go off to visit and you come home and eat without saying anything and take your books and drive alone to Wapiti School."

Thom said, knowing her prayers for him, "The quartet did come last Sunday." After a moment, reaching for another bun, "But it's all over."

"Why?" unsurprised, head bent.

"Mr Block has bought Moosomins out. And he will the others too, before spring."

She asked, on the superficial level both of them knew held no meaning, "What does he, with one son, want with all that bush? There's no decent acre of breaking in the lot."

"Just to get rid of them! He told me as much on Thursday when I talked with him in the hay-meadow. Louis's being in jail just proves his point that nothing can be done with them. They'll just—somehow—infect us with their sin. He didn't outrightly mention Herman, but there's obviously the beginning. And my teaching those—" Thom stopped.

"What did he say to you?"

Thom hesitated, fearful for her as he had been, and was, for himself. But there was no avoiding it. He said, baldly, "Could we have half-breeds joining our church?"

She said nothing. Thom, drawing his finger through a bump of flour on the oil-cloth, pushed on, "What have I been doing? Trying to salve my conscience for a half a year with a salve that doesn't exist?"

She spoke then, quietly, considering only his first question. "I cannot see how it would work, either. Perhaps we would—somehow—be fit to cross that bridge once it had faced us for a time."

"But Mom, can you see Old Rempel—or Unger—Block—"

She interrupted his groping. "No. Look at yourself—or me—" She shook her head, almost shuddering. "Too many things would have to break. It would be fearful."

Eyes unseeing on her work, she murmured, "And Christ left us no easy way out. Only love. Hard. Probably impossible. After having seen as good an example of impossible love as ever there was in the world. Elizabeth. For all the unhappiness that came to her; all that one may think her father did wrong towards her, she loved him to the end. Her whisper as she lay dying."

"Mom!" The question leaped up in Thom, "What really happened to her?"

He saw his mother start, as if his presence, forgotten, had betrayed her. She did not look up at him, hands forming buns for which there was no room on the pans. "Was I speaking aloud? What do you mean—what happened?"

"What did Elizabeth die of so suddenly?"

"You said the doctor had told you, not?" she wearily evaded.

"He said 'of an internal disorder that got out of hand'—which could mean anything except that she was knocked down by a falling tree." As he stared at his mother's mute figure, he suddenly comprehended that somehow Elizabeth was vital for unsnarling his confusion. Intensely, "Mother, I don't want to know because I'm curious or because I want to blame anyone. I *have* to know for myself."

She silently opened the oven door to her baking. He could not know that she saw nothing there as she bent to look. His eyes followed her into the tiny pantry and out, while she placed another pan on the table. She stooped to her work, wordless.

"Mother," in his need he used the strange word a second time, speaking in heat no longer, "I talked to her—that day. I had to eat dinner late, and so did she. When she came with the lunch and coffee later, I was all alone with her at the box and she said, 'Thom, get out of Wapiti!' And I had never once talked to her alone before that day! I can't comprehend why she said it; she just told me that I would be buried by rules if I stayed and I could only stare at her worn face. Then she burst out; Mother, it was like her death-cry, 'God in Heaven, can't you see what's happened to me?' I still hear it sometimes, at night, even though I helped bury her. What did happen to her?"

"Thom, my son—"

"I have to *know*!" He was standing now at the refusal in her tone, like a giant above her, hands clenching massively on the table, crumbs dribbling. "On Thursday—I was angry—I told Mr Block to take care of his own children instead of bothering about other people's, and he turned white to fainting." The black hair seemed to bristle on his fists. "You have no right not to tell me. How can you keep me ignorant when everything is falling in ruins? There is something wrong and I must know!"

She stared mutely at his face above her, and she was the child before his tyrannically grasping maturity. She did not cry easily, but now her sobbing fell uncontrolled in the hot kitchen as she stood before him, tears pushing down her cheeks. Dumbfounded, he took her stooped shoulders in his hands and pulled her tight to him. "Mom." The top of her head reached the middle of his chest. "Mom, why do you cry so much?"

She pushed away, not using her hands for they were white with flour, and returned blindly to her work. "Thom, I promised never to tell. But for you I must say: what happened to Elizabeth was brought on her by her father's strictness as well as her own falling. It cannot matter to you what it was. They were both partly to blame."

"Okay. They were both partly to blame. But no one in Wapiti has heard Mr Block say that he had a large share in bringing his daughter to her grave. He is still the great man, getting rid of undesirables, running church, store, school, all our business with the government: he is Deacon; everyone's quiet and peaceful when he speaks. He—"

"Thom. I did not say that for you to get angry. He did get us a farm here, all of us, when we came from Russia with not a cent but only debts to our name. And he has been right—"

"So he helped us! We would have survived somehow in this land without him. Others did. Even if he is a great business man and can run this district like no one else, does that mean that on every subject he must place the only word in every man's mouth and they go home and re-chew it for their family? What has he done to own us? He tells us what is good and what isn't good for us. He keeps us behind this bush away from all the world as if he were one of those mind-scientists who takes rats and puts them in cages and sees how they jump when he sticks them with pins. Behind all this bush, do we have to be the rats of Block and our forefathers? Whenever they jab us, we know what to believe? We don't owe them our souls!"

"Thom—it's because he shows us how to live the Bible—"

"Everyone keeps saying that! But where does the Bible say you must torture your daughter to death if she wants to mix her sacred Mennonite blood with—"

"Thom!" his mother cried, distraught in the face of his raging, "It was because she did just that that she—" she gagged at the dawning comprehension on his features.

"Oh." What he experienced at that moment drove too deeply for anger. He said, slowly, "And who else but Louis could it have been? Right on their farm. Elizabeth, bound by her father's will—"

In the dreadful silence of their thoughts, they heard the ring of the harness outside.

Mrs Wiens no longer wept. Her eyes followed her son as he strode to the living room, ashen-faced. She said, "Yet she loved him. Thom, she said that as she lay dying. If she could forgive, surely you can."

The drapes twitched.

The outside door was jerked open and a small body bumped against the inner. Hal crashed in, tugging a huge drab-covered parcel with a familiar red-and-white sticker in one corner. Margret's laughter spilled into the room after him. She was trying to hold the other end of the parcel while gripping a huge box under her arm as Carlo leaped against her on the porch. All was laughter and cold air and shouts and barks.

Hal's voice flew above Margret's joy, "We got the Parcel! Look—bi-i-i-g! An' Hank Unger's comin' home for Christmas —Danny Unger told me at the store. Maybe he'll bring his big plane along for us to see—come on Margret! Let's get the string off!"

The flurry and shouts drowned all else, for Wiens was pushing in behind them with another armload of boxes and Margret was gasping, "Oh, what a crowd of people at the store!" Thom sat in the rocker beyond the drapes, dazed, his nursed suspicions never having hinted such horror.

His reason told him this should not affect him so, but as remembered details fitted into the design only too smoothly, he could not deny that something had crashed within him. In the past six months he had questioned almost the man's every act: surely his own Christian faith should not now be affected. But the one log that held the jam had been jarred and he could sense within him only the numb void that remained after the rush had vanished. Distantly he heard Margret's clear voice, "Yes, Mom, Hank Unger is coming for Christmas on leave," and he thought vaguely, Well, the War is finally coming home to Wapiti. Good. We'll find out what it's like—not just imagine things.

He could not bear his emptiness. He twisted the dial of the radio and it slid in immediately with a smooth voice:

"We have a news bulletin just handed to us. Reports from the

Allied Front in France would indicate that a German counter-offensive has begun. Reports are still vague and unconfirmed, but it is clear that in the Ardennes area of the Western Front massive offensives are now taking place. American troops in the area have been caught off balance and the Germans, moving in massive armoured thrusts, could possibly break through back into Belgium. The stalemate of the war would appear to be over, one ranking military observer commented upon hearing the reports. He added that a major break-through to the Allied supply depots in Belgium and western France might well prolong the war another year. Our eventual victory however, he concluded, is certain. This is the German last gasp. We shall have peace within the year.

"Stay tuned to this station; we will keep you informed as reports come in.

"To return to the regular news. The dreaded V-2 buzz-bomb attacks against London are becoming steadily worse. Loss of life and property are now reaching greater proportions than during the height of V-1 blitz last August . . ."

Thom did not listen. He was thinking of the new German offensives, the first in many months, and a pattern shaped in his mind. They announced full overseas conscription in Ottawa at the end of November. They need another 60,000 men to send over to get shot; my number is coming now. Probably next Friday—three days before Christmas. What a present! Three months to train, and then just in time to get into the thick before it's over. To move at last in harmony with all the world. After the summer of futile and, in the light of what he now knew, evasive thought and action, the answer in his blackened mind seemed reasonable, finally.

Hal's voice quavered from the kitchen: "Ain't there anythin' in here for me—at all?"

CHAPTER SEVENTEEN

In the frozen air around the Wiens family bundled in the rocking cutter the harness-bells rang. His face livid from the cold, Thom stood to guide Star and Duster in their steady trot, their breath like clouds erupting from their nostrils. As they crested the hill, the far lights of the school, sharp in snow-dazzled moonlight, winked in the valley. The winter sun was long gone; in the north-west the Northern Lights glimmered faintly; the trees on the roadside slid by in the silver-black world, weighted, cracking in the iron frost. Cold burning in their noses, the family was caught up in the old tradition of a frigid drive to the Christmas concert. The world was white, purified by snow: a world into which it could be believed the warmth of Heaven had once come at Bethlehem. Thom almost forgot his dull resignation.

With a whirl they drew around the gate and into the schoolyard. By the number of sleighs, Thom could see that nearly everyone must be there. Despite muffling scarfs, Hal was again explaining the marvel of the temporary stage. As he scrambled over the heavy robes, his voice rose, "See Mom! There's the stairs we made so we can go in through the window and we don' have to use the door at all when we've dressed in the teacherage. Nobody'll see us till we're on the stage. Miss Tan'amon' figured it'd be a bigger surprise if—" and in his speech and untangling of himself, Hal caught his toe on the edge of the cutter, tipped, and sprawled face-first in the snow.

"Boy, keep quiet and get out," Wiens rapped in Low German, grasping him by the bottom of the parka and, as it appeared to Thom in the half-light that gleamed from curtained windows tossing the rest of Hal's body after his head.

Mrs Wiens said, "Pa, be careful!" to which Wiens grunted pulling himself up. Hal was already standing, wiping his face with a sweep of his hand. "And anyway, it's lots better than last year when all us Brownies had to get dressed behind the stage—"

Thom said, "Get going—you're late already."

"Oh—" and he was off, dumpy in all the wrapping of his clothes, running towards the stairs that almost overshadowed the adventure of the Christmas program itself. After years of entering school the same old way, to be allowed to go in through the window!

Thom unhitched at the barn and walked slowly through the snow back to the school. He would as soon not have come, but how could Hal understand? His feet sinking with each step, he saw the lights of the teacherage beyond the school; the excitement of the carefree children dressing for their evening laughed distantly at him. You couldn't tell a child's skin colour from its laughter—just as you couldn't tell the difference between Jackie Labret and Johnny Lepp by the way Hal talked about them. Give him a few years. Thinking of Jackie, he knew the boy had been puzzled Sunday afternoon. As for himself, he could but count it a blessing that the afternoon had been planned as program practice. What he would have taught them in a regular lesson he did not bother to consider. As the school-steps creaked under his weight he thought, Face it. Block, one way or another, has his way. He reached for the door-knob.

As he opened the door and edged in among the young men crowded there, he sensed, puzzled by his acute perception, an "atmosphere" in the school. He pushed back the frost-rimmed hood of his parka, eyes struggling with the invading light, and then the grey-blue back of a figure just before him emerged, and he knew why he felt the oddness. There was no murmur of conversation. Though the curtains were still unopened in the crammed hall, only one person was speaking in a voice that had pulled the attention of all present around him like a bunch of calves on a string. Hank Unger was really home on furlough from Overseas.

"—twenty-seven of the Huns. An' I wasn't scratched! Not once—though about roasted twice before I could land. Never lost a plane." The voice stopped, as though half surprised that its loudness had hushed all other sounds in the room. Every face faced him. After the fire of the Luftwaffe, it was like balm. They had never before listened to him. He was only Hank Unger, son of obviously the poorest farmer in the district, just the younger of the boys who in winter carried sandwiches to school filled with rabbit meat of their own snaring, on whose doorstep on Christmas Eve they left bundles of old clothing that their family had outworn and glowed with benevolence next day because they had done their Christian duty, while he out-stared the laughter of the brats who recognized him in their cast-offs. Let them squirm now in their non-resistance!

His hand reaching inside his jacket, he dropped his voice in the quietness. "As I told that *Record* reporter in Montreal—here—read it," and he pulled out the dog-eared paper, folded at the page where his picture grinned, and held it up before the eager eyes of the young men about him. For an instant a smile curled his lips; not one person in the whole building had even known that the *Record* existed, or now knew that it was the largest weekly newspaper in the world. "When I shoot down a Nazi pig, it's strictly fun for me. Only one question crosses my mind, watchin' them make that slow loop down, as they blaze. 'Will he blow or fry?' "

Without inflection, the five words dropped upon their consciences. Above Hank's cropped head, on either side of the starred tip of the tree, Thom caught the angels' message, in bold red: Peace on Earth, Goodwill towards Men.

The scuffling of children's feet and hissing whispers behind the curtain were the only sounds in the schoolroom. Horror congealed on the faces of the Mennonites as they looked at the slim figure in the Air Force uniform, at his familiar blonde hair and eagle-cut features. Herb, standing beside Hank, his face agrin like a satyr—he should be the one telling atrocities about himself—not Hank, who had always been so carefully polite to his elders. It was the War. In a shudder that seemed to pass over them physically, the older people felt these two as the incarnation of sin among them. Though crowded beyond possible motion, in the silence some of the younger men seemed to draw closer to Hank, the world like an aura about him, and then Thom noticed that the frosty air around his legs ebbed through the door he himself was still holding open. The door slammed as he jerked.

Hank, slightly awed by the effect he was having on the people who had seen him grow up, turned at the sound and all eyes shifted with him. Tall above them all against the door, Thom's weathered face darkened as he pulled off his cap in their stare. Though only three feet away, Hank's voice rolled at him like a circus barker. "Well, well, who have we here? Thomas Wiens! How's the milkin' goin', big boy? Always told the Old Man that I wasn't wastin' my life doing what any calf could do better," and the roar filled the room. Thom could not think, mumbling a "Hello Hank," which no one heard. The picture on the glossy paper someone was holding before him and the row of ribbons on Hank's chest gleamed dully at Thom as he fumbled through his mind for something to say, but Herb bellowed, "Oh Thom, he carries on the good traditions of the fathers. He'll be milkin' for quite a while yet." Then Block's loud tapping near the front of the room was heard and all turned from the baiting towards the curtained stage. Hank said, reaching, "The show's on, I guess—let's have that paper. You can see afterwards." As he turned, Thom, opening his parka, slowly rammed his thoughts away, looking steadily at the legend crowning the tree.

The curtain twitched. At its motion, Hank whispered sideways at Herb, "You say this teacher's called Razia Tantamont?" In the two hours the air ace had been home, Herb had barely muttered her name to his direct question. Since learning of Hank's furlough, he had often considered the effect a uniform and blonde hair would have on the teacher. He grunted. "A real stunner?" Hank persisted. "I think maybe she's one of the little jobs I—ah—met—ha ha—while training near the Hub—everyone called her Razz—" and then the pupils stood revealed on the stage, in three rows, each child holding a lighted candle. At the far side poised Razia, in a smooth green dress. Hank suppressed an ejaculation. "Wheww—that's her, all right. I didn't dream of *that,* here in old Wapiti—" At his brother's reaction, Herb's hatred sank deep in his soul. He might have known!

A nod from the teacher and little Katie Martens, the smallest child in school, stepped timidly forward and, her candle-flame flickering against her best blue dress, spoke fearfully into the hush:

To each one that has come tonight
To join our Christmas cheer,
We lift up high our candles bright
And say, "Be welcome here!"

At the last line, each distinct in the tot's recitation, the children lifted their candles and spoke the welcome in unison. A sigh of happiness swept the listeners as the intrusion of the world and the War vanished like a thought at the innocence of the children's voices and little Katie's low bow over her thickly stockinged bow legs.

Thom stretched himself against the door, leaning heavily. There was no possibility of his finding a seat. About ten men were standing around the door with him, but he noticed that Pete had found a seat in the last row, sitting crammed into the desk. He appeared oblivious of all save the activities on stage.

The stage had been built against the windows on the left side of Wapiti School. Thom could look at it only at an angle, but directly faced the black-boards and the festive tree at the front of the building. All the people of the district seemed pressed into the room, with Beaver families also present to compare this program with their own the following Thursday evening. Side by side, Mennonites and Métis sat or leaned where they could, eyes intent, listening. Thom looked about for an instant before turning back to the stage, the craggy faces known about him, and then his eyes caught the hope he had been looking for without having admitted the fact even to himself. Just over Pete's head, at the far end of the room among some older girls, was the auburn sheen of Annamarie's hair.

She was home for Christmas, sitting where, with a slight turn of her head, he would see her face to face, He had not imagined how her presence would fill all his mind as a light the empty darkness. He had no moment even to wonder at this, now. He could see her profile as she watched the stage, and the words of the nine smaller children paraded there caught his ear, the large green letters which they held before them hanging on the edge of his vision:

C is for Christ who was born on this day,
Laid as a baby to rest on the hay.

She looked just as she always had done, but far away, as if there was now little hope of his nearing her. She was inexpressibly beautiful. The gathering heat, with its vagrant smells from the crowding people, did not exist for him.

Looking at her in what he rigidly disciplined himself to believe were inconspicuous intervals, he smiled to remember how he had once, fleetingly, paused to ponder if Razia might be almost as pretty. Even in that smooth green dress on the stage corner she—

—Mary the virgin so mild,
Singing a song to her heaven-born child.

Herb, turning slightly, saw Thom's glance shift. Eyes glinting, he tilted backwards and hissed at Thom in his confidential undertone, "Easy on the heat, boy—only one apiece. Wanna start a whole stud?"

The eight children were marching, chanting,

S is for Steps as we follow our Lord,
They lead us heavenward to our reward.

Thom's muscles knotted. Only the crowd and the occasion checked him.

Then ramrod-rigid against the door, forcibly breaking his thoughts, revulsion swept him. Repelled at Block's dogmas that had hounded Elizabeth to death, he had existed five days in fearful vacuum. What difference did it all make anyway? Live as you could and die when you must. And he had the example before him. The brothers held to no law of the fathers: they were animals. Worse, for he could think of no animal that, at the mere sight of a female, could only slaver in anticipation; or killed for the pleasure of seeing the victim writhe in his last throes. But even Hank paled before Herb. The body, the body, the body. It was impossible to think of Annamarie in that way, but Razia—abruptly he found that if he allowed his mind a corner of leeway he could think in unison with Herb. The realization staggered him. His mind, strange to such thoughts, went fumbling after the tantalizing figure in the tight green dress. Such wells of depravity yawned in his empty self that he could only shudder and pray for diversion.

The children sang, voices high and happy:

Christmas Day is coming soon,
Now you dear old man,
Listen what I say to you
Softly, if you can.

When the clock is striking twelve,
When I'm fast asleep,
Down the chimney broad and black,
With your pack you'll creep . . .

Lying on the straw tick, Hal limp in sleep beside him, Thom had thought of Annamarie, studying and working, far away. He glanced back at her profile. Away from her, he could never remember what she looked like exactly, for he thought of her as a person and not as a figure. She was to him beautiful, but beauty which had little to do with her shape. Her beauty reached beyond her appearance into her purity. For Herb to drag Annamarie and Razia together in one obscenity was—his mind could articulate no word; he felt rasped to his soul. But the question stood. Pete, sitting in the desk looking steadily at the stage; what helped him control his thoughts against a woman who flaunted her body like a flag? He turned on his father's principles. "We Mennonites teach," and so on.

—what to give the rest,
Choose for me, dear Santa Claus,
What you think is best.

The curtain closed on its wires to the clapping of the audience. Thom clapped in imitation, hazily comprehending some of the people about him. To his right, Old Moosomin glared, non-committal, at the stage. never turning his head. Herman and his wife were beyond him in one corner with their little bundle, talking to Margret in the pause. Mrs Mackenzie, proud beside her sombre husband, caught Thom's eye with a smile. He smiled and looked away. The Rempel twins were gazing about for something to laugh at, and Hank, stretching prodigiously, his short jacket pulling up to show the blue shirt, said, "That was a long flight out to 'Battleford. Could do with some sleep. Wonder what 'dear old Santa' will bring *me!*" and everyone laughed with the twins. Herb laughed too, forcedly.

The program went on smoothly, the children reciting and singing and marching as Razia directed. Whatever she thought as she announced, prompted, conducted, the teacher gave no outward indication. In training herself, Razia had been thorough. She could succeed in anything she wanted to, no matter what she thought of it, and pride welled in her at the way she had trained the children for this program without a single person knowing what she thought of the semi-religious doggerel Christmas concerts that, under Mennonite teachers, seemed tradition at Wapiti School. Unknowing half-breeds and innocent Mennonites! In her power she had gone even a step further towards religion than was usually the case. There would be no usual "Santa and Brownies" affair. If they liked religion, she could dish it up.

And Hank Unger! She had rigidly resisted the pull of her look towards the door where the younger men stood: only after the program. But as item after item slipped smoothly by and success drew towards triumph, her mind, aroused, began to tense under that pull. If he really was that Hank from the air-base! What did it matter, a few minutes. As Linda Giesbrecht recited "The Shepherd's Welcome," Razia turned abruptly from her prompting papers—Linda never made a mistake—and fingered a slit through the side curtain. The door was twenty feet away—and Pete Block, staring about for her, smitten as a moon-calf. She barely smothered a laugh at his remembered stutter on her doorstep a week before. Where had he groped up the nerve to sneak away from his father that late at night to

—then the edge of her eye caught, she shifted, and there he was.

As she remembered him: face sharp, clipped blond hair, but the ribbons were now like the scar of gigantic potency across his chest. Knowing him unconscious of her look, his manhood ranted through her. After a time, she realized that the clean boyish lines of his face seemed smudged, somehow, by the weight of what he had encountered. He had done his share, and more: twenty-seven German planes shot down. What a welcome he'd get here! A small hand twitched her dress, "Miss Tantamon'—" and she could barely restrain from brushing it away as she would an insect. What a beautiful man! She forced herself to let the curtain slip, and turned.

Linda stepped behind the curtain. Thom shifted his position against the door in the pause that lengthened to hurried scurrying on the closed stage. It must be the "Surprise" under which Hal had laboured so manfully. Block was leaning forward in his chair, face as ever noncommittal. Consummate! After a moment, Razia stepped through the curtain and Thom jolted his mind to concentrate on her words.

"Dear parents and school friends, we have what we think a special attraction for you tonight. The children have tried not to speak about it at home, though it was hard for them. Instead of the usual type of short play, we decided to write one completely on our own, and, with the whole school working at it—and everyone very hard, I assure you—we wrote a play which we call 'The Star and the Three Kings.'" She paused, everyone held by her smile. As the people understood the title, Reimer, near the front with Block nodded to Pastor Lepp beside him, smiling. Thom, glancing back at the green figure, saw her look sweep over the schoolroom and waver for one instant toward the door. But she did not see him, of that he was certain. Her glance seemed to hesitate on some man before him and in that flick of time he thought her face was transformed. He blinked, puzzled, but then her look was away again and she announced, her voice slightly roughened, "The Star and the Three Kings, written by Wapiti School."

She vanished. The curtain opened slowly on a transformed

stage. The Mennonites, never having seen a real stage show, and content, in their short teaching plays, to imagine all the properties, since the front of the church in which these were usually held could allow no real setting, were bewitched in one glance. The stage was a room in a palace. Blanket rugs hid the floor. A palm of crepe-paper reached in through a huge window. The walls were hung with blanket tapestries. In the centre, bright paper flared like flames in a short-legged grate.

But what held everyone's eye were the three men in long robes and beards, their turbaned heads stirringly strange. One squatted while poring over a thin scroll rolled out on his knees, another made careful measurements on a map of the stars stretched wide against the wall, while the third looked steadfastly through a long mounted telescope past the reaching palm-tree into the farthest distance of the heavens. There was no sound, until slow whispers in the audience revealed that some mother had recognized her son. And only then did the bundle near the grate stir to show, fleetingly, Hal Wiens's face, now calm as if in sleep beside the fire. They were in the Far East.

The silent figure at the telescope turned to the others. "I cannot believe it. It cannot be true."

"But see here—the record in the scrolls. It is the Star. How can you doubt?" The man seated on the rug spoke with the conviction of his soul.

"It would seem to be so," the other bearded patriarch left the stars mapped on the wall. "There is no other star possible in that region. Never has a star been seen there before. It would seem to be as the old scroll says."

The first left his instrument and went towards the window, staring out into the heavens. He stood alone with his doubt. The audience could barely hear his murmur, "So bright, even to the naked eye. As no star has ever been! Why so bright? Why?"

The second leaped up as no old man had ever leaped, but the audience heard only his words: "We must go. The scroll tells us that when the Star appears, the Saviour of Mankind will have been born. We must go to worship Him, bearing gifts with us. Up, we must go! Samuel," stirring the sleeping bundle by the fire, "out with you! Get the camels watered and the men to load the packs." The little boy uncoiled and ran out, bare feet padding on the blankets. The third man turned with the second and all three stood in their slender robes, gazing steadily out into the heavens. The third said, in a deep voice, "Yes, we must follow the Star. Wherever it leads."

As the curtain closed, Thom saw the Deacon, face shining, looking up beyond the ceiling. He looked away, but the point of that first scene pierced him. A man must live on something. And Truth must be followed as a Star, though the road is sometimes superhumanly difficult. But did Block have this Truth—from the fathers? Abruptly, Thom could not avoid the conviction that Elizabeth had faltered; his compulsion against Block could not forever hide the fact that, despite her father's rigidity, she still had to consent personally to that act. If she was not really responsible, then Block was not either, because then he also had been, helplessly, moulded by his training. Following that back, you arrived at Adam: what then? You blame God. And you go through life doing what you do because you can do no else. No. There was no need to follow your body with its every impulse, or acclaim yourself a murderer before your fellow men and brandish ribbons and medals like scalp-locks strung across your chest. So where was the Truth that must be followed? Was there only the old Block or the young Unger way?

The curtain was opening. Erect by the half-opened door, he saw the long journey of the Kings and slowly, as he saw, he began to follow, praying unconsciously in his longing. He followed the three step by step as they plodded where they could see only the stretching misery of land and sand before them; while they crouched in their kingly robes exhausted under the tents at night as the storm raged about; while their men deserted them and they grew deathly weary of the quest, the very end of which was unknown, while they doubted but struggled on. Finally, he was with them in Jerusalem where the murderous Herod gave them their last directions for a divine reason he himself would have scorned to understand. And then, the final scene.

The curtain opened to an empty stage. There was an outline of hills and domed houses in the background. In one corner stood an old barn that appeared about to collapse at any moment. A hole gaped in one of its walls, and light shone from inside upon a scattering of straw that led from the hole. There was nothing else for a moment, and then the three Kings entered, bedraggled now and footsore in their walking, with only little Samuel to accompany them. But there was a holy look on their faces and each carried a gift carefully held before him. As they approached the building, they hesitated, gazing up at the sky and then back at one another, questioning. There was a stir inside the hovel, and then, bending low, a young shepherd emerged and stood before them, his crook in his hand. The first man said, quietly, "Is this the place?" And the shepherd—Thom recognized Jackie Labret—smiled and said,

"It is. Enter with me, O Kings—and kiss the feet of God."

And bowing low, they followed him, one by one, with little Samuel entering last of all.

The listeners awoke slowly to reality. They stared before them, as if still gazing at remembered holiness. For Thom the marvel that Razia should initiate such a play was drowned in his own conflict. He could follow the kings in their quest, but when they bent and entered he was blocked. They found the answer of their search in that barn in Bethlehem, but his answer? He needed it—this evening—in Wapiti. The War was there before him. The huge German break-through back into France would demand a vast recruitment of those eligible to receive calls; his own letter could not but already be in the mail. What—and as he raised his head, his eye centred on old Moosomin, face folded in the same inflexible lines. There was more than one war to be faced in Wapiti.

On the instant the door jerked wide behind him and a dumpy red figure whooped as it crashed in. Santa Claus. As Thom tried to move aside, the curtains opened to the pupils on the platform, smiles as wide as their faces would stretch, Razia behind them, face enraptured. Santa bulled his way through the crowd, dragging his bulging bag and laughing to burst his seams. In a moment, all was confusion of laughter and talk.

The movement of people and the shouting of children pushing towards their parents erupted into the glory of happiness at Christmas. Caught in the eddies of the crowd, Thom, despite his longing to get outside and alone with himself, was jostled farther from the door. Everyone recognized him, he was forced to answer their friendly questions. Then cauldrons of coffee were carried in from the teacherage, and soon all were eating candies and sandwiches and nuts and apples and drinking scalding coffee as faces split in glistening laughter under the hissing lamps. The Deacon inched his way inconspicuously from one family father to the next, speaking a few words and then edging on. When at long last Santa had roared his way into the snow and the litter of wrappings and crunching nutshells underfoot indicated that the evening was drawing to a close, Block, as head trustee, stepped quietly to the front of the stage and waited for the tumult to quiet. Thom had finally, evading all coffee-cups, worked his way almost to reaching the door-knob when he noticed the Deacon. He stopped then. After an evening such as they could not remember before, the Wapiti people hushed quickly.

"This has been a wonderful evening—an evening such as we will not forget. To be happy at the approaching feast of our Lord, undisturbed by the world, that is when we understand what those words mean, first spoken at His birth." The Deacon pointed to the tree-top. "Peace on earth, goodwill toward men. When, some day, Christ will return and the world have the peace we experience here now, then that prophecy will be completely fulfilled."

Thom was numbed. To say that!

"We are happy about this evening. Our children have worked hard and have received many presents which they have already enjoyed." The smiling munching faces beamed up at him from among the press. "Now, our teacher, Miss Tantamont, has also worked very hard. She planned one of the best programs we have ever seen. While we sat here, we as trustees decided that we should give her a little present. Christmas is a good time to give gifts—to acknowledge our gratitude to others. Our teacher is new here, and yet has done a good work among the peculiar people that we are," and the Deacon smiled broadly while pulling a heavy envelope from his coat-pocket.

Thom thought, the half-breeds don't exist in Wapiti any longer. They never have—for him—except when Eliz—he listened. "It was a surprise to you men to be asked to contribute, but in giving you all showed that you enjoyed and received a spiritual blessing from the program given here tonight. So this gift, small as it may be," the Deacon hefted the heavy envelope in his hand, "comes as a surprise to both giver and receiver—which is certainly the best way it could be. If Miss Tantamont will come forward—" and he paused, smiling his rare smile. All shifted and craned to see the young teacher's face as she pushed through the crowd. She did not appear. Block, scanning, repeated in a louder voice, "Miss Tantamont." Every sound vanished in the crammed building. "Isn't she here?"

Everyone stared about, smiles frozen, as if looking would suddenly reveal her. There was a scurry at the door, and all turned to see Pete Block slam the door behind him. Thom saw Herb before him, the bachelor's crooked face registering nothing but a gaping question, and then he noticed that Hank was gone also. He stared about, and Herb, catching his glance, awoke to Hank's absence at the same moment. As people stood up here and there, one or other voice aloud with, "Well, what's this?", Thom stretched for the door-knob and in two strides was outside. On the edge of the steps he paused, irresolute. Where had Pete gone? And Hank?

It was very cold.

If Hank and Razia—or something—he could not quite think, yet that look kept nagging. The teacherage was lit and two bigger pupils in heavy coats came from it. He called, as the door closed and he sensed Herb behind him, "Hey, is Miss Tantamont there?"

The teen-agers stopped, startled in the moonlight. Then one said, slowly, "Huh? Uh—no, we haven't seen her."

There was sound from the direction of the barn.

He and Herb whirled, and both saw the light flick across the tiny window of the barn as if flung in a searching arc, and then they were off the steps and running—Herb slipping in the criss-crossed sleigh-tracks, cursing his shoes, Thom with long moccasin strides soundless in the softer snow. His mind was blank with no thought but the physical necessity of getting to that barn-door. He could hear the sounds of people behind him as he jerked the door open on its leather hinges. His glance leaped between the two rows of nervous horses to the barn's far wall. He stood, rocked.

The yellow beam of Pete's flashlight transfixed a blue figure sprawled limp on the straw and the blonde head of the girl in the green dress kneeling over it. As Thom opened the door, her face jerked back up to the blackness that was Pete. The straw in her hair and the look like acid on her face trapped Pete's stammer, "I'm sorry that such a brute—" in his teeth. And her voice.

"You should have asked *Papa* what to do!"

Her hiss hung like stench in the air. Herb barged in without pause, "What's go—" the scene stunned him. Hank gestured groggily, trying to sit up, his hand at his face where the blood pushed a gleaming line from his mouth.

"He hit me. Pete, he—"

He tilted sideways against the girl. Only the horses stirred; the thudding footsteps, which none heard, raced nearer. To the two, silhouetted like marble in the shadows by the open door, the words filtered to consciousness through the habitual pattern of their thinking. Hank, in numbed amazement, stumbled a curse.

Herb's righteous rage erupted as he moved, "Pete, you damn hypocrite—" and his long unreleased hatred against his brother for ever gaining in a moment what he himself had never won in a lifetime of desire, against the Mennonites whose actions and looks had always condemned him, spilled from him in a flood of filth as he leaped. Pete turned, his light waist high, with no motion towards defence. Herb never touched him.

Pete! Thom's mind gasped the cry as into his void of splintered dogmas violence surged to brute strength. His left hand clamped on Herb's shoulder and yanked him round.

It was the first time he had hit a man with his fist. Herb crumpled, pole-axed, on the straw beside his brother.

On the instant the barn was full of men, hundreds it seemed, with more jamming and craning in the doorway. Lights probed.

The horses reared in their stalls, terrified, but the men put out strong hands to calm them, staring at the tableau in the aisle. Pete's flashlight still held the group unknowingly, but now the added light showed Herb twisting over on the scattered straw with Hank sitting as half-bemused between him and the crouching Razia. Thom and Pete stood on either side, the presence of the men slowly registering on their faces as they turned towards the door. Backed against the barn-wall, at first glance they looked like a group of friends casual for the photographer.

Block rammed his way through the crush. Breathing heavily, he spoke like thunder as he stepped forward. "What's going on here?"

Razia began to laugh. She was convulsed. She leaned over Hank, then tilted up towards the sod roof, her high laughter lashing the dumbfounded men. She staggered to her feet, straw in her hair and sticking to her crumpled dress, face abandoned. "What went on here! You're too late for this show—" and the laughter flared through again, and then, between gasps, "Pete found things not quite Mennonite! *You* hadn't told him what to do—so he smashed Hank—and then Thom smashed Herb—all these loving Mennonites smashing!" She could not gasp another word, her laughter a howl, and then it ebbed abruptly and snapped. She saw the light of a dozen flashlights poking at every wrinkle on her dress, the shadowed men, faces blank in staring silent amazement, and her figure seemed to shrink into its shame. Her look flashed about, frantic for escape. With a bursting sob she hid her face in her hands and ran towards the one door. The men parted before her like a wave, not one touching her, and her crying could be heard as she floundered out of hearing. In the barn there was only the breathing of men, the stamp of horses, and Block's half-whisper, like a cry, "Peter, Peter."

Pete had not said a word since he had started to speak to Razia. He had stood looking steadily at his father after he entered. His voice sounded as if he was speaking for the first time. "Pa, you have to do what you think right."

The Deacon bowed his scarred grey head to his hands, and the men of Wapiti community, Métis and Mennonite, standing in an old barn, heard the sobs of a great strong man, suddenly bereft, and broken. They heard, terrified.

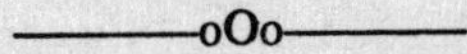

The two horses swung into the road, muscles straining at going home. As he stood in the cutter, the packed snow from their hooves thudding on the dash, Thom sensed dimly other teams trotting behind them. There was no hint of the carols that usually rang from sleigh to sleigh. The half-breeds had vanished quietly, awed in incomprehension yet sensing a great break. No Mennonite had looked at another. Shame acknowledged and bare on each face, they had hitched their teams, gathered up their families, hushing the jolly children with one clipped word, and driven off as from a funeral where each had contributed the corpse of his silent agreement with Block. Thom's only mind-controlled act had been to speed his hitching so that the Lepps would not be out before he drove up to the school.

Block had been led away by Pastor Lepp, with Pete following silently.

Thom drove, reins clenched in his left fist, his right throbbing dully, forcing his thoughts back. His body revolted in barely controllable nausea at the remembered crash on Herb's face, the oozing blood. Beastly. One taste eclipsed a thousand imaginings. He, with his months of oh-so-noble questionings, had plumbed the pit.

He gazed unseeing between the greys' heads, nodding in their trot. The evening overwhelmingly upon him, it would be long before he could conceive of how much had been sloughed aside that night in Wapiti. Then, Jackie Labret, bending down to lead the way to the manger, stood before him. There must lie the way. Not the paths of conscienceless violence or one man's misguided interpretation of tradition. They brought chaos. But the path of God's revelation. Christ's teachings stood clear in the Scriptures; could he but scrape them bare of all their acquired meanings and see them as those first disciples had done, their feet in the dust of Galilee. He must. And, seeing Jackie again, a long-forgotten statement by Joseph rose to his memory. "We are spared war duty and possible death on the battlefield only because we are to be so much the better witnesses for Christ here at home." Comprehending suddenly a shade of those words' depth, he realized that two wars did not confront him; only one's own two faces. And he was felled before both.

No. If in suppression and avoidance lay defeat, then victory beckoned in pushing ahead. Only a conquest by love unites the combatants. And in the heat of this battle lay God's peace. "My peace I give unto you: not as the world giveth."

Wiens was praying. "God have mercy on me, a sinner—in silence."

Hal cuddled against his mother. They were all so quiet. Even Margret only stared at the blankets. The boy said, for the tenth time, "Mom, what happened in the barn?"

Her voice was old. "You'll know, some day. Now we'll soon be home." She held him close, weeping without a sound, for it had come as hard, and harder than she had feared, and the end was not yet.

Hal's mind flew. "Anyway, I sure liked our concert. 'Specially the Three Kings. We sure worked on that. You know what part I like best? Just the last where we all follow Jackie into the barn one by one to see the baby Jesus—'course there's nothin' really in there, but after the four fellas go I always feel like there was." The horses turned east into the poplars and scattered pine of the Lepps' south quarter. The pines were massive. "Mom, 'member I used to believe it when you said there were pines all 'round the edge of the world?"

"We just said that because you were too little to know about it."

"Yah. The world's really round, eh?"

"Yes."

After a pause, "They're nice and green—like in spring. It's sure cold. Wish it was spring so we could go lookin' for frogs' eggs again."

"Yes," Mrs Wiens said, holding her little boy tightly. Thom stood huge before her, staring skyward. As she looked up at him, it seemed momentarily that he was driving them towards the brightest star in the heavens.

Harness ringing, they drove on, late in the winter night. Around the world the guns were already booming in a new day.

The Author

Rudy Henry Wiebe's Mennonite parents came to Canada from Russia in 1930, having finally received permits to make the journey. Rudy was born four years later in a one-room log cabin in Saskatchewan. Later he attended school in the local improvement district called "Speedwell," and proceeded to read his way through every book in the small library.

The family moved to Coaldale, Alberta, in 1947 and Wiebe continued his education at the Alberta Mennonite High School, where his English teacher recognized and encouraged his writing potential. With the help of a major scholarship he enrolled at the University of Alberta in a medical course after Hugh Buchanan, Editor of the *Lethbridge Herald*, advocated an academic career in lieu of one in reporting. In the second year he switched to English and found his true métier in creative writing. His output of short stories and poems won him publication in anthologies and first prize in the National Federation of Canadian University Students' short story contest as well as a Rotary International contest to study at the University of Tuebingen.

Rudy Wiebe's first novel, *Peace Shall Destroy Many* (1962), was followed by *First and Vital Candle* (1966) which was adapted for radio in 1967. His articles have been published in many magazines, more recently in *Tamarack Review*, *Fiddlehead*, and *Mosaic*. In 1963 he accepted a position as assistant Professor of English at Goshen College, Indiana, and in 1964 he studied creative writing at the University of Iowa. At present he holds the post of assistant Professor of English at the University of Alberta. Professor Wiebe is married and has three children. His most recent novel was *The Blue Mountains of China* (1970).

THE NEW CANADIAN LIBRARY LIST

n 1. OVER PRAIRIE TRAILS / Frederick Philip Grove
n 2. SUCH IS MY BELOVED / Morley Callaghan
n 3. LITERARY LAPSES / Stephen Leacock
n 4. AS FOR ME AND MY HOUSE / Sinclair Ross
n 5. THE TIN FLUTE / Gabrielle Roy
n 6. THE CLOCKMAKER / Thomas Chandler Haliburton
n 7. THE LAST BARRIER AND OTHER STORIES / Charles G. D. Roberts
n 8. BAROMETER RISING / Hugh MacLennan
n 9. AT THE TIDE'S TURN AND OTHER STORIES / Thomas H. Raddall
n10. ARCADIAN ADVENTURES WITH THE IDLE RICH / Stephen Leacock
n11. HABITANT POEMS / William Henry Drummond
n12. THIRTY ACRES / Ringuet
n13. EARTH AND HIGH HEAVEN / Gwethalyn Graham
n14. THE MAN FROM GLENGARRY / Ralph Connor
n15. SUNSHINE SKETCHES OF A LITTLE TOWN / Stephen Leacock
n16. THE STEPSURE LETTERS / Thomas McCulloch
n17. MORE JOY IN HEAVEN / Morley Callaghan
n18. WILD GEESE / Martha Ostenso
n19. THE MASTER OF THE MILL / Frederick Philip Grove
n20. THE IMPERIALIST / Sara Jeannette Duncan
n21. DELIGHT / Mazo de la Roche
n22. THE SECOND SCROLL / A. M. Klein
n23. THE MOUNTAIN AND THE VALLEY / Ernest Buckler
n24. THE RICH MAN / Henry Kreisel
n25. WHERE NESTS THE WATER HEN / Gabrielle Roy
n26. THE TOWN BELOW / Roger Lemelin
n27. THE HISTORY OF EMILY MONTAGUE / Frances Brooke
n28. MY DISCOVERY OF ENGLAND / Stephen Leacock
n29. SWAMP ANGEL / Ethel Wilson
n30. EACH MAN'S SON / Hugh MacLennan
n31. ROUGHING IT IN THE BUSH / Susanna Moodie
n32. WHITE NARCISSUS / Raymond Knister
n33. THEY SHALL INHERIT THE EARTH / Morley Callaghan
n34. TURVEY / Earle Birney
n35. NONSENSE NOVELS / Stephen Leacock
n36. GRAIN / R. J. C. Stead
n37. LAST OF THE CURLEWS / Fred Bodsworth
n38. THE NYMPH AND THE LAMP / Thomas H. Raddall
n39. JUDITH HEARNE / Brian Moore
n40. THE CASHIER / Gabrielle Roy
n41. UNDER THE RIBS OF DEATH / John Marlyn
n42. WOODSMEN OF THE WEST / M. Allerdale Grainger
n43. MOONBEAMS FROM THE LARGER LUNACY / Stephen Leacock
n44. SARAH BINKS / Paul Hiebert
n45. SON OF A SMALLER HERO / Mordecai Richler
n46. WINTER STUDIES AND SUMMER RAMBLES IN CANADA / Anna Brownell Jameson
n47. REMEMBER ME / Edward Meade

n48. FRENZIED FICTION / Stephen Leacock
n49. FRUITS OF THE EARTH / Frederick Philip Grove
n50. SETTLERS OF THE MARSH / Frederick Philip Grove
n51. THE BACKWOODS OF CANADA / Catharine Parr Traill
n52. MUSIC AT THE CLOSE / Edward McCourt
n53. MY REMARKABLE UNCLE / Stephen Leacock
n54. THE DOUBLE HOOK / Sheila Watson
n55. TIGER DUNLOP'S UPPER CANADA / William Dunlop
n56. STREET OF RICHES / Gabrielle Roy
n57. SHORT CIRCUITS / Stephen Leacock
n58. WACOUSTA / John Richardson
n59. THE STONE ANGEL / Margaret Laurence
n60. FURTHER FOOLISHNESS / Stephen Leacock
n61. SAMUEL MARCHBANKS' ALMANACK / Robertson Davies
n62. THE LAMP AT NOON AND OTHER STORIES / Sinclair Ross
n63. THE HARBOR MASTER / Theodore Goodridge Roberts
n64. THE CANADIAN SETTLER'S GUIDE / Catharine Parr Traill
n65. THE GOLDEN DOG / William Kirby
n66. THE APPRENTICESHIP OF DUDDY KRAVITZ / Mordecai Richler
n67. BEHIND THE BEYOND / Stephen Leacock
n68. A STRANGE MANUSCRIPT FOUND IN A COPPER CYLINDER / James De Mille
n69. LAST LEAVES / Stephen Leacock
n70. THE TOMORROW-TAMER / Margaret Laurence
n71. ODYSSEUS EVER RETURNING / George Woodcock
n72. THE CURE OF ST. PHILIPPE / Francis William Grey
n73. THE FAVOURITE GAME / Leonard Cohen
n74. WINNOWED WISDOM / Stephen Leacock
n75. THE SEATS OF THE MIGHTY / Gilbert Parker
n76. A SEARCH FOR AMERICA / FrederickPhilip Grove
n77. THE BETRAYAL / Henry Kreisel
n78. MAD SHADOWS / Marie-Claire Blais
n79. THE INCOMPARABLE ATUK / Mordecai Richler
n80. THE LUCK OF GINGER COFFEY / Brian Moore
n81. JOHN SUTHERLAND: ESSAYS, CONTROVERSIES AND POEMS / Miriam Waddington
n82. PEACE SHALL DESTROY MANY / Rudy Henry Wiebe
n83. A VOICE FROM THE ATTIC / Robertson Davies
n84. PROCHAIN EPISODE / Hubert Aquin
n85. ROGER SUDDEN / Thomas H. Raddall
n86. MIST ON THE RIVER / Hubert Evans
n87. THE FIRE-DWELLERS / Margaret Laurence
n88. THE DESERTER / Douglas LePan
n89. ANTOINETTE DE MIRECOURT / Rosanna Leprohon
n90. ALLEGRO / Felix Leclerc
n91. THE END OF THE WORLD AND OTHER STORIES / Mavis Gallant
n92. IN THE VILLAGE OF VIGER AND OTHER STORIES / Duncan Campbell Scott
n93. THE EDIBLE WOMAN / Margaret Atwood
n94. IN SEARCH OF MYSELF / Frederick Philip Grove
n95. FEAST OF STEPHEN / Robertson Davies
n96. A BIRD IN THE HOUSE / Margaret Laurence

n97. THE WOODEN SWORD / Edward McCourt
n98. PRIDE'S FANCY / Thomas Raddall
n99. OX BELLS AND FIREFLIES / Ernest Buckler
n100. ABOVE GROUND / Jack Ludwig
n101. NEW PRIEST IN CONCEPTION BAY / Robert Traill Spence Lowell
n102. THE FLYING YEARS / Frederick Niven
n103. WIND WITHOUT RAIN / Selwyn Dewdney
n104. TETE BLANCHE / Marie-Claire Blais
n105. TAY JOHN / Howard O'Hagan
n106. CANADIANS OF OLD / Philippe Aubert de Gaspé. Translated by Sir Charles G. D. Roberts
n107. HEADWATERS OF CANADIAN LITERATURE / Archibald MacMechan
n108. THE BLUE MOUNTAINS OF CHINA / Rudy Wiebe
n109. THE HIDDEN MOUNTAIN / Gabrielle Roy
n110. THE HEART OF THE ANCIENT WOOD / Charles G. D. Roberts
n111. A JEST OF GOD / Margaret Laurence
n112. SELF CONDEMNED / Wyndham Lewis
n113. DUST OVER THE CITY / André Langevin
n114. OUR DAILY BREAD / Frederick Philip Grove
n115. THE CANADIAN NOVEL IN THE TWENTIETH CENTURY / edited by George Woodcock
n116. THE VIKING HEART / Laura Goodman Salverson
n117. DOWN THE LONG TABLE / Earle Birney
n118. GLENGARRY SCHOOL DAYS / Ralph Connor
n119. THE PLOUFFE FAMILY / Roger Lemelin
n120. WINDFLOWER / Gabrielle Roy
n121. THE DISINHERITED / Matt Cohen
n122. THE TEMPTATIONS OF BIG BEAR / Rudy Wiebe
n123. PANDORA / Sylvia Fraser
n124. HOUSE OF HATE / Percy Janes
n125. A CANDLE TO LIGHT THE SUN / Patricia Blondal
n126. THIS SIDE JORDAN / Margaret Laurence
n127. THE RED FEATHERS / T. G. Roberts
n128. I AM MARY DUNNE / Brian Moore
n129. THE ROAD PAST ALTAMONT / Gabrielle Roy
n130. KNIFE ON THE TABLE / Jacques Godbout
n131. THE MANAWAKA WORLD OF MARGARET LAURENCE / Clara Thomas
n132. CONSIDER HER WAYS / Frederick Philip Grove
n133. HIS MAJESTY'S YANKEES / Thomas Raddall
n134. JEAN RIVARD / Antoine Gérin-Lajoie
n135. BOGLE CORBET / John Galt
n136. A CHOICE OF ENEMIES / Mordecai Richler
n137. RESPONSES AND EVALUATIONS: ESSAYS ON CANADA / E. K. Brown
n138. THE MASTER'S WIFE / Sir Andrew Macphail
n139. THE CRUELEST MONTH / Ernest Buckler
n140. THE ATONEMENT OF ASHLEY MORDEN / Fred Bodsworth
n141. WILD ANIMALS I HAVE KNOWN / Ernest Thompson Seton
n142. SCANN / Robert Harlow
n143. ON POETRY AND POETS / A. J. M. Smith

n144. CRACKPOT / Adele Wiseman
n145. SAWBONES MEMORIAL / Sinclair Ross
n146. THE DIVINERS / Margaret Laurence
n147. HIGH BRIGHT BUGGY WHEELS / Luella Creighton
n148. BIG LONELY / James Bacque
n149. WOODEN HUNTERS / Matt Cohen
n150. GOD'S SPARROWS / Philip Child
n151. THE OUTLANDER / Germaine Guèvremont
n152. THE GREAT COMIC BOOK HEROES AND OTHER ESSAYS BY MORDECAI RICHLER / edited by Robert Fulford
n153. BEAUTIFUL LOSERS / Leonard Cohen
n154. THE EMPEROR OF ICE-CREAM / Brian Moore
n155. GARDEN IN THE WIND and ENCHANTED SUMMER / Gabrielle Roy
n156. THE SCORCHED-WOOD PEOPLE / Rudy Wiebe
n157. THE LOST SALT GIFT OF BLOOD / Alistair MacLeod
n158. LORD NELSON TAVERN / Ray Smith
n159. EVERYTHING IN THE WINDOW / Shirley Faessler
n160. THE CAMERA ALWAYS LIES / Hugh Hood
n161. THE SELENA TREE / Patricia Joudry
n162. WATCHERS AT THE POND / Franklin Russell
n163. TWO IN THE BUSH AND OTHER STORIES / Audrey Thomas
n164. BLOODY HARVEST / Grahame Woods
n165. THE NEIGHBOUR AND OTHER STORIES / Naim Kattan
n166. THE MANUSCRIPTS OF PAULINE ARCHANGE / Marie-Claire Blais
n167. SANDBARS / Oonah McFee
n168. SELECTED STORIES / John Metcalf
n169. THE ANGEL OF THE TAR SANDS AND OTHER STORIES / Rudy Wiebe
n170. THE INNOCENT TRAVELLER / Ethel Wilson
n171. THE SWEET SECOND SUMMER OF KITTY MALONE / Matt Cohen

POETS OF CANADA

o 1. VOL. I: POETS OF THE CONFEDERATION / edited by Malcolm Ross
o 2. MASKS OF FICTION: CANADIAN CRITICS ON CANADIAN PROSE / edited by A. J. M. Smith
o 3. MASKS OF POETRY: CANADIAN CRITICS ON CANADIAN VERSE / edited by A. J. M. Smith
o 4. VOL. III: POETRY OF MID-CENTURY 1940-1960 / edited by Milton Wilson
o 5. VOL. II: POETS BETWEEN THE WARS / edited by Milton Wilson
o 6. THE POEMS OF EARLE BIRNEY
o 7. VOL. IV: POETS OF CONTEMPORARY CANADA 1960-1970 / edited by Eli Mandel
o 8. VOL. V: NINETEENTH CENTURY NARRATIVE POEMS / edited by David Sinclair
o 9. THE POEMS OF BLISS CARMAN / edited by John Robert Sorfleet
o10. THE POEMS OF AL PURDY
o11. THE DAMNATION OF VANCOUVER / Earle Birney
o12. THE POEMS OF IRVING LAYTON / edited by Eli Mandel